16TH MYSTERY ANNUAL

NOVELS BY ELLERY QUEEN

The Roman Hat Mystery
The French Powder Mystery
The Dutch Shoe Mystery
The Greek Coffin Mystery
The Egyptian Cross Mystery
The American Gun Mystery
The Siamese Twin Mystery
The Chinese Orange Mystery
The Spanish Cape Mystery
Halfway House
The Door Between
The Devil to Pay
The Four of Hearts

The Dragon's Teeth
Calamity Town
There Was an Old Woman
The Murderer Is a Fox
Ten Days' Wonder
Cat of Many Tails
Double, Double
The Origin of Evil
The King Is Dead
The Scarlet Letters
The Glass Village
Inspector Queen's Own Case
The Finishing Stroke

BOOKS OF SHORT STORIES BY ELLERY QUEEN

The Adventures of Ellery Queen
The *New* Adventures of Ellery Queen
The Case Book of Ellery Queen

Calendar of Crime
Q.B.I.:
    Queen's Bureau of Investigation

EDITED BY ELLERY QUEEN

Challenge to the Reader
101 Years' Entertainment
Sporting Blood
The Female of the Species
The Misadventures of Sherlock Holmes
Rogues' Gallery
Best Stories from *EQMM*
To the Queen's Taste
The Queen's Awards, 1946
Murder by Experts
The Queen's Awards, 1947
Twentieth Century Detective Stories
The Queen's Awards, 1948
The Queen's Awards, 1949
The Queen's Awards, 5th Series

The Literature of Crime
The Queen's Awards, 6th Series
The Queen's Awards, 7th Series
The Queen's Awards, 8th Series
Ellery Queen's Awards: 9th Series
Ellery Queen's Awards: 10th Series
Ellery Queen's Awards: 11th Series
Ellery Queen's Awards: 12th Series
Ellery Queen's 13th Mystery Annual
Ellery Queen's 14th Mystery Annual
Ellery Queen's 1960 Anthology
Ellery Queen's 15th Mystery Annual
Ellery Queen's 1961 Anthology
Ellery Queen's 16th Mystery Annual
Ellery Queen's 1962 Anthology

Ellery Queen's Mystery Magazine (21st Year)

CRITICAL WORKS BY ELLERY QUEEN

The Detective Short Story

Queen's Quorum
In the Queens' Parlor

UNDER THE PSEUDONYM OF BARNABY ROSS

The Tragedy of X
The Tragedy of Y

The Tragedy of Z
Drury Lane's Last Case

ELLERY QUEEN'S 16th MYSTERY ANNUAL

The Year's Best

from *Ellery Queen's Mystery Magazine*

Edited by ELLERY QUEEN

RANDOM HOUSE · NEW YORK

ACKNOWLEDGMENTS

The Editors hereby make grateful acknowledgment to the following authors and authors' representatives for giving permission to reprint the material in this volume:

Lurton Blassingame for *The Symbolic Logic of Murder*, by John Reese.

Brandt & Brandt for *To Die with Decency*, by Geoffrey Household; and *Who Wants To Be a Dead Hero?* by Hugh Pentecost.

Curtis Brown, Ltd. for *Beidenbauer's Flea*, by Stanley Ellin.

James Brown Associates, Inc. for *The Scent of Murder*, by Frances and Richard Lockridge.

Harold R. Daniels for *The Master Stroke*.

Ann Elmo Agency, Inc. for *The Man in the Next Cell*, by Henry Slesar.

Don Knowlton for *For Sale—Silence*.

Harold Matson Company for *The Exploit of the Embalmed Whale*, by Jacob Hay.

MCA Artists, Ltd. for *A Man Named Thin*, by Dashiell Hammett.

Scott Meredith Literary Agency, Inc., for *Crime on Mars*, by Arthur C. Clarke; *The Back Stairway*, by Hal Ellson; and *Easy Money*, by Evan Hunter.

Paul R. Reynolds & Son for *Family Affair*, by Margery Allingham.

June McMahan Roy for *A Visit from Brother Thomas*.

Elaine Slater for *The Way It Used To Be*.

Rogers Terrill Literary Agency for *The Town That Will Never Forget*, by Norman Daniels; *Where Do You Live, Queen Esther?* by Avram Davidson; and *A Gift for Antonietta*, by Rick Rubin.

Esther Wagner for *Miss Weird-O*.

Willis Kingsley Wing for *The Ultimate Clue*, by Anthony Boucher; and *Too Clever for Scotland Yard*, by Edmund Crispin.

CONTENTS

16TH MYSTERY ANNUAL

Frances and Richard Lockridge

The Scent of Murder

Ronnie Beede, escaped from a psychiatric ward, had
already killed twice. The net was closing in around him
—but not before murder struck again . . .

Ronnie Beede had been free for forty-eight hours and he had a
gun and he was a killer. Throughout Westchester and Putnam
counties people locked their doors against Ronnie Beede.

He had escaped from the psychiatric ward of an upstate hospital
and since then he had murdered twice. First he had killed a salesman who had picked him up on the road, and after that a girl of
sixteen who had been baby-sitting in a house he had broken into
for food and clothes. The police were sure of the first: his finger-
prints had been found on the salesman's car, which Beede had
abandoned when it ran out of gas. They were not so sure about
the girl. But her killing had been needless, wanton, and that looked
like Ronnie Beede.

They knew a good deal about Beede—almost everything except
where he was. A big blond man in his middle twenties; a good-
looking man with a friendly face and a wide, agreeable smile, and

a slow, rather diffident way of speaking. The sort of attractive young man anyone might have picked up, even a person who should have known better. Probably the salesman had been bored and lonely when he stopped for Ronnie on a road above Peekskill. Ronnie had slugged him, then strangled him and thrown his body by the roadside. That was needless, too, but it was Ronnie's way. The gun he had now had been in the glove compartment of the salesman's car.

The girl had been killed in Mt. Kisco, and geography as well as wantonness made the police think of Ronnie Beede. If he was working his way home—killing his way home—Mt. Kisco would be on his route—on the route to a small, unpainted farmhouse on a back road between Brewster and Pawling. His mother waited there—a frail woman with a drawn face who had trembled uncontrollably when Captain M. L. Heimrich of the New York State Police spoke to her, although Heimrich spoke gently, believing that Ronnie was no fault of hers. She thought the fault the army's. "He was always a good boy until he went into the army. The best son a mother ever—" She had been unable to finish.

There was no telling whose fault Ronnie was, but that was not Heimrich's problem—except that, as well as a policeman, he was a man, and mankind worried him. It was easy enough to put a word to Ronnie. He was a paranoic, knowing the world was against him and killing to defend himself against the world. *Mad Killer Strikes Again*—that was the way a New York City tabloid had headlined it that July morning, after the girl's body had been found. The fault? It was not for the police to decide. Their problem was to catch Beede—before he killed again.

The news came on the car radio at four thirty-one in the afternoon. The car, with Sergeant Charles Forniss driving, was two miles east of Katonah on NY 22, heading west toward the barracks at Hawthorne. Forniss set the siren going and the car leaped —leaped through Katonah, with other cars flinching to the curbs; screamed its way north and west for three miles and a little more, and onto a side road and then, almost at once, up a winding driveway between trees.

Forniss knew the way. The Franklins were well-known thereabouts—Arthur Franklin was on the town planning board and the library committee, and Martha Franklin had been active in the garden club, although less lately than in the recent past. It was hard to believe that a thing like this could happen to people like the Franklins.

Their house was isolated, deep in ancient trees. It was probably the isolation and quiet that had brought murder there.

Heimrich and Forniss were the first of the police to arrive. The front door of the house stood open; the screen which had shielded it had been gashed near the knob. In the square hall beyond the door, Arthur Franklin was sitting on a bench—sitting with his wrists resting on his knees and his hands dangling between them. He sat staring at the floor, which was in deep shadow. When Heimrich and Forniss crossed the porch, he got up slowly, heavily, then came to the door and looked at them with almost blank eyes.

"He killed her," Arthur Franklin said. He spoke, Heimrich thought, as if for sometime he had been saying the same words over and over in his mind. "For no reason at all. Anything he wanted—" Franklin did not finish; he pressed the palm of his right hand against his forehead and moved it slowly up his forehead. The hand ground dirt into the skin. He was a handsome man—heavy and in his late forties, but still handsome. He wore stained walking shorts and a blue shirt; he had been kneeling in earth and his knees were grimed with it. "For no reason at all," he repeated, and stepped back so that they could enter the hall.

Martha Franklin lay on the floor, on her back, in blood. She had been a tall woman and looked older by some years than her husband. The dead face was bony—even in death, austere and dominating. Up to now, Heimrich thought, looking down at her, she probably had always got her way. She must, Heimrich found himself thinking, have died in furious surprise that she—*she*— could thus be flouted. She had been shot through the head, from close in. She had fallen with her head toward a marble fireplace.

"I was down in the garden," Franklin said, without being asked. "If only I had been here—" He shook his head, then looked hard at Heimrich. "How many more are you going to let him kill?"

"Him?" Heimrich said.

"This—maniac," Franklin said. "The one in the newspapers. On the radio. What's his name?"

"Beede," Heimrich said. "Ronnie Beede."

"We'd have given him whatever he wanted," Franklin said. "Food, money—anything he wanted. To kill somebody for—for *nothing.*" He looked down at the body of his wife, stunned, moving his head slowly from side to side.

There was no use staying in the hall where death was so visible. There was nothing immediately to be done there, and the others were on their way. Through the open door they could hear sirens, not far off. Gently, Heimrich guided the heavy man from the hall into a living room. "You were in the garden?" Heimrich said. "You didn't see anyone?"

"I heard somebody running," Franklin said. "And a shot. I didn't pay any attention to the shot. You hear them in the country, and it sounded a long way off. But then—somebody running off through the field. From the house." He stopped and stood shaking his head, as if in disbelief. "I was staking up the tomatoes," he said. He repeated it—"staking up the tomatoes"—as if this incongruity was monstrous.

"The garden," Heimrich said. "It's some distance from the house, I take it?"

"Over the hill," Franklin said. "Only place there's enough sun. If—if I'd only been here with her. I—" He shook his head quickly, this time as if to shake shadows out of his mind. "She was resting, probably," he went on. "Heard him break in—you saw the screen?"

"Yes," Heimrich said.

"Went to see what it was," Franklin said. "She would have. She was like that. And he shot her. Just like that. For no reason at all. For no—"

"Now Mr. Franklin," Heimrich said. "The man you heard running. He ran past the garden?"

"Through the next field," Franklin said. "I was kneeling down among the vines. Had my back to the field. By the time I looked around he was gone. It was this man Beede, wasn't it?"

Heimrich said he supposed so. It had been done Ronnie

Beede's way—wantonly, for no reason. "We're doing all—" he began, and stopped, because Arthur Franklin was swaying on his feet. Heimrich moved quickly and caught Franklin around the shoulders. For an instant the man was dead weight in his grasp. Heimrich helped him to a chair, lowered him into it, holding the heavy man's wrists as he let him down, being pulled forward by Franklin's weight. Heimrich's nostrils were pinched.

"All right," Franklin said, after a moment. "It's nothing. Dizzy. Too much sun, maybe. Too much—everything."

"Naturally," Heimrich soothed. He heard a car door slam outside, heard feet on the porch. And then brakes squealed, and another car door opened and closed. The others were showing up. "Just sit and rest a minute, Mr. Franklin," Heimrich said, and went back to the hall.

They were getting cameras out. That came first. "Beede?" Forniss said, and Heimrich said, "Looks like it, doesn't it, Charlie? Mrs. Franklin surprised him and he killed her. And ran. Down past Mr. Franklin's garden. I'll go and have a look."

He went along a path, in the shade first, over a rise and down again, and then into the sun—the full sun a garden needs. It was a fine neat garden. Some day, Heimrich thought, he would like to have a garden like it—with bush limas ripening in long rows and tomato vines tied carefully to stakes. To his right, as he faced the garden, there was a stone fence, and beyond it a field of tall grass and blueberry bushes.

Heimrich went into Mr. Franklin's vegetable garden and squatted among the tomatoes. Mr. Franklin kept the vines trained to three stems by pinching off unwanted shoots. The stubs of many such were on the ground, withering in the sun. Franklin had missed some and Heimrich snipped two or three between thumb and forefinger. He smelled his fingers, nodded, and walked back to the house. He went through the now crowded hall and into the living room. Franklin sat where Heimrich had left him.

Heimrich went up to the seated man, lifted Franklin's right hand, and looked at it, while Franklin stared at him, then began to pull his hand away. The hand was grimed. Heimrich bent down and smelled it.

"What the hell?" Franklin said, and his voice was no longer dull—it was sharp, alert.

"Now Mr. Franklin," Heimrich said. "You say you were working with the tomato plants?"

"I told you—" Franklin began, then stopped.

"Smell your hands yourself," Heimrich said. "Go on, Mr. Franklin."

But Franklin did not smell his hands. He began to stand up.

"No," Heimrich said, and Franklin sank back.

"Then," Heimrich said, "smell *my* fingers, Mr. Franklin," and held thumb and forefinger in front of Franklin's nose. "Very pungent odor tomato vines have, haven't they?" Heimrich said. "Quite unmistakable. When you handle them, the odor gets on your hands and stays. Until you wash the sap off, and then the water you wash in turns green. You know that, naturally. But—*it's not on your hands now, is it?* I noticed that when you were dizzy and I was helping you. No tomato smell. But—you hadn't washed your hands, had you? You dirtied them, yes—and your knees too—to show you'd just come from the garden. Took advantage of the fact there was a killer on the loose and—*why did you kill her, Mr. Franklin?* Merely because she was hard to live with? Or did she have the money?"

Franklin did not answer. But something happened to his eyes.

That sort of thing occurs now and then—a flaw in a lie is exposed and the lie falls, and the liar with it. Franklin had been careless, Heimrich pointed out to Sergeant Forniss somewhat later. If he had said he was in the garden hoeing beans he might easily have got away with it.

They trapped Ronnie Beede that evening. The trap was his mother's house and they let him walk into it. He was on his knees, with his face buried in his mother's lap, when they took him. He was shaking so hard that the frail woman shook with him.

Edmund Crispin

Too Clever for Scotland Yard

How a man, alone in his prison cell, was murdered—the "impossible crime," the "locked room mystery," with a new and most ingenious solution . . . Cheers!

From The Assistant Commissioner
Criminal Investigation Department
Metropolitan Police

To H.M. Secretary for Home Affairs
PRIVATE AND CONFIDENTIAL

New Scotland Yard,
London, S.W. 1
May 12th, 1960

Dear Mr. Clunes,

Thank you for your letter dated yesterday. Needless to say, the nature of the questions regarding the Wynter case which Opposition Members are proposing to ask in the House of Commons comes as no particular surprise to me. I have in fact dealt somewhat disingenuously with this matter, as you will see; but to suggest that I have avoided arresting Gillian on account of my personal acquaintance with him is absurd.

The outline of the case which follows will, I hope, be sufficient to secure a withdrawal of the questions. If this fails, I shall of course be glad to offer the Members concerned a full and free opportunity to question me, as well as the officers who have conducted the investigation, in whatever fashion they think fit.

Their suspicions are the more ironical in that Gillian was actually arrested yesterday morning, on my personal instructions. Since the Department of Public Prosecutions regards the evidence against him as insufficient, the arrest was made without a warrant; and within a couple of hours Gillian was inevitably once again a free man.

My action did, however, succeed in its intended purpose: Gillian and Mrs. Wynter had planned to be married yesterday afternoon; as a result of the scene that occurred in my office the marriage will not now take place.

You will say, and rightly, that it is no business of the police to discourage people who wish to marry murderers. Nonetheless, when one partner is completely unsuspicious, there is, I believe, a good deal to be said on humane grounds for at least dropping a hint. In fact, the simple ruse we employed succeeded handsomely, thereby confirming the theory we had formed as to the only possible method by which this perplexing murder can have been committed.

Gillian's arrest was so contrived that Mrs. Wynter would be with him at the time; she was "allowed" to accompany him to Scotland Yard, and on arrival both of them were brought to my office. Also present were Superintendent Colleanor (in charge of the case), Detective-Inspector Pugh (who made the arrest), and a shorthand writer (P. C. Clements). Despite Mrs. Wynter's urgings, Gillian declined to send for a solicitor; his attitude was fatalistic throughout, and he looked ill.

I need hardly say that if Gillian's arrest had been anything other than a trick there would have been no question of my confronting him personally. As it was, I was able to use our previous acquaintance as a pretext for the meeting: I told him, quite untruthfully, that I had just returned from leave, and was anxious for old times' sake to hear an account of the circumstances which had resulted in the Deputy A.C.'s ordering his arrest, and to look into the matter in person; and it is the measure of the queer, apathetic state he was in that he apparently swallowed this preposterous tale without turning a hair.

The proceedings opened with Colleano's giving me a summary of the case. From our point of view this was mere camouflage; but it is necessary to repeat it here for the purpose of clarifying what happened subsequently.

Approximately two years ago Dr. Harold Wynter, a general practitioner working in the Somerset town of Midcastle, was tried for, and convicted of, the manslaughter of a patient through gross negligence. The evidence against him was by no means decisive, but both judge and jury seem to have been influenced by the fact that the doctor himself was a morphine addict. He was adjudged guilty and sentenced to imprisonment for three years.

At Nottsville Prison—to which Gillian had a year previously been appointed Governor—Wynter's first few weeks were spent in the infirmary, where he was weaned of his addiction before being transferred to the cells. Very shortly afterwards, however, he began to suffer from attacks of angina pectoris. Accordingly he was excused from all serious exertion; and in addition—since he proved a model prisoner—was allowed a cell to himself, so that he mingled with the other prisoners only on the occasions when he took light exercise in the yard.

His wife, Ellen Wynter, wrote to him regularly and seems to have visited him as often as she could; these visits were, however, restricted in number owing to the fact that for financial reasons she had been obliged to take a job some considerable distance away.

In the ordinary course of things—taking into account remissions for good conduct—Wynter would have been released in October of this year.

On April 23rd he died in his cell.

This was discovered when luncheon was brought to him at noon on that day. In the absence of contra-indications, the death was ascribed to the angina—for although a man suffering from this complaint may, and often does, live on for a great many years, there is no guarantee that any single attack may not finish him. As with all prison deaths, however, an inquest was held. But there was no post mortem, since none seemed to be called for, and on April 27th Wynter was buried in the prison cemetery, his death being certified as due to his heart disease.

There the matter might well have rested. Three days later, however, we received here at Scotland Yard an anonymous letter which accused Gillian of having poisoned Wynter with a plant spray containing nicotine; Gillian's motive, the writer added, was infatuation with Wynter's wife.

I myself ordered that this accusation be investigated, and there proved to be sufficient plausibility in it to justify us in exhuming Wynter's body. The stomach was shown to contain a small but sufficiently lethal quantity of nicotine; in consequence of this, a full-scale examination of the circumstances was at once put in hand.

The writer of the anonymous letter was traced easily enough. He was a warder at Nottsville named Parker, who conceived himself to have a grudge against the Governor, and who purely by chance had come to hear of the irregular association which did in fact exist between Gillian and Mrs. Wynter; the nicotine, he said, was only a guess, based on the fact that he knew this type of plant spray was used occasionally on the Governor's shrubbery.

It was a suspiciously good guess, and Superintendent Colleano devoted plenty of time and energy to investigating whether Parker himself had opportunity or motive for poisoning Wynter. In the end, however, it was established that he had neither. A second possibility was that Wynter's death had some connection with the death of the patient he was alleged to have neglected; but this again proved unlikely, if not impossible.

To cut a long story short, the closest checking and counter-checking failed to establish a motive for Wynter's death in any of the prison staff—except Gillian.

Gillian's motive, however, was undeniably a strong one: he was in love with Mrs. Wynter. There is no doubt, by the way, that Wynter was devoted to his wife, to the extent that—in her view—he would never have agreed to divorce her; and in spite of his illness he might well have lived for many years after his release from Nottsville.

As to the manner in which Gillian and Mrs. Wynter became acquainted, that, I think, calls for no detailed description here. It is worth noting, however, that Gillian's obsession with the woman was by no means a happy one. The husband was a prisoner in his personal charge, undergoing a relatively savage sentence for a crime of which he may quite possibly have been innocent; moreover, Wynter loved his wife; and finally, he was an incurable invalid.

To a man with Gillian's record for probity these considerations may well have been horribly distressing; he himself has said that they worried him deeply—and his anxiety was naturally compounded by the fact that from the official point of view his surreptitious relationship with Mrs. Wynter was an unforgivable offence for which his resignation would certainly be demanded as soon as the truth became known. As you are aware, that resignation was tendered, and accepted, a fortnight ago.

Since Gillian is a wealthy man in his own right, his financial position will not be affected; at the same time, for a man with his long and devoted connection with the penal service, the wrench must have been considerable.

Was Gillian's passion for Mrs. Wynter sufficiently strong to override all these considerations? Unquestionably it was; and if so, we may not unreasonably assume that it was strong enough to impel him to the act of murder. He had motive, he had means.

Unfortunately, what he seems quite definitely not to have had was opportunity.

The medical evidence as to the time of Wynter's death, and how long he took to die, is regrettably uncertain; but there is a definite consensus of opinion to the effect that Wynter could not have ingested the poison earlier than breakfast time—that is to say, 7:30 A.M. on the day of his death. It seems equally certain, however, that the nicotine was not in Wynter's breakfast; two warders (perfectly reputable men) were concerned in the serving of this, and moreover they were, as it happened, accompanied on this occasion by one of H.M. Inspectors of Prisons, who had been staying in Nottsville overnight; without going into the matter in detail, I can assure you that short of a conspiracy among these three it is absolutely impossible for the poison to have been administered in Wynter's breakfast.

But if not at this time, when? On the morning of his death Wynter did not, as it chanced, require fresh materials for the work he performed in his cell; and the result of this was that the next visit paid to him was at lunch-time—when his dead body was discovered. It is certain that between 7:30 and noon Wynter was alone in his cell in E block, and that during this period he came in contact with no one—neither with Gillian nor with anyone else.

These circumstances would seem to point either to suicide or to murder by trickery—for example, Wynter might previously have been given a preparation of nicotine under the guise of medicine, and have consumed it of his own volition some time on the morning of his death. There exists, however, an insuperable objection to both assumptions: before breakfast on that particular morning a snap search of the cells in E block was carried out. These searches are routine, but they are nevertheless thorough; and because of the recent suicide of Pickering at Tawton Prison, special attention is currently being paid to the possibility of concealed poison.

The upshot, as it applies to Wynter, you will guess: no pills or powders or capsules or fluids were found in his cell other than the small supply of trinitrini tablets which he was allowed to keep by him in case of an angina attack. Of these, at the time of the search, there were three, in a sealed container; and there is irrefutable evidence to prove that this same container was still there, still sealed and intact, when Wynter's body was discovered (it was, of course, noticed particularly for the reason that at the time Wynter's death was assumed to be the result of an angina attack sufficiently disabling to have prevented him from getting at the tablets).

Now, Gillian's last direct encounter with Wynter had taken place more than a week before the death; and on that occasion, as always, another member of the prison staff was present—this precaution is so invariable in dealing with convicts that if Gillian had at any time departed from it in his dealings with Wynter, the fact must inevitably have become known to us.

How, then, can Gillian possibly have committed this murder?

Or if it was suicide, how can Gillian or anyone else possibly have supplied Wynter with the means?

The three warders who conducted the search on the morning of the death might conceivably have conspired together to make Wynter a present of poison; but in view of their excellent record this was not a possibility which Colleano felt able to accept so long as another, and likelier, explanation of the circumstances remained open to him.

And such an explanation did exist.

Despite the external appearances of what thriller-writers describe as an "impossible murder" or a "locked-room mystery," the ingenious yet simple way in which Wynter had been murdered was easily deduced from the facts I have given above.

Unluckily, proving it in court is quite another matter. The D.P.P. has refused to sanction a prosecution, and I cannot blame them; here, I am sorry to have to say, is one murderer who has been too clever for us.

In reconsidering what I have written, I realise that I have left Mrs. Wynter unduly in the background; for in returning Gillian's affection (as she admits she did) she too had cause to wish Wynter dead—a motive all the more powerful in that Gillian is a rich man, while Wynter was not. This motive, however, is offset by the fact that, on the face of it, Mrs. Wynter had even *less* chance of conveying the poison to her husband than Gillian did: the prison staff is convinced that Mrs. Wynter cannot have transmitted the nicotine to her husband either through the post—which naturally is strictly censored in Nottsville as in all prisons—or in the course of a visit; and even if this conviction were mistaken, there would still remain the problem of how the poison thus supplied could possibly have escaped notice during the search of Wynter's cell on the very morning of his death.

I return now to the scene in my office yesterday morning.

As soon as Colleano finished his account of the case, Mrs.

Wynter, acutely distressed, urged that her husband's death was almost certainly a suicide. She was unable to give any coherent idea of how he could have obtained the poison, or secreted it so effectively as to defy expert search; but she propounded the theory that although she had never explicitly mentioned her association with Gillian to Wynter, he might have come to hear of it through prison rumor, emanating, presumably, from the warder Parker. In support of this theory she mentioned the fact—which she had learned from Colleano's account—that Wynter had destroyed all but a single page (this, presumably, having accidentally escaped his attention) of the many letters she had written him. Also—

But at this point there came an interruption—in the form of a short report addressed to me by the head of our forensic laboratory.

After scanning this report, I proceeded to read it aloud.

The single page surviving from Mrs. Wynter's correspondence with her husband has been mentioned above; and it was with this that the laboratory report was concerned. The page was a part of the last letter which Wynter received from his wife, delivered to him two days before his death. Its news and messages were commonplace; but one of Colleano's subordinates who handled it had been struck by something unusual in the texture of the paper, and had therefore passed it on to the laboratory.

The laboratory's report, though technical in its phraseology, was clear and conclusive: the paper on which the letter was written had been impregnated with a nicotine solution identical with the plant spray that Gillian used on his shrubbery.

When Mrs. Wynter heard the contents of the report, she seemed to shrivel. I make no apology for stating her reaction in such melodramatic terms, for never in all my experience have I seen anyone display such plain physical evidences of guilt.

This was satisfactory to us, of course, but an actual confession, induced by the shock, would have been more satisfactory still. The D.P.P., however, had already advised us that such a confession would be worthless in court so long as it was unsupported by other evidence, so that we were not unduly cast down by its failure to materialize. Since Mrs. Wynter remained silent, Gillian presently asked, in a bewildered fashion, for an explanation. With as much as I could manage of the air of one to whom the truth had at last miraculously been made plain, I gave it.

When Wynter's arrest became imminent (I said), he must have arranged with his wife that in the event of his being sent to prison she should keep him supplied with morphine by the medium of what are known to United States prison authorities as "satch" letters—that is, letters written on paper which has been previously saturated in the drug required. So long as these arrive regularly, the chewing and swallowing of them will keep even a confirmed addict fairly happy during the period when his normal sources of supply are cut off.

This program Mrs. Wynter was evidently scrupulous in carrying out. But then she met Gillian, perceived his infatuation for her, noted that he was a rich man, and became aware of the existence of the plant spray in his potting-shed. At once she saw not only how her husband could be murdered, but also how in the process the victim could effortlessly be induced to *destroy the evidence against his murderer.*

Inevitably, her principal intention was that the death should be ascribed to the angina; and but for Parker's grudge against Gillian, that is precisely what would have happened. In case this first line of defense failed, however, Mrs. Wynter took a further precaution: she used a poison which could be linked or traced to Gillian, arguing that even if he were to be accused, arrested, and convicted, her hold over him was such that she could persuade him at least to make arrangements for keeping her in comfort during the period of his imprisonment; there might even, she thought, be a fair chance of marrying him before the warrant for his arrest was implemented.

There was little more that I needed to say. Gillian could scarcely have avoided noticing Mrs. Wynter's terror; and his own reaction, as the details of this cruel murder plot were unfolded, was everything I had hoped for—he will be careful, I am confident, never to see or communicate with the woman again.

What remained was the question of whether or not Mrs. Wynter would call our bluff. For of course it *was* bluff. The wretched

Wynter undoubtedly chewed up every fragment of the final, poisonous letter precisely as he had chewed up every fragment of the preceding ones.

As you know, a confession obtained by trickery is not inadmissible in court; but we were aware that in the absence of confirmatory evidence such a confession would be hopelessly inadequate for the purpose of a prosecution. In any case, we never got it: Mrs. Wynter challenged us to produce the sheet of paper which had supposedly been subjected to laboratory examination, and to that challenge we naturally had no reply.

For a few moments, Mrs. Wynter seemed confusedly to suppose that this circumstance would exonerate her in Gillian's eyes. But the signs of her guilt had been plain to him. They left Scotland Yard separately.

Like the majority of policemen I detest murderers, and accordingly it would be no sorrow to me if you were driven to expound Mrs. Wynter's guilt in detail in the privileged circumstances of the House of Commons. The Opposition, however, is notoriously solicitous regarding the sensibilities of criminals; consequently I have no doubt that if the truth is made known to them in private they will exert themselves most strenuously to prevent its going further.

Hoping that this letter supplies as much detail as you require,

I am, Sir, yours truly,

JOHN KIRKBRIDE.

Stanley Ellin

Beidenbauer's Flea

*Meet the impresario of Beidenbauer's Mighty Mites—
a grand and glorious character out of the past,
wandering over the face of the earth, doomed to suffer
and search, search and suffer . . . an extraordinary
story.*

I was seated on a bench in Central Park, half drowsing in the
autumn sunlight, when a strange figure approached—the cadaver-
ous figure of a man who bore himself with the grandeur of an
ancient matinee idol. As he walked, he swung a malacca stick
with practiced ease. His hair was snowy-white and swept back almost to his collar, and on it was cocked with indescribable pa-
nache a battered homburg. His tight-waisted, velveteen-collared
overcoat was long out of fashion and badly frayed at the cuffs.
His narrow-toed, patent-leather shoes were scuffed and down at
the heels. Yet, so noble was his demeanor and so profound the
sorrow written on his lined face that I found myself pitying his
curious garb, rather than being moved to scorn by it.

He sat down beside me, propped his stick between his legs, and
said, "It is a beautiful day, is it not?"

"Yes," I said, "it is." Then I felt a sudden apprehension. I am too easy a mark for the wayfarer's sad story, his melting eyes, his extended palm. I have never learned to say no to the humble derelict who stops me with hat in hand and asks for carfare to places he never intends to visit. Now I had the feeling that I knew what was coming, and I drew a tight rein on my susceptibilities. This time, I silently resolved, I would escape before it was too late.

But there was no escape. As I started to rise, my companion placed a hand on my shoulder and gently pressed me back into my seat. "It is a beautiful day," he said, "but what does that matter to one who is doomed to suffer and search, search and suffer through every day of his life, fair or foul?"

I was resigned to my fate, but in a bitter mood. He might tell his story to the end, but when he held out his hand for the expected offering he would get nothing more than a handshake. That much I took my oath on.

"Evidently," I said, concealing my true emotions with an effort, "you are spending your life in a search for something. What is that something?"

"A flea."

"A flea?"

The aged curio nodded somberly. "Yes, strange as it seems, that is the object of my search. But perhaps you will understand more readily if I reveal my name to you. It is Beidenbauer. Thaddeus Beidenbauer. There, does that enlighten you?"

He looked at me eagerly, but the light in his eyes faded when I shook my head. "No," I said, "I'm sorry to say it doesn't."

"It doesn't?"

"I'm afraid not."

Beidenbauer sighed. "Well, such is fame. A bubble—a glittering, weightless thing that one holds briefly in hand, and then—but let me tell you my story. There is pain and heartbreak in it, true, but I am inured to that now. I have lived my tragedy over and over so many times in my waking dreams that I can bear to talk about it freely when the occasion arises. I will tell it all to you just as it happened."

"I am sure you will," I said.

There was a time (Beidenbauer said) when my name was known in every mighty city of the world, when I was petted and sought after by the great, when I was drunk each day with my youth and wealth and the joy of my lot. Ah, I should have thought then how the gods destroy those who are too proud, but I did not. I lived only with the happy realization that I was the proprietor of Beidenbauer's Mighty Mites, the greatest flea circus on earth, the one that did more to honor the vast and unsung talents of the flea than any other before or since.

There have been flea circuses before mine and after mine, but always shabby affairs, dismal two-penny entertainments with none of the true glamor of the stage invested in them. But mine was different. It was superlative theater. Whether performed before the bumpkins who attend touring carnivals or before a soiree of society's bluest blue bloods, it never failed to stir the audience to its depths, to bring it to its feet shouting for endless encores. And all because as a mere child I had learned the secret of the relationship between the flea and its trainer, and with infinite patience had put the secret to work.

I can see you are wondering what the secret is; you will be astonished to learn of its simplicity. There is a strange and wonderful symbiosis between flea and man. The flea feeds from its trainer's arm and thus strengthened goes into the arena to perform. The money earned this way is then used by the trainer to buy him his dinner, to enrich his blood, that the performer may feed and return to his performance. So we have a perfect cycle, flea and man feeding off each other, each contributing to their mutual existence.

That is all there is to it, but I was the one to discover that there must be more than mere food involved in this relationship. There must be a symbiosis of emotions as well. Respect, sympathy, understanding, and love—yes, love—must be there, for the flea, a quivering mass of sensitivity, needs them desperately. And unlike all other trainers I provided them. Cruelty was the rule elsewhere. The harsh word, the heavy hand—these were all my confreres knew in trying to master and instruct the flea. But kindness was my rule, and for that reason I soared to success while all others remained mired in failure.

But enough of myself; after all, it was not I who entered the spotlighted ring every day to perform, to act the clown so that the crowd roared with laughter, to risk my neck in acrobatics so that it gasped, to woo it with grace so that it sighed in rapture. All this was done by the fleas, and it is they who must get the lion's share of admiration.

There were twenty-four members of the troupe, hand-picked, trained for weary hours on end, and it is impossible to imagine the range of their talents. But the unchallenged star of the show, and, sorrow of sorrows, the star of the tragedy I am unfolding, was a flea named Sebastian. Small, volatile, full of riotous wit and invention, he was our featured clown. And he was a true star in every respect. Tense and withdrawn before a performance, he was at ease the instant the spotlight fell on him and in absolute command of the audience.

I can see him now, waiting behind the scenes as the white silk handkerchief was laid on the table and tacks driven into each of its four corners to moor it securely. Then, as the darning hoop which was our main ring was set on it, Sebastian would fretfully start to pace up and down, his mouth drawn tight, his eyes far-away, fighting the fears reborn in him at every performance. I knew those signs, and I would give him a little nod—just one small nod—to make clear my confidence in him. And he would respond with a little nod of his own to show that he understood. It was our private ritual, those two almost imperceptible gestures, and it was all that was ever needed to assure another sterling performance from him. That, and the knowledge that the prima ballerina of our company, an enchanting, doe-eyed little flea named Selina, had eyes only for him and would stand worshipping from afar while he held the spotlight. For Selina, I think, was the only one on earth other than myself to whom he gave his unquestioning devotion.

But, alas, what he did not know at the time, and what I did not know—such is the cruel deviousness of the female heart—was that Selina worshipped only at the altar of his success. She loved him not for himself, but for the glory that was his: the laughter and applause of the crowd, the featured billing given him, and the favored place on my forearm at feeding time. She was a great dancer, but like too many of her kind she had no true warmth in her heart. Only a fanatic adoration of success.

Had I known that at the time I would have made a different turning somewhere along the road to disaster which lay ahead. But how could I know, how could anyone know, when Selina dissembled so brilliantly? When she looked at Sebastian with melting eyes she almost turned my head as well as his. She clung to him, comforted him in his times of doubt, let him know in a hundred different ways that he was her hero. And he, befuddled by her airs and graces, was completely her slave.

It was an apparently meaningless episode—meaningless at the time it occurred—that brought on the inexorable crisis. Hercules, our flea who performed feats of strength, had become old and stifflegged, and one night while lifting a grape seed over his head before a hushed and awestruck audience he suddenly fell to the floor in a writhing agony. The veterinarian who diagnosed the case did not mince words. It was a serious rupture, he said grimly, and Hercules would perform no more.

It was shocking beyond measure to me, that news. Not only because of my warm regard for Hercules, but because it left me without one of my featured acts. I instantly gave orders to agents to scour the world, look high and low, pay any price for a flea who could duplicate Hercules' feats, but I did so with a heavy heart. I had already garnered the best there was in the entire world. What chance was there to find a replacement I had not previously considered and found unworthy?

But miracles can and do happen. I had rejected scores of applicants in despair when suddenly a cable arrived from an agent in Bulgaria. The length of the cable alone suggested his state of emotions, and what it said made them even more vivid. By pure chance he had entered a broken-down café in Sofia where the guests were being entertained by a flea circus. Not even a circus. A few acts badly performed by sullen, half-starved fleas. But one flea there—! Nothing would do, save that I come at once and see for myself.

I did not believe him, because I knew he was inordinately

proud of his native fleas who are, at best, temperamental performers; but I went. When a man is desperate he will do anything, even to putting his faith in the potentialities of a Bulgarian flea. So I went. And to paraphrase the saying: I came, I saw, I was conquered.

The flea was named Casimir, and even the unspeakable surroundings in which he performed could not dim his luster. Barrel-chested, bull-necked, glowing with health, and with a frank, open face that gave clear evidence of an honest nature and willing heart, he dwarfed the fleas around him to insignificance. I saw at a glance that I might be looking at a born star. I waited for his performance in a fever of impatience.

At last the motley acts that preceded his were finished, and the café loungers crowded close around the table, I in their forefront. The trainer, a wizened wretch, placed two small wooden blocks on the table, one of which had a series of steps carved into it. Between the blocks I could see a single strand of dark hair—evidently from the trainer's head since it shone greasily in the dim light around me—which was stretched taut from block to block. The trainer then placed Casimir on the table, and before the flea he placed a gleaming pin two inches long which he drew from his lapel.

I could not believe my eyes. To a flea that pin was as a length of railroad track would be to me, yet Casimir stooped low, got a grip on it, and with bulging muscles suddenly lifted it overhead. I gasped, but I had not yet seen the full capabilities of this magnificent creature. Holding the pin overhead he made his way to the steps of the block, climbed them, and then slowly, cautiously, he stepped onto the hair itself. The hair sagged under the weight on it, and Casimir balanced himself with an effort. Then with precise steps, secure as if he were affixed to that hair, he walked its full length, the pin held high overhead throughout and never wavering in his grip. Only when the other block had been reached and the pin laid down could you detect in the convulsive tremors of his body and the heaving of his chest what the strain must have been.

I knew even before the applause started that my search was over. Six hours later, after passionate bargaining and endless rounds of slivovitz, I paid for Casimir's contract more money than anyone on earth would ever have dreamed of paying for a flea. And at that I felt I was fortunate.

I took my prize home with me. I allowed time for him to become accustomed to our American ways; I filled his starved soul with my affection and trust; and only when I was sure that he was accepted by the rest of the company and felt at ease with them did I put him on the stage. That night was his night. When the final curtain fell he was the unchallenged star of the show. It was clear that he, simple, honest, unassuming, would not permit this honor to inflate him; but there was no question about it, he was the star. And Sebastian, the great Punchinello, the unparalleled clown, was in second place.

What were Sebastian's feelings then? What could they have been but anguish at having to yield his place to another. But whatever the torments he suffered, he was a trouper through and through. To him the show was the thing, and if he were asked to sacrifice himself to it, he would do so like a stoic. The quality of his performances remained superb. If anything, they were better than ever. Each time he entered the spotlight he flung himself into his role with an abandon, a virtuosity, far beyond the powers of most fleas.

No, it was not the loss of his commanding place in the company that finally shattered him; it was the loss of his beloved. Selina had seen his glory transferred to Casimir. She watched with narrowed eyes as a new star rose on the horizon. And with cold-blooded deliberation, never heeding the consequences, she turned from the old to worship the new. She had eyes only for Casimir now, comfort only for him, flattery only for him, and he, poor, simpleminded male, accepted this at first incredulously, then eagerly, then with rapture.

That was what destroyed Sebastian. The sight of the couple together transfixed him like a needle. And there was no escaping the sight, no turning away from it. Selina was unabashed in her pursuit, and Casimir nakedly reveled in it. The outsider might have seen this as a stirring romance; to Sebastian it would be an obscenity. Selina was his; what right did some burly stranger have to fondle her before his very eyes? He must have brooded himself into a state of madness over this.

The end came with shocking suddenness. It was during an evening performance, and the show had gone well until Casimir undertook his master feat. The audience leaned forward with bated breath as he lifted the pin over his head. It hummed with excitement as he climbed the block and set forth on his journey across the taut hair which stretched no less than a foot above the table. And it cried out in alarm when, as he reached the middle of the hair, it suddenly parted, and he plummeted to the table, the pin following him and crushing his chest.

I had leaped forward wildly when I saw the hair part, but I was too late. All I could do was remove the oppressive weight of the pin and turn my head away to conceal my tears from the expiring Casimir. He had his own pains to bear; I would spare him mine. But when my misted eyes fell on the broken strand of hair my grief turned to blazing rage. The hair had not worn through; it had been deliberately cut part of the way. I was looking, not at an accident, but at murder!

I knew at once who the murderer was. And I could tell from the shock on Selina's face and the growing comprehension on the face of every flea huddled there that the story was clear to all of them. But before I could wreak vengeance on the criminal my glance fell on Casimir, lying there, breathing his last. He looked at me with lustrous eyes full of pain; he tried to smile—oh, pitiful sight —and with a great effort he shook his head at me. He understood, too, noble soul, and he was telling me that vengeance was not for him. Only pity for the malefactor, and forgiveness. It was his last gesture on earth, and the lesson struck me to my heart. It wiped the thirst for vengeance out of me on the spot. I felt only a great need to find Sebastian, to tell him that I alone was the cause of the sorrows that had befallen us. Obsessed by pride in the show I had put another in his place, had deprived him of his beloved, had driven him at last to insanity and crime.

But when I looked for him I could not find him. Filled with horror at his deed he had fled into the night. And with his disappearance, with Casimir's death, with the company's morale destroyed, there was nothing left. I cancelled my bookings, broke up the company, and set forth with only one thought in mind—to find Sebastian, to face him as a penitent, and to win forgiveness from him.

It has been a weary search. I have walked the lonely streets day and night, combed dog shows and zoological parks, looked every place where a wanderer like Sebastian might take refuge. But all to no avail. I am old and poor now. I must rely on alms from strangers to help me on my way, but I will never give up my search until I am successful in it. There is no other way for me. I am doomed to suffer and search, search and suffer until then.

Beidenbauer's voice ceased and his narrative ended on this plaintive note. We sat together in silence for a long while, contemplating the pigeons burbling on the grass beyond, and then I said, "I have heard tell that the life span of the flea is extremely brief. Is it not likely that by now, in some unmarked grave—?"

"I do not allow myself to think of that," said Beidenbauer with deep feeling. "It would be the final blow."

"Yes," I said, "I can see that it would be."

We sat in silence again, and then with resignation I took a coin from my pocket and offered it to him. He only looked at it reproachfully. I sighed, put the coin away, and offered him a dollar bill. This he took.

"You are kind," he said, getting to his feet. "I am only sorry that you never saw my circus in its glory. You would better understand then how far I have fallen."

"Well," I said, "that's life."

"No, my friend," said Beidenbauer gravely, "that's show business."

Hugh Pentecost

Who Wants To Be a Dead Hero?

*It takes a big man to do a really big job, especially
against ruthless racketeers. Banty Towers was all of five
feet two and 110 pounds, and he had a game leg; but
he had in him the seeds of a big man . . .*

Banty Towers limped toward the far opening on the north side of
Pier X to where he knew the McNab family was gathered. They
couldn't hear his awkward, lurching approach over the noise of
the winches and the Hi-Lo machines and the orderly confusion
attendant upon the discharge of cargo from the *Orient Princess*.
Nor could the McNabs see Banty's approach because the exit to
the stringpiece was hidden behind great stacks of green-striped
coffee bags from Brazil, waiting for the buyers and their trucks.

Michael "Big Mike" McNab sat on one of the bollards on the
stringpiece, holding court. His three sons listened with respect.
Terry "Trigger" McNab stood at the edge of the stringpiece looking
out at the river, busy with tugboats and lighters and the slow approach of the *Queen Elizabeth* being nudged toward her berth a
few blocks north. Oscar "The Ox" McNab, his muscles seeming to
bulge out of his work clothes, leaned against the siding of the pier,
a cigarette dangling from his lips. Louis "The Lawyer" McNab,

squatted at his father's feet like a Hindu idol smiling, always smiling—but listening.

From behind the barricade of coffee bags Banty Towers could now hear Big Mike's deep, Irish-flavored voice.

"Between now and Friday nothing goes off the pier," Big Mike was saying. "We play it open and aboveboard—till Friday." He chuckled. "We even work!"

"And after Friday?" Trigger asked, without looking at his father.

"We call the piper's tune, any way we like," Big Mike said. "But until then it's Sunday school."

"How do you figure the cut?" The Ox asked.

Big Mike's massive, weatherbeaten face wrinkled in a broad grin. "Fifty Gs," he said. "Ten apiece—counting in Gander."

Behind the pile of coffee bags a helpless rage surged through Banty Towers. There was a big take coming up, and as always he would have to stand by, helpless, useless. He kicked savagely at one of the coffee bags with his crippled foot.

The lawyer, squatting on his haunches, pursed his lips. He whistled—a long high note and then a lower note. "The Bantam," he said softly.

Banty heard the whistle and knew he'd given himself away with that angry kick. He felt the cold sweat break out inside his clothes, and it increased his anger. He was afraid, and the fear made him hate himself. He straightened up, all five feet two and one hundred and ten pounds of him. Once he'd been as quick on his feet as a ballet dancer. That was before a case of artificial flowers had toppled out of a sling and fallen on his foot in the hold of a Mitsui Line freighter. Now the foot dragged and thumped.

Still sweating, Banty moved around the stack of coffee bags to the McNabs. He moistened dry lips.

"You guys aren't supposed to be out here," he said.

Big Mike looked at Banty, smiling, and there was a sham amiability in his voice when he spoke.

"Why, it's the little watchman!" he said in mock surprise.

The Lawyer, squatting at his father's feet, chanted softly:

"Georgie Porgie pudding and pie,
Kissed the girls and made them cry . . ."

Despite the clammy sweat on his body, Banty felt the hot, angry flush rising in his cheeks.

"You'll have to get back off the stringpiece," he said.

"In my day," Big Mike said in a conversational tone, "the watchmen didn't take so much on themselves. Enforce the no-smoking rule was about all."

"You better duck that butt, Oscar," Banty said.

The Ox smiled at Banty, sweetly, and enjoyed an extra deep drag on his cigarette.

Banty moistened his lips. "I can't take you on single-handed," he said. "You know that, Mike. So you're getting a breath of air on the stringpiece. It's against the rules, but no one would help me enforce it. It's against the rules to smoke, but unless the dock super saw it with his own eyes he wouldn't back me up. But I'm warning you, Mike. I've been watching and putting the pieces together. I'm warning you!"

Trigger McNab turned slowly, so that his eyes, cold as two newly minted dimes, rested on Banty.

"And what have you put together, little man?" he asked.

"I need to tell you only this," Banty said. "There were cameras missing from that Dutch freighter last week—and cheeses, and more than a case of Holland gin. I'm licensed by the Commission to guard against pilferage. I'm about ready to report where the cameras and the cheeses and the gin got to."

"Who cares about a camera or two, or some cheeses, or a crock or two of Holland gin?" Big Mike asked. "It's been custom and practice for years, Banty. The shipper expects it; the dock super expects it; the stevedore expects it; the insurance company expects it. All the watchmen expect it, Banty—all but you. So who'd listen to you?"

"The Commission!" Banty said, sweating.

"The Commission!" Trigger spat over the edge of the stringpiece. "The working man's friend!"

There was a moment of awful silence. Banty knew he'd struck out with that crack. He'd so desperately wanted to take at least one trick in the game of words.

Then it happened so quickly, and apparently quite by accident.

The Lawyer rose abruptly from his squatting position. In doing so he bumped against Banty. Banty, his balance never secure on his gimpy foot, staggered and fell against The Ox. There was a roar of anger.

"Who you think you're pushin'?"

A huge fist, half open, acting like the swipe of a bear cub, knocked Banty spinning. He fell and his head struck heavily against the bollard on which Big Mike was sitting. An explosion of lights went off before Banty's eyes, and the last thought he remembered was: "Here it is! Into the river!"

When Banty opened his eyes, he lay where he had fallen, and there was the salty taste of blood in his mouth and a terrible ache in his head. The McNabs were gone.

Banty struggled to his feet. He felt dizzy and he steadied himself on the bollard—the iron hitching post for ships. Then he turned and limped back into the pier. He'd bitten into his lower lip when The Ox struck him and the blood ran out of the corner of his mouth.

There was a washroom at the head of the pier and he made for it, unsteadily, to repair the damage. He was fifty yards from it when he heard the whistles—the high note, followed by the low note. It was the ancient signal running the length of the pier meaning "stranger" or "cop."

As he approached the head, Banty saw young "Muddy" Waters, the Commission investigator, on his daily round. That explained the warning whistle. A college-type young man, Muddy Waters. All the Commission investigators were college-type young men these days. Banty had wondered if they were the kind to deal effectively with the McNabs of the waterfront.

"Hey, what happened to you, Banty?" Waters asked cheerfully.

Banty turned his head and saw Tough Tony Minelli, a Hi-Lo driver, standing by the coke machine. Tough Tony made a gesture with his forefinger—a throat-cutting gesture. "Cop! Choke up! Don't talk!"

Banty looked straight at Waters and the habit of years took over. "I tripped on a pineapple crate and hit my head on the edge of a Hi-Lo machine," he said.

"Tough," Waters said. "I'll be on the pier for half an hour. Take the time to get yourself fixed up."

They might laugh at the college boy behind his back, but they'd work while he was there, and even the McNabs wouldn't risk smoking a cigarette while he was on the pier. You had to be registered with the Commission to work on the waterfront, and the college boy could suspend your registration for any infraction at all. A peace officer he was, too, with the power to arrest. But a watchman like Banty, charged with the security of the pier, had no such authority. He was no more than a licensed stool pigeon—*if* he chose to do his job.

Banty went into the washroom and locked the door behind him. He soaked his handkerchief in cold water and held it to his bruised head. He looked at himself in the cloudy mirror.

"You got no guts!" he snarled at himself. "You got no guts at all! Why didn't you tell Waters what you know, what you heard about Friday?"

It was all very well to shout at himself in the glass, but he knew what having guts meant. The guts to die for something. And the next question was, "Die for what?"

When he'd been a water boy on the piers in the early thirties —nine years old—the answer had been the union. There was the Wagner Act, and new locals were springing up. The union would protect the longshoremen from the racketeers, the murderers, the extortionists, the bribe-givers and the bible-takers, the loan sharks, the bookmakers, the numbers boys. The union would end the kick-backs, end the uncertain employment. The union was something to die for. And then who was suddenly heading the union locals? The same racketeers and murderers and extortionists.

You still paid to work. You still kept your mouth shut—or else. You still kept your mouth shut and worked when you could. That was the only safe answer.

Now there was the Commission, set up by the two States of New York and New Jersey, to end all this. Longshoremen were regis-tered, watchmen were licensed, the old shape-up was gone, the kickbacks had been pushed undercover, the bribes were handled more adroitly to confuse the Commission auditors. The big shots were in the shadow—but they were there!

The Commission is your friend, the men were told. But if you talked to them—was it safe? Or would you still wind up in the river with your feet in a barrel of cement? Or beaten up in a doorway and left to die? Time would tell, and who wanted to be a dead hero? Until you knew the Commission wouldn't sell you out, you still had to ask, "Die for what?"

Banty's own personal troubles had begun at a church supper. The McNabs were a great church-going family, and it happened that Banty went to the same church. Banty was a reasonably popular young man with overtones of comedy attached to him because of his size. He was a good man in the hold of a ship. If a crate or a box was jammed, Banty could climb over a pile of cargo like a monkey and pry it loose. He was thirty years old at the time of that church supper, and he wasn't a boy inside, although most of them treated him warmly enough, as if he were still carrying a water bucket like in the old days. But there were hungers in him that hadn't been properly answered because of his size. Women wanted to take him in their laps and muss his hair.

Now at this church supper was a girl Banty had never seen before—a girl with red hair, skillfully applied make-up, and a rounded body that seemed somehow to be constantly writhing. She was no waterfront housewife. No ring on her finger—so she seemed unattached.

After the supper there was a showing of a film taken by Father Cain on a trip to Ireland he'd made the previous summer. To Banty's surprise when the lights were lowered for the film, the red-haired girl sat next to him on a folding chair. She smelled wonderful. All at once Banty's nerves were like supercharged electric wires. The girl's warm hand had moved over to cover his. He didn't dare turn his head. Then he felt her knee against his and he began to tremble all over. Then he heard a soft whisper in his ear.

"Should we go out in the kitchen for a cup of coffee?"

There'd be no one in the kitchen.

Her hand tightened in his and they slipped out of the darkened room, the sound of their movement covered by the hearty voice of Father Cain describing the film as it unwound. And then they were in the kitchen, garish in the light of a single naked bulb.

There were no words. She was suddenly all over him, her arms around him, her lips pressed against his. A great surge of excitement swept through Banty—something he'd never felt before. This was a woman behaving toward him as if he were a man—a real man. His arms closed round her.

And then suddenly she wrenched free of him, screaming. She hit him viciously across the mouth with the back of her hand. Her enameled fingernails tore at his cheek.

"You dirty little—little rooster!" she shouted at him.

Banty staggered away from her, dazed and shaken. And there in the doorway, smiling, always smiling, was Louis The Lawyer.

"This bum make a pass at you, Sis?" he asked softly.

Sis! The sister of Louis and Oscar and Terry McNab—the daughter of Big Mike!

"The dirty little wolf! He tried to paw me!" Miss McNab cried out.

The scream had brought others, and suddenly the room was dark with McNabs. It was The Ox who reached him first. A blow on the side of the head sent Banty reeling into the arms of Trigger. A knee in the groin sent Banty stumbling and screaming with pain into the arms of Big Mike. Like a bean bag they kicked and punched him around the room. Through the red fog of agony Banty heard The Lawyer chanting:

"Georgie Porgie pudding and pie,
Kissed the girls and made them cry . . ."

This beating could have gone on until he was dead of it. But as he was hurled against the wall right by the door, Banty dived through and ran—doubled over with pain, screams of laughter ringing in his ear, and the Lawyer's voice calling after him: "Georgie Porgie ran away!"

It was the next day that disaster overtook Banty. Working in the hold of a Mitsui Line freighter, his body still aching from the McNabs' beating, he wasn't himself. He wasn't thinking about the job. He was thinking about Miss McNab. She'd asked for it, hadn't she? She'd initiated it, hadn't she? And then when he'd been caught at it by The Lawyer she'd been too frightened of her brothers to speak up for Banty.

The crate of artificial flowers from Japan fell on Banty's foot as he thought of Miss McNab.

That was the end of Banty as a longshoreman. He couldn't walk right, even after months in the free ward of the hospital. He might have looked elsewhere for work, but the waterfront was all he knew. Somehow, when you've been brought up there, you don't leave it. He applied to the Commission for a license as Port Watchman. Most watchmen were older men, no longer able to do their accustomed work. Banty was in the same boat with them, and the Commission granted his license.

He got a job on Pier Y, and a week later he began to see what was in store for him. The McNabs came to work on that pier. Big Mike was a checker, The Ox was a dock man on the hatch gang, and Trigger was a cooper. Banty saw how the McNabs worked. A crate containing something valuable—say, watches or cameras or silks or liquor—would be swung out of the hold to the dock. Somehow The Ox would manage to drop the crate and break it open. He'd call for a cooper to mend it. The cooper would be Trigger. The checker, on hand to see that all was properly handled, would be Big Mike. Trigger would mend the crate—but not before some of its contents had been deftly removed.

Banty watched this for several days and then he reported what he knew to Waters, the Commission investigator.

It was The Lawyer who opened Banty's eyes to the future. The Lawyer protested to the investigator in outraged tones.

"This little punk tried to attack my sister," he said, apparently shocked at the memory. "My brothers and I—and my father— gave him a good hiding for it. Naturally, he's out to get us—"

"Better keep your personal life out of your job, Banty," Waters had advised.

They would cry "he attacked my sister" and use him forever, Banty saw. He could stop a McNab at the head of the pier with some pilfered object under his coat. The McNab would be suspended from the longshoreman's register for a short time—and Banty would be beaten to a pulp in some back alley by an "unknown assailant"—named McNab.

Banty got a transfer to Pier X. A week later the McNabs were working there, pulling the same old game, the same triple play.

"Cooper!" The Ox's voice would shout, and there would be Trigger with his hammer and his other tolls, and Big Mike to check, and another bit of cargo was gone—to be paid for by the insurance company. These days there was a fourth member of this thieving gang, one Frank Gander, naturally called "Goosie," who seemed to be in on the systematic pilferage . . .

Muddy Waters was waiting outside the washroom when Banty came out.

"Feeling better?" he asked.

"Yeah. Thanks."

Waters looked at the lump on Banty's forehead and the swollen lower lip. "Pineapple crate, eh?"

"Yeah," Banty said.

Waters smiled, but his eyes were very bright. "Everything else going okay?"

Banty looked down the crowded tunnel of the pier. A $50,000 haul coming up Friday! If he opened his mouth, the cry wouldn't be "he attacked my sister." There'd be no cry at all—only a quiet killing. Banty echoed his own question: "Die for what?" Let the Commission fight its own battles, he thought.

"Everything okay," Banty said.

About nine o'clock that night Banty lay on the bed in his room at Mrs. O'Loughlin's. His landlady was a widow who supported herself and her three kids by boarding Banty and three other longshoremen and by taking in laundry.

Deep anger had been seething in Banty all day. It had been one thing when he was working in the hold: you could do your job and take your pay; you could even steal a little if you wanted to. Or you could play it straight—so long as you didn't talk. But Banty's foot had made him a watchman, and he was supposed to talk. He was paid to talk. Only he couldn't if he wanted to survive. It made the juices bitter inside him.

The phone in the hall outside Banty's room shrilled loudly. He knew Mrs. O'Loughlin was working in the laundry in the basement, so he went out to answer it.

"Hello?"

"Mr. Georgie Porgie Towers, watchman on Pier X?"

The small hairs rose on the back of Banty's neck. He'd know that voice anywhere. The Lawyer!

"Yes."

"If it wasn't for my persuasiveness, Georgie Porgie, you'd be floating down the river just about now. So listen good, sucker. Stay away from the pier and keep your mouth shut till after Friday, or you will be in the river with your feet wrapped in cement."

Banty tried to speak, but the black bile of anger choked him. Making sure, they were. He was being told he couldn't work, couldn't take his pay. He was being told they controlled his right to eat, his right to do his job.

"Got it, Porgie?" the soft sinister voice asked. "We'll be watching you, little man, day and night—just to make sure."

Click! The receiver was hung up at the other end.

Banty turned back toward his room, shaking from head to foot. This was it! He had no choice left. They weren't going to let him decide whether he would or wouldn't do his job. They were deciding that for him. He pounded his fist against the door jamb of his room.

"No! No! *No!*

Keep your mouth shut because you chose to—yes! Keep your mouth shut because it was the ancient code—yes! But keep your mouth shut because some murdering hoodlums meant to steal the port blind and make you an accomplice in it—*no!*

He went into his room and walked over to the window, his teeth chattering. He didn't want to die. Most of all, he didn't want to wait for it, wondering when and how.

And then he froze, staring across the street. In the doorway of an old warehouse he saw the figure of a man, the red end of a cigarette glowing in the darkness. The pulsing neon sign on Garrity's saloon down the block made the man's hiding place alternately dark and light. The man was Goosie Gander, the McNabs' stocky confederate. They *were* watching him!

Sweat beaded Banty's forehead as he turned away from the window. "All right," he muttered between his chattering teeth. "All *right!*"

He rummaged in the drawer of his bureau until he found a little black notebook. Then he sat down at the table with the notebook and a pad of paper. He began to write with a kind of frenzied haste, referring from time to time to the black book. After he'd covered several sheets of paper he read them over, folded them, and put them in an envelope which he sealed. He wrote the full address in a bold hand.

Mr. Daniel Gebhardt
Chief of the Division of Investigation
Waterfront Commission . . .

He put the letter in his pocket and walked over to the window, humming tunelessly. Gander was still in the warehouse doorway across the street.

Banty looked around the dingy little room. It had been his home for a long time. Not much to leave behind, he thought. He clumped along the narrow hallway to the front door and went out onto the concrete steps. Instantly he saw movement across the street. The red end of a cigarette arched into the gutter.

It was only about ten yards to the mail box on the corner. Gander would have to be a Jessie Owens to reach it before Banty did, game leg and all. He struck out as fast as his awkward gait would allow. He saw Gander move quickly, but not quickly enough.

Banty reached the mail box, dropped in his report. He let the handle swing back with a metallic clang. Then he turned and walked east, without looking back.

It was only a block to his destination. He walked up the front steps of an old brick house and rang the doorbell. He heard a sharp voice call out behind him.

"Banty!" It was Gander, running toward him.

The door of the house opened and Trigger McNab stood there,

his pale eyes narrowed, his right hand in the pocket of his work jacket.

"Well, well, well," he said softly.

Banty, his fists clenched so tightly they ached, said, "I've just mailed a complete report of all I know to Gebhardt at the Commission—all I know about the past, and what I know about Friday. Now I came to get it over with."

"You damn little fool!" Gander said from behind him. He was breathing hard from running.

"Check?" Trigger asked, looking over the top of Banty's head at Gander.

"He mailed something," Gander said.

Trigger pulled Banty into the house and gave him a push that sent him staggering along a dark hallway into a room where Big Mike and The Ox and The Lawyer sat around a table drinking beer.

"A visitor," Trigger said in a savage voice. "He claims he's mailed a report to Gebhardt—including what he heard us say about Friday."

"I came to get it over with," Banty said to Big Mike. "You'll kill me for this, and there's no point in my waiting!"

The Ox stood up and his chair fell over backward.

"A big hero!" Big Mike said softly.

"Somebody's got to have the guts to fight for the Commission," Banty said. "They're our only chance for a decent life. So I elected myself."

"The Commission!" Trigger exploded. "You crazy jerk! They got their price, just like anyone else."

"Not the Commission!" Banty yelled. "I feel good for about the first time in my life, Mike. Somebody's gotta fight you guys, no matter what!"

"So he wants us to get it over with!" The Ox said. "So let's get it over with!" He took a big step toward Banty and his enormous hand came down on Banty's shoulder, staggering the little man to his knees.

"Hold it!" Gander said sharply. "There may be a way out of this yet. Gebhardt won't get that letter till the first mail—maybe about nine thirty in the morning. If Banty was there at eight o'clock, say, when the office opens, and told Gebhardt it was all a fake— he was just trying to pin something on you guys because he hates you so—"

"Not a chance," Banty said, wiping the sweat out of his eyes with the back of his hand. "You drove me to it, you McNabs, and I'm not backing down."

Gander smiled faintly. "Maybe you will back down by morning, Banty. Maybe, after you think about it all night, you'll decide it's not so sweet and noble to die. Maybe, after you've sweated a little—"

The Ox drew back his hand, an angry grumble in his throat.

"No marks on him," Gander said. "Gebhardt might not believe him if he was marked up. Just let him sweat out the night. Living looks better by daylight. He's all screwed up to be a hero now. Maybe by morning—"

"Get him out of here," Big Mike said. "And Banty! You be in Commission office by eight o'clock if you don't want to die slow."

Banty's legs shook under him. The wave of courage was begin- ning to leave him. "I'll be waiting for you in my room," he said, trying to keep his voice steady.

The Ox threw him out.

Banty walked unsteadily to Garrity's saloon, where he ordered a double shot. Gander, the slick hood! He knew what waiting would mean. He knew Banty would think of changing his mind a thousand times in the next few hours. But he wouldn't. *He wouldn't!*

After the second double shot Banty left Garrity's and headed back toward the room he thought he'd left forever. A car drove past him and then pulled up at the far corner on the opposite side of the street. Banty recognized that car with a surge of relief. It was the blue sedan that Muddy Waters drove on his daily rounds.

Banty quickened his pace. The neon sign showed him Waters behind the wheel, lighting a cigarette. Banty hurried. He'd go to Waters and tell him the whole story before the poison of waiting worked on him.

He was half a block from Waters in his parked car when another figure came around the corner opposite him. Gander! Gander walked straight up to the car and spoke to Waters. The car door opened and Gander got in.

Banty stopped where he was, trying to suck in air.

Gander and Waters!

They sat there in the car, chatting together like old friends. Waters held his lighter for Gander's cigarette. Banty turned toward the wall of the building and buried his face in the crook of his arm. *"They got their price, just like anyone else!"* Trigger had said.

Bitter salty tears ran down Banty's cheeks. He thought he'd found the answer to the question: "Die for what?"—and here was the same rotten disease that had eaten away at the harbor for a hundred years.

After about ten minutes Gander got out of the car. Banty saw Waters give him a friendly pat on the shoulder before he drove away. Gander disappeared around the far corner without seeing Banty.

It was a long night, during which Banty lay on his bed, arms locked behind his head, staring up at the ceiling. At a quarter past seven he got up, doused his face with cold water, brushed his hair, and went out onto the street. Standing quite openly in the warehouse doorway was The Ox. He smiled when he saw Banty, a sly, relieved smile. Banty smiled back at him and shrugged, as much as to say, "Gander was right."

Downtown on Park Row, just outside the building that housed the Commission's offices, Banty saw Trigger a few yards away studying the merchandise in a hardware store window. The Trigger turned, looked straight at Banty, and smiled. Banty could feel his amused contempt.

It might be hard to get in to see Gebhardt, he thought. But when he gave his name to the cop on duty in the reception booth, he was waved to an unmarked office at the end of the hall.

Banty opened the door and went in. A white-haired man with a lined, weary face and bright dark eyes sat behind a big desk.

"Mr. Gebhardt?" Banty asked, moistening his lips.

"Yes."

"My name is Banty Towers, sir."

"Hello, Banty, I—"

Banty only half heard, and the words flowed out of him. "I wrote you a letter last night, Mr. Gebhardt, but I don't think you're going to get it. In it I reported the pilferage that's been going on at Pier X, and a big deal that's coming up Friday, engineered by the McNabs and a man named Gander. After I mailed it to you I went to the McNabs and told 'em to do their worst. I was fighting on your side, I told 'em, and I wasn't scared to die in the fight. They laughed at me. They said the Commission had its price like anyone else. I knew it wasn't so—for about ten minutes!"

"Banty, listen—"

"Your man Waters—he's up to here in it! I saw him with my own eyes, friendly and palsy-walsy with Gander. He'll see you don't get the letter. He'll see I get what's coming to me. But you got to know before he gets me, or the McNabs get me—"

"Shut up!" Gebhardt said sharply. He'd been ringing a bell on his desk while Banty was talking. Now the door opened. Two men came in. One of them was Waters. The other was Gander.

Hot tears welled up into Banty's eyes, but he was laughing—a hysterical, high-pitched laugh. "They were right!" he cried. "All of you in it! Even you, Gebhardt. Crooked, lousy, graft-taking— Well, I told the McNabs—get it over with, I told them. I say the same to you, Mr. Crooked Gebhardt—get it over with!" He was breathing hard when he finished.

Gebhardt spoke quietly. "You know this man as Goosie Gander, Banty. His real name is Frank Taylor. He's one of my best undercover men."

Gander, or Taylor, grinned at Banty. "You're a gutsy little guy, Banty," he said. "I didn't think I'd ever get you away from the McNabs last night without their working you over."

Gebhardt's office began to spin slowly around Banty, but he could hear the Chief Investigator's voice clearly. It was gentle and penetrating.

"We've had to pass by your reports, Banty, had to laugh you off a little because of the big deal coming up Friday. So you'll

go back to work on the pier this morning, and you'll let the Mc-
Nabs know you retracted what you wrote in the letter, and that
I believe it and let you off with a reprimand. You'll take the
kidding and maybe even a little pushing around. Nothing serious
will happen to you, because Taylor here will be watching you
every minute. On Friday they'll be discharging cargo from the
Liebestadt. We know from our contacts abroad there'll be a special
case of tweeds from Scotland. It'll get into Oscar McNab's hands
because it's specially marked, and he'll drop it like always and
yell for a cooper to mend it. It'll be Trigger who'll come, and Big
Mike to check. Taylor here will be helping Oscar. There'll be a
small package passed from the crate into someone's pocket. You'll
see it happen, Banty, and so will Taylor. And then we make the
pinch. About a hundred and fifty thousand dollars worth of heroin.
We hope to find it in Trigger's pocket, because we want him out of
the way most of all. But they'll all go up for a long stretch, thanks
to your reports confirming Taylor's testimony."

"Heroin!" Banty whispered. "So that was it!"

"A long stretch," Gebhardt said. "After the brush you had with
the McNabs yesterday morning they wanted you off the pier till
after Friday. They were afraid of your honesty, Banty."

"You knew about that?" Banty asked.

Waters laughed. "Pineapple crate my foot!" he said. He laughed
again. "College boys aren't as dumb as they look, Banty." He
yawned. "I'm for a little shut-eye, Chief. We watched Banty's
place all night, just in case he did what he said and waited there
for the McNabs."

Gebhardt looked straight at Banty with those bright black eyes.
"This isn't always a gratifying job, Banty. You've got no idea how
badly we need people like you on the waterfront—people who believe in us and who will fight for what we stand for. I'm sorry
you had to lose your trust in us, even for a night."

It was crazy, but Banty felt the sting of tears in his eyes. "Don't
worry about that, Mr. Gebhardt. I feel great," he said. "Just
great!"

Evan Hunter

Easy Money

The author of THE BLACKBOARD JUNGLE *and*
STRANGERS WHEN WE MEET *gives us a highly charged
story of one of the dirtiest of con games—a filthy racket
that the men of the 87th Precinct would have loved to
crack down on with all their might* . . .

Jeffrey Talbot knocked on the door and waited. He stared at the metal numerals stuck to the wood, noticing that one of the screws was missing in the numeral 2. Inside, he heard a faint rustling.

He knocked again.

"Just a minute," the voice came, muffled, low.

He straightened his tie, putting the heavy valise on the floor near the door. Briefly, he went over the pitch in his mind. He looked at the name written on the slip of paper he held in his hand: O'Connor.

He smiled and put the slip of paper back into his jacket pocket. Why didn't she hurry? Or he? Or whoever was rustling around inside?

Patience, Mr. Matthews had said. A little patience goes a long way. Just remember that these people want what you have to offer. It's your job to give it to them. Be patient. But make the sale.

The door opened a crack, and Jeff edged his toe slightly forward, ready to jam into the opening should the door begin to close. Just the way Mr. Matthews had showed him.

"Yes?"

The woman was small and old—at least, she looked old. He sensed immediately that she wasn't really as shrunken as she appeared. If only she would pull back her shoulders and stand erect; if only there wasn't that tired, pained expression in her eyes; if only her mouth would . . .

"Yes?" she asked again, her blue eyes widening slightly.

Now the pitch. Once the door is open the rest is easy, Mr. Matthews said. Just get the door open, that's the big thing.

"How do you do, Mrs. O'Connor?" he said, touching his hand to the brim of his hat.

The woman looked slightly puzzled. A thin network of frowns, spidery, lacelike, etched its way across her forehead.

"I'm from the Home Bible Company," he announced, a pleasant smile on his face.

"Oh?" the woman said.

He sensed her confusion, sensed it sweeping into the hallway, almost overpowering him. There was the smell of panic, and he remembered the smell and tried to put it out of his mind. Why on earth didn't she stand up straight?

"May I come in?" he asked.

"Well, I . . ." she hesitated.

He smiled tenderly, his eyes pleading with hers, the way Mr. Matthews had showed him. Mr. Matthews was smart, all right.

"Well," she said, clutching her housedress at the neck, her thin hand working nervously at the collar, "I suppose it would be all right." She opened the door wider and then added hastily, "I really can't afford . . ."

Jeff stepped through the door into a living-room. The shades were drawn and the room was dim.

"What a pleasant room," he said.

Mrs. O'Connor walked rapidly to a battered green couch, its upholstery worn and faded. She fluffed a cushion and said, "It's really a mess. I haven't felt too much like cleaning since . . ."

"Nonsense," Jeff lied. "It's spic and span."

He was beginning to feel it. He was doing all right. His first approach, and he was doing all right. Now was the time to move in.

He sat down on the couch while Mrs. O'Connor went to the windows and lifted the shades. The couch was hard. He could feel the springs when he sat down.

He glanced briefly around the room. A radio set stood in the corner. It was an old-fashioned set, with a cabinet that had sliding doors. Both doors were closed, as if the radio hadn't been played for a long while. On top of the radio a photograph in a leather frame smiled across at Jeff.

The man in the photograph had white hair and a broad grin. His jaw was solid, like a square slab of marble. His eyes held a gay twinkle under the shaggy white brows.

"Now," Jeff began, turning away from the picture.

"I do hope you're not going to sell me anything," Mrs. O'Connor said, and Jeff noticed the faint Irish brogue for the first time, like a charming splash of green on her tongue. He wished again that she would straighten her shoulders, perhaps smile out of her tired blue eyes. "I haven't any money to spare."

Jeff opened the suitcase and took out the Bible. He held it on the palm of his hand, the way Matthews told him to, the gold letters facing Mrs. O'Connor.

The Holy Bible.

He paused a moment for effect. The Bible was black, bound in handsome leather, the gold lettering done in Old English stamped deep into the cover.

"It's very nice," Mrs. O'Connor said, "but I don't think I need . . ."

Jeff flipped open the cover quickly and showed Mrs. O'Connor the flyleaf.

There, in attractive script, carefully hand-lettered on the heavy paper was the name: *John O'Connor.*

Mrs. O'Connor's mouth rounded into a little "O," but no sound escaped her lips. Her hand went to her throat, and he watched it flutter there in panic. She gasped, then passed her hand over her eyes, as if clearing away a dreadful vision.

"It's beautiful, isn't it?" he said in awed tones.

Mrs. O'Connor shook her head meaninglessly, and then she nodded.

"Your husband ordered it," Jeff said. That was what Mr. Matthews said would always clinch it.

"My husband," she whispered. There was no expression in her voice. A mist had risen to her eyes, moistening the blue, lending an artificial sparkle where there was none.

"Yes," Jeff also whispered. "Before he died."

It was almost as if he'd told her for the first time that her husband was dead. She jerked back involuntarily, the thin hands completely out of control now, the tears springing to her eyes.

"John," she said, her voice breaking, the sobs overwhelming her.

"There, there," Jeff said. He rose and put his arm around her quaking shoulders. "There, now. There." He felt rather foolish—felt, too, that he was watching a stranger go through the routine, almost as though he were watching Mr. Matthews when he'd gone through the same act with the Italian woman.

"There," he consoled.

She drew away from him. "I'm . . . sorry. It's difficult to . . . get used to."

The Bible. Never let them forget the Bible.

"He wanted this," Jeff said, placing the Bible on the couch. "He ordered it. Before he died."

He watched her eyes again, waiting for the tears. But there were none this time. Instead, she touched the Bible with reverent fingers, almost caressing it.

"Thank you," she said. "Thank you so much for bringing it."

He cleared his throat uncomfortably.

"Only ten dollars," he said.

She didn't understand. He hadn't said it correctly. He hadn't said it the way Mr. Matthews taught him, the way Mr. Matthews had said it to the Italian woman.

"John saved," she said, misunderstanding. "He probably saved."

In a quiet voice Jeff said, "It isn't paid for yet, Mrs. O'Connor."

He felt momentary panic, and then guilt. He struggled against the feelings and deliberately put them down. This was easy money.

The Bible was worth ten dollars any day of the week. And he got five out of every ten. Easy money.

Mrs. O'Connor touched the Bible once more, lovingly. "Ten dollars," she crooned.

"There's no obligation, of course," he said, reaching for the book. "That is, if you don't want it, we couldn't possibly . . ."

"Oh, I'll take it," she protested. "He ordered it. It was what he wanted."

"Well, yes, but if . . ."

"No, no, I'll pay for it." She paused. "Only, well, you see I haven't that much just now."

"You can pay it in four weekly payments, if you like. Two fifty each time."

"Yes," she said, as though he had just offered her salvation. "Oh, yes!"

He busied himself with his order pad, writing her name and address. He checked a box marked "Installment."

"That'll be two fifty," he said.

She walked into the next room, and he heard the protesting squeak of a drawer, the faint click of a purse being opened. He heard the jingle of coins. Then silence.

He waited.

Another drawer squeaked open, and he heard the rustle of clothing, then a tin can being pried open. The drawer shuffled shut, and Mrs. O'Connor returned.

"Here," she said, and she reached for the Bible.

He took the money in his left hand and casually covered the book with his right.

Then he slipped the money into his pocket and picked up the book. She stared at him, the fear working its way into her eyes again. He saw what was mirrored there, and turned away.

"I'll be back next week," he said pleasantly. He gave her the receipt. "I'd like to leave the book, but you understand, Mrs. O'Connor. So many people have . . . well, no scruples. We're forced to take precautions, you know."

"Yes," she said, disappointment in her voice and in her eyes.

"I'll see you next week," Jeff said putting the Bible back in the suitcase.

She held the door open for him, and as he started down the stairs he heard it close like a whimper behind him.

The following Monday, after a week of selling, he sat in the big leather chair in the reception room, waiting to see Mr. Matthews. The receptionist was working on a crossword puzzle, her legs crossed, one shoe swinging back and forth, back and forth.

It's a job, Jeff thought. It's a better job than any I've ever had. It pays well. It's a job.

And then, abruptly, he thought, "But I'd quit if I were half a man."

His own thought startled him, and he glanced up nervously, almost expecting the receptionist to be watching him. She was still busy with the puzzle, her pencil stuck thoughtfully between her lips.

"How much longer?" he asked, twisting in the chair.

"Keep your shirt on," she said. Her voice had a twang in it. He didn't like her voice. She glanced up at the clock.

"Jeepers," she said, "time for lunch." She got up quickly, perching a little hat atop her head. "Be a dear and take any calls, will you?" she said over her shoulder.

I should have said no, he thought after she was gone. That's her job, not mine. My job is selling Bibles. Easy money. The easy way out.

Well, so what? he asked himself. If I don't take these suckers, somebody else will. So it's the easy way, the coward's way.

The word burned in his mind.

Coward.

It was funny the way a man could forget. Or did he really forget? Somewhere, deep in the folds of memory, the picture would always persist, dimly sometimes, but it was always there, always quick to flare up.

A sudden cold sweat broke out over his upper lip. He fumbled for his handkerchief and wiped the sweat away. But he couldn't wipe away the picture in his mind. He looked at the reception desk, at the clock ticking on the far wall, at Mr. Matthews' closed door.

The picture was still there . . .

"Jeff!" MacC. was yelling, "Jeff, you can't stay here. They're raking the beach."

A sprinkle of slugs playfully kicked up sand three feet before their eyes.

"Leave me alone!" Jeff shouted.

The machine gun began probing in earnest, the sand rising in angry spurts around them. MacC. dropped his gun in the sand and stood up, his tall form towering over the protection of the dune. He rolled Jeff over, struggling for a firmer grip. Jeff stared up into his face, watched the sweat there, the strain.

And then, magically, he watched in fascination as the dust spouted on MacC.'s blouse. Just little spurts of dust—ping, ping, ping, right across his chest. And right behind the dust the red blossomed, spreading from the little holes like flowers opening in the morning.

MacC.'s mouth opened. He looked at Jeff with accusing eyes that suddenly rolled and went lifeless.

The machine gun kept chattering ceaselessly just beyond the dune . . .

"Well, Jeff!" It was Matthews' voice. "Sorry to keep you waiting. Come in, come in."

Jeff mopped his face with the handkerchief, gripped Matthews' hand and pumped it vigorously.

In the office Jeff sat next to Matthews' desk.

"Eighteen sales in one week," Matthews said. "Good work, my boy!"

"Thanks," Jeff said. He was thinking again of the fear in Mrs. O'Connor's eyes. He shrugged the thought away and tried to concentrate on what Matthews was saying.

"And this is only the beginning, Jeff, only the beginning. You'll be lighting your cigarettes with dollar bills soon."

He chuckled, the fat on his jowls wiggling.

Suddenly he became very businesslike. "You understand, of course, that it's to your advantage to get all the money the first time."

"It's not easy," Jeff said. Again he heard Mrs. O'Connor rummaging through her dresser, looking for two dollars and fifty cents.

"Of course not," Matthews agreed smoothly. He was puffing a cigar, the band still on it. The gold of the cigar band rested against the gold of the signet ring on his finger. A ring on a cigar, a ring on a fat finger.

"You should play up the leaving a little more," Matthews suggested. "Make them feel that if they don't give you the whole ten right then and there, it's all off. Get me?"

"I'd lose the sale that way," Jeff argued.

"Possibly. But a lot of these people are holding out on you. They've got the sawbuck, but they just don't want to part with it."

Did Mrs. O'Connor have the sawbuck?

"Well, I'll try," Jeff mumbled uncomfortably.

"I know you will," Matthews said, a grin flashing across his fleshy features.

The next day Jeff got five new customers. And then he went to collect the second installment from Mrs. O'Connor.

He stood in the narrow hallway, the same feeling of oppression bearing down on him. Across the hall, behind a closed door marked 2F, angry voices shouted at each other. Jeff knocked again, and the door next to Mrs. O'Connor's opened.

"She ain't in," the boy said. He had rumpled blond hair and a nose spattered with freckles.

Jeff smiled and asked, "Do you know when she'll be back?"

"Nope."

"Did she leave any messages?"

"Nope."

Jeff stroked his chin thoughtfully. "Have you got any idea where she went?"

"Sure."

"Well, where?"

The smell of boiling cabbage drifted up the stairwell.

"To work," the boy said, and he started to close the door.

Jeff's foot darted out and jammed itself in the crack.

"Where does she work, sonny?" he asked.

"Next door. She helps the landlady. Mrs. Canning."

"Thanks," Jeff said.

"That's all right," the boy answered.

Jeff started down the stairs, the cabbage smell growing stronger when he reached the ground floor. He walked into the street hastily and looked to either side of the tenement. A small grocery store, its windows packed with fat, round salamis and colorful beer ads, was on the left, and another tenement on the right. He walked to the latter and climbed the steps, past a woman sitting on the stoop rocking a baby carriage.

He glanced at the doorbells and rang the one marked "Superintendent."

"You looking for Mrs. Canning?" the woman with the carriage asked.

"Indirectly," Jeff said. "I'm really looking for Mrs. O'Connor."

"Mary O'Connor?" the woman asked.

"Yes," Jeff said, almost astonished that Mrs. O'Connor had a first name, even though he had written it on the receipt.

"You'll find her on the third floor."

"Thanks."

The baby in the carriage began to cry as he walked into the dark interior and started up the stairs. The building was pretty much like the one he'd just left: the stairway was narrow, the banister wobbly, the walls full of cracks, and here and there huge chunks of plaster had fallen down leaving large gray holes in the ceiling. Assorted smells of crowded living reached out to embrace him as he winced slightly and climbed the badly lit stairs.

On the third floor he found Mary O'Connor.

She was on her hands and knees. Her hair was stuck to her forehead. She dipped her brush into the bucket and sloshed water onto the floor.

Wearily, she bent over her work. Jeff watched her, embarrassed, and then he cleared his throat.

Mary O'Connor looked up, and puzzlement crossed her face.

Then her eyes grew large, and Jeff thought she was going to cry. Instead, she smiled eagerly, scrambled to her feet, and began drying her hands on her apron.

"Hello," she said, "I've been waiting for you."

"Hello," Jeff said. "I had quite a time finding you."

"I took a job," she said. "I . . ." She seemed to debate telling him more than she had to. "I took a job."

"That's nice," Jeff said.

" 'Tisn't much," she explained, "but it helps. John, he didn't leave much. I mean, not that it was his fault."

"Of course not," Jeff agreed. He reached into his pocket for his receipt pad.

"Five dollars a day, Mrs. Canning gives me," Mary O'Connor said.

Jeff's fingers fumbled with the pad. Five dollars a day!

She reached into the pocket of her apron and pulled out two crumpled dollar bills and two quarters.

"Here it is," she said, "just the way you said."

Jeff took the money, still thinking of her salary. Quickly he made the entry on his pad and handed her a receipt.

"Thank you," he mumbled.

Mrs. O'Connor smiled weakly. "You'll be sure to be back next week?"

"Yes. Of course."

"And then there'll be just one more week until I get the Bible."

"Yes."

She smiled in satisfaction, got down on her knees again, and dipped the brush into the water.

Jeff left her that way—on her hands and knees over a wet floor. He walked down the three flights of stairs, not looking back. He couldn't chase a persistent thought out of his head.

Mrs. O'Connor scrubbed floors for a full day to get five dollars. To earn the same amount all he had to do was sell her a Bible that her husband never ordered.

That week his new sales went up to twenty-three.

Once—just once—he thought of quitting. And then he thought

of the money again. It was too easy. He'd been a shoe clerk for a time, holding sweaty feet in his hands, flattering customers, cursing them when they were gone. And once he worked in an office, and the boss would come out every ten minutes, look over his desk, clear his throat, and go back into the office again. And then the restaurant job, washing dishes, and the stock clerk job, and driving the truck, and the countless other jobs since the Army.

No, it was too much. He was tired of sweating, tired of being afraid. He was going to take it easy now. He was going to light his cigarettes with dollar bills . . .

Matthews was in rare form that Wednesday.

"How do you like the job?" he asked.

"Fine," Jeff said in a low voice.

"One hundred and fifteen dollars in a single week! That's mighty nice money, boy, mighty nice money."

"Is it?" Jeff asked.

"I'll say it is," Matthews assured him. "And this is only the beginning, boy, only the beginning. Wait'll I tell you the latest wrinkle."

Jeff sat in the leather chair beside Matthews' desk.

"Yes, my boy, a new wrinkle. The obituaries in the morning papers are fine, and we'll still use them, of course. People are dying every day, you know." He chuckled noisily.

Jeff knew someone who had died—on a slug-spattered beach.

Matthews puffed on his cigar, warming up to his news.

"I guarantee a hundred sales a week, Jeff. With this new wrinkle there'll be no more duds. These people will think you're doing them a favor, a big favor."

Suddenly Jeff didn't want to hear Matthews' new scheme. He wanted to be left alone. He didn't want any more pep talks. He'd heard a pep talk once, a pep talk punctuated with machine-gun bursts. He'd quit then, and he was quitting now, but he didn't want to be told about it.

He was nothing but a con man—a swindler and cheat playing on sympathy and respect for the dead.

"The casualty lists," Matthews announced proudly. "More and

more are being released every day. The War Department is really just catching up with itself."

Casualty lists. Somewhere in the back of Jeff's mind staccato chattering began. Casualty lists.

"Killed in action," Matthews said. "As soon as the names are released we snatch them up—and bingo!"

Ping, ping, ping, right across his chest. Little spurts of dust.

"Your son ordered this, ma'am, asking us to collect for it over here." Matthews grinned and winked at Jeff.

Jeff gripped the sides of his chair, his knuckles white.

"What?" Matthews continued in mock surprise. "Your son was killed in action? Oh, I'm terribly sorry, I had no idea. Then we spring the Bible with the kid's name in it and . . ."

Matthews stopped suddenly.

"What's the matter, boy?"

Jeff reached out and grabbed Matthews by the lapels of his coat.

"You filthy pig," he snarled. "Your dirty filthy pig. Casualty lists!"

With sudden fury he threw his fist into Matthews' jaw, staggering him backward, smashing him into the desk, knocking his box of expensive cigars to the floor.

"Just a minute, boy," Matthews squealed, his hands out in front of him. "Just a minute now, Jeff."

Jeff's eyes blazed. His hands ripped at the lapels again, and he lifted Matthews and threw him against the wall.

"I quit, you stinking scum! I quit, do you hear? I'm through, finished! I've stopped doing your filthy work, do you understand?"

Jeff was shouting now. He threw open the black suitcase and began searching among the books, finally coming on what he wanted. He stood up then and faced Matthews who was crouching in the far corner of the room.

"Expect the police," he said simply. Then he left.

He felt a little happier as he gave the boy the envelope with the five dollars, and the Bible. The note said, "A mistake has been made, Mrs. O'Connor. This Bible was already paid for. A long time ago."

Perhaps he was still a coward. A more courageous man would have gone up to face Mary O'Connor personally. But when he saw the boy disappear into the building, he felt a lot happier.

Happier than he'd felt in a long time.

Margery Allingham

Family Affair

What happened at 29 Chestnut Grove was a remarkable parallel to the famous old "Mary Celeste" mystery— with two differences: 29 was a house, not a ship; and Mr. Campion was called in to solve the modern mystery.

The newspapers were calling the McGill house in Chestnut Grove "the villa Mary Celeste" before Chief-Inspector Charles Luke noticed the similarity between the two mysteries and that so shook him that he telephoned Albert Campion and asked him to come over.

They met in the Sun, a discreet pub in suburban High Street, and stood talking in the small bar-parlor which was deserted at that time of day.

"The two stories *are* alike," Luke said, picking up his drink. He was at the height of his career then, a dark, muscular man, high-cheek-boned and packed with energy; and as usual he was talking nineteen to the dozen forcing home his points with characteristic gestures of his long hands. "I read the rehash of the *Mary Celeste* mystery in the *Courier* this morning and it took me to the fair. Except that she was a ship and 29 Chestnut Grove is a semi-detached suburban house, the two desertion stories are virtually the same—even to the half-eaten breakfast left on the table in each case. It's uncanny, Campion."

The quiet, fair man in the hornrimmed glasses stood listening affably, as was his habit. And as usual, he looked vague and probably ineffectual; in the shadier corners of Europe it was said that no one ever took him seriously until just about two hours too late. At the moment he appeared faintly amused. The thumping force of Luke's enthusiasms always tickled him.

"You think you know what has happened to the McGill couple, then?" he ventured.

"The hell I do!" The policeman opened his small black eyes to their widest. "I tell you it's the same tale as the classic mystery of the *Mary Celeste*. They've gone like a stain under a bleach. One minute they were having breakfast together like every other married couple for miles around and the next they were gone, sunk without trace."

Mr. Campion hesitated. He looked a trifle embarrassed. "As I recall the story of the *Mary Celeste* it had the simple charm of the utterly incredible," he said at last. "Let's see: she was a brig brought into Gib by a prize crew of innocent sailormen who had a wonderful tale to tell. According to them, she was sighted in mid-ocean with all her sails set, her decks clean, her lockers tidy, but not a soul on board. The details were fascinating. There were three cups of tea on the captain's table and they were still warm to the touch. There was a trunk of female clothes, small enough to be a child's, in his cabin. There was a cat asleep in the galley and a chicken ready for stewing in a pot on the stove." Campion sighed gently. "Quite beautiful," he said, "but witnesses also swore that with no one at the wheel she was still dead on course and that seemed a little too much for the court of inquiry. After kicking it about as long as they could, they finally made the absolute minimum award."

Luke glanced at him sharply.

"That wasn't the *Courier's* angle last night," he said. "They called it the 'world's favorite unsolved mystery.'"

"So it is!" Mr. Campion was laughing. "Because nobody wants a prosaic explanation of fraud and greed. The mystery of the *Mary*

Celeste is a prime example of the story which really is a bit *too* good to spoil, don't you think?"

"I don't know. It's not an idea which occurred to me." Luke sounded slightly irritated. "I was merely quoting the main outlines of the two tales—1872 and the *Mary Celeste* is a bit before my time. On the other hand, 29 Chestnut Grove is definitely my business and you can take it from me no witness is being allowed to use his imagination in this inquiry. Just give your mind to the details, Campion."

Luke set his tumbler down on the bar and began ticking off each item on his fingers.

"Consider the couple," he said. "They sound normal enough. Peter McGill was twenty-eight and his wife Maureen a year younger. They'd been married three years and got on well together. For the first two years they had to board with his mother while they were waiting for a house. That didn't work out too well, so they rented a couple of rooms from Maureen's married sister. That lasted for six months and then they got the offer of this house in Chestnut Grove."

"Any money troubles?" Mr. Campion asked.

"No." The Chief clearly thought the fact remarkable. "Peter seems to be the one lad in the family who had nothing to grumble about. His firm—they're locksmiths in Aldgate, he's in the office —are very pleased with him. His reputation is that he keeps within his income and he's recently had a raise in salary. I saw the senior partner this morning and he's genuinely worried, poor old boy. He liked the young man and had nothing but praise for him."

"What about Mrs. McGill?"

"She's another good type. Steady, reliable, kept on at her job as a typist until a few months ago when her husband decided she should retire to enjoy the new house and raise a family. She certainly did her housework. The place is still like a new pin and they've been gone six weeks."

For the first time Mr. Campion's eyes darkened with interest. "Forgive me," he said, "but the police seem to have come into this disappearance very quickly. What are you looking for, Charles? A body? Or bodies?"

Luke shrugged. "Not officially," he said, "but one doesn't have to have a nasty mind to wonder. We came in to the investigation quickly because the alarm was given quickly. The circumstances were extraordinary and the family got the wind up. That's the explanation of that." He paused and stood for a moment hesitating. "Come along and have a look," he said, and his restless personality was a live thing in the confined space. "We'll come back and have another drink after you've seen the setup—I've got something really recherché here. I want you in on it."

Mr. Campion followed him out into the network of trim little streets lined with bandbox villas, each set in a nest of flower garden.

"It's just down the end here and along to the right," Luke said, nodding toward the end of the avenue. "I'll give you the rest of it as we go. On the twelfth of June, Bertram Heskith, a somewhat overbright specimen who is the husband of Maureen's elder sister—the one they lodged with, two doors down the road before Number 29 became available—dropped round to see them as he usually did just before eight in the morning. He came in at the back door which was standing open and found a half-eaten breakfast for two on the table in the smart new kitchen. No one was about, so he pulled up a chair and sat down to wait."

Luke's long hands were busy as he talked and Mr. Campion could almost see the bright little room with the built-in furniture and the pot of flowers on the window ledge.

"Bertram is a toy salesman and one of a large family," Luke went on. "He's out of a job at the moment but is not despondent. He's a talkative man, a fraction too big for his clothes now, and he likes his nip—but he's sharp enough. He'd have noticed at once if there had been anything at all unusual to see. As it was, he poured himself a cup of tea out of the pot under the cosy and sat there waiting, reading the newspaper which he found lying open on the floor by Peter McGill's chair. Finally it occurred to him that the house was very quiet and he put his head round the door and shouted up the stairs. When he got no reply he went up and found the bed unmade, the bathroom still warm and wet with steam, and Maureen's everyday hat and coat lying on a chair with her familiar brown handbag on it. Bertram came down, examined the rest of the house, then went on out into the garden. Maureen had been doing the laundry before breakfast. There was linen, almost dry, on the clothesline and a basket lying on the grass under it, but that was all. The little rectangle of land was quite empty."

As his deep voice ceased, he gave Campion a sidelong glance.

"And that, my lad, is that," he said. "Neither Peter nor Maureen has been seen since. When they didn't show up, Bertram consulted the rest of the family and after waiting for two days, they went to the police."

"Really?" Mr. Campion was fascinated in spite of himself. "Is that *all* you've got?"

"Not quite but the rest is hardly helpful." Luke sounded almost gratified. "Wherever they are, they're not in the house or garden. If they walked out they did it without being seen—which is more of a feat than you'd expect because they had interested relatives and friends all round them—and the only things that anyone is sure they took with them are a couple of clean linen sheets. 'Fine winding sheets,' one lady called them."

Mr. Campion's brows rose behind his big spectacles.

"That's a delicate touch," he said. "I take it there is no suggestion of foul play?"

"Foul play is becoming positively common in London. I don't know what the old Town is coming to," Luke said gloomily, "but this setup sounds healthy and happy enough. The McGills seem to have been pleasant normal young people and yet there are one or two little items which make one wonder. As far as we can find out, Peter was not on his usual train to the City that morning, but we have one witness—a third cousin of his—who says she followed him up the street from his house to the corner just as she often did on weekday mornings. At the top of the street she went one way and she assumed that as usual he went the other, but no one else seems to have seen him and she's probably mistaken. Well, now, here we are. Stand here for a minute."

He had paused on the pavement of a narrow residential street, shady with plane trees and lined with pairs of pleasant little houses, stone-dashed and bay-windowed, in a style which is now a little out of fashion.

"The next gate along here belongs to the Heskiths," he went on, lowering his voice a tone or so. "We'll walk rather quickly past there because we don't want any more help from Bertram at the moment. He's a good enough chap but he sees himself as the watchdog of his sister-in-law's property and the way he follows me round makes me self-conscious. His house is Number 25— the odd numbers are on this side—29 is two doors along. Now Number 31, which is actually adjoined to 29 on the other side, is closed. The old lady who owns it is in the hospital; but in 33 there live two sisters who are aunts of Peter's. They moved there soon after the young couple.

"One is a widow," Luke sketched a portly juglike silhouette with his hands, "and the other is a spinster who looks like two yards of pumpwater. Both are very interested in their nephew and his wife but whereas the widow is prepared to take a more or less benevolent view of her young relations, the spinster, Miss Dove, is apt to be critical. She told me Maureen didn't know how to budget her money and I think that from time to time she'd had a few words with the girl on the subject. I heard about the 'fine linen sheets' from her. Apparently she'd told Maureen off about buying something so expensive but the young bride had saved up for them and she'd got them."

Luke sighed. "Women are like that," he said. "They get a yen for something and they want it and that's all there is to it. Miss Dove says she watched Maureen hanging them out on the line early in the morning of the day she vanished. There's one upstairs window in her house from which she can just see part of the garden at 29 if she stands on a chair and clings to the sash."

He grinned. "She happened to be doing just that at about half-past six on the day the McGills disappeared and she insists she saw them hanging there—the sheets, I mean. She recognized them by the crochet on the top edge. They're certainly not in the house now. Miss Dove hints delicately that I should search Bertram's home for them!"

Mr. Campion's pale eyes had narrowed and his mouth was smiling.

"It's a honey of a story," he murmured. "A sort of circumstantial history of the utterly impossible. The whole thing just can't have happened. How very odd, Charles. Did anybody else see Maureen that morning? Could she have walked out of the front door and come up the street with the linen over her arm unnoticed? I am not asking *would* she but *could* she?"

"No." Luke made no bones about it. "Even had she wanted to, which is unlikely, it's virtually impossible. There are the cousins opposite, you see. They live in the house with the red geraniums over there, directly in front of Number 29. They are some sort of distant relatives of Peter's. A father, mother, five marriageable daughters—it was one of them who says she followed Peter up the road that morning. Also there's an old Irish granny who sits up in bed in the window of the front room all day. She's not very reliable—for instance, she can't remember if Peter came out of the house at his usual time that day—but she would have noticed if Maureen had done so. No one saw Maureen that morning except Miss Dove, who, as I told you, watched her hanging linen on the line. The paper comes early; the milkman heard her washing machine from the scullery door when he left his bottles but he did not see her."

"What about the postman?"

"He's no help. He's a new man on the round and can't even remember if he called at 29. It's a long street and, as he says, the houses are all alike. He gets to 29 about 7:25 and seldom meets anybody at that hour. He wouldn't know the McGills if he saw them anyhow. Come on in, Campion—take a look round and see what you think."

Mr. Campion followed his friend up a narrow garden path to where a uniformed officer stood on guard before the front door. He was aware of a flutter behind the curtains in the house opposite and a tall, thin woman with a determinedly blank expression walked down the path of the next house but one and bowed to Luke meaningly as she paused at her gate before going back.

"Miss Dove," said Luke unnecessarily, as he opened the door of Number 29 Chestnut Grove.

The house had few surprises for Mr. Campion. It was almost exactly as he had imagined it. The furniture in the hall and front room was new and sparse, leaving plenty of room for future acquisitions; the kitchen-dining-room was well lived in and conveyed a distinct personality. Someone without much money, but who liked nice things, had lived there. He or she—and he suspected it was a she—had been generous too, despite her economies, if the "charitable" calendars and packets of gypsy pegs bought at the door were any guide. The breakfast table had been left exactly as Bertram Heskith had found it and his cup was still there.

The thin man in the hornrimmed glasses wandered through the house without comment, Luke at his heels. The scene was just as stated. There was no sign of hurried flight, no evidence of packing, no hint of violence. The dwelling was not so much untidy as in the process of being used. There was a pair of man's pajamas on the stool in the bathroom and a towel hung over the edge of the basin to dry. The woman's handbag and coat on a chair in the bedroom contained the usual miscellany and two pounds three shillings, some coppers, and a set of keys.

Mr. Campion looked at everything—the clothes hanging neatly in the cupboards, the dead flowers still in the vases; but the only item which appeared to hold his attention was the photograph of a wedding group which he found in a silver frame on the dressing table.

He stood before it for a long time apparently fascinated, yet it was not a remarkable picture. As is occasionally the case in such photographs, the two central figures were the least dominant characters in the entire group of vigorous, laughing wedding guests. Maureen, timid and gentle, with a slender figure and big dark eyes, looked positively scared of her own bridesmaid, and Peter, although solid and with a determined chin, had a panic-stricken look about him which contrasted with the cheerfully assured grin of the best man.

"That's Heskith," said Luke. "You can see the sort of chap he is—not one of nature's noblemen, but not a man to go imagining things. When he says he felt the two were there that morning, perfectly normal and happy as usual, I believe him."

"No Miss Dove here?" said Campion, still looking at the group photograph.

"No. That's her sister though, deputizing for the bride's mother. And that's the girl from opposite, the one who thinks she saw Peter go up the road."

Luke put a forefinger over the face of the third bridesmaid. "There's another sister here and the rest are cousins. I understand the pic doesn't do the bride justice. Everybody says she was a very pretty girl . . ." He corrected himself. "Is, I mean."

"The bridegroom looks like a reasonable type to me," murmured Mr. Campion. "A little apprehensive, perhaps."

"I wonder." Luke spoke thoughtfully. "The Heskiths had another photo of him and perhaps it's more marked in that—but don't you think there's a kind of ruthlessness in that face, Campion? It's not quite recklessness—more, I'd say, like decision. I knew a sergeant in the war with a face like that. He was mild enough in the ordinary way but once something shook him he acted fast and pulled no punches whatever. Well, that's neither here nor there. Come and inspect the clothesline and then, Heaven help you, you'll know as much as I do."

Luke led the way to the back and stood for a moment on the concrete path which ran under the kitchen window separating the house from the small rectangle of shorn grass which was all there was of a garden.

A high hedge and rustic fencing separated it from the neighbors on the right, and at the bottom there was a garden shed and a few fruit trees; on the left, the greenery in the neglected garden of the old lady who was in the hospital had grown up high so that a green wall screened the garden from all but the prying eyes of Miss Dove who, at that moment, Mr. Campion suspected, was standing on a chair and clinging to a sash to peer at them.

Luke indicated the empty line slung across the grass. "I had the linen brought in," he said. "The Heskiths were worrying and there seemed no earthly point in leaving it out to rot."

"What's in the shed?"

"A spade and fork and a lawn mower," said Luke promptly. "Come and look. The floor is beaten earth and if it's been disturbed in thirty years I'll eat my hat in Trafalgar Square. I suppose we'll have to dig it up in the end but we'll be wasting our time."

Mr. Campion went over and glanced into the tarred wooden hut. It was tidy and dusty and the floor was dry and hard. Outside, a dilapidated pair of steps leaned against the six-foot brick wall which marked the boundary.

Mr. Campion tried the steps gingerly. They held firmly enough, so he climbed up to look over the wall to the narrow path which separated it from the fence in the rear garden of the house in the next street.

"That's an old right of way," Luke said. "It leads down between the two residential roads. These suburban places are not very matey, you know. Half the time one street doesn't know the next. Chestnut Grove is classier than Philpott Avenue which runs parallel with it."

Mr. Campion descended and dusted his hands. He was grinning and his eyes were dancing.

"I wonder if anybody there noticed her," he said. "She must have been carrying the sheets."

Luke turned round slowly and stared at him.

"You're not suggesting she simply walked down here and over the wall and out! In the clothes she'd been washing in? It's crazy. Why should she? And did her husband go with her?"

"No, I think he went down Chestnut Grove as usual, doubled back down this path as soon as he came to the other end of it near the station, picked up his wife, and went off with her through Philpott Avenue to the bus stop. They'd only have to get to Broadway to find a cab, you see."

Luke's dark face still wore an expression of complete incredulity.

"But for Peter's sake *why?*" he demanded. "Why clear out in the middle of breakfast on a washday morning? And why take the sheets? Young couples can do the most unlikely things—but there are limits, Campion! They didn't take their savings bank books, you know. There's not much in them but they're still there in the writing desk in the front room. What in the world are you getting at, Campion?"

The thin man walked slowly back to the patch of grass.

"I expect the sheets were dry and she'd folded them into the basket before breakfast," he began slowly. "As she ran out of the house they were lying there and she couldn't resist taking them with her. The husband must have been irritated with her when he saw her with them, but people are like that. When they're running from a fire they save the oddest things."

"But she wasn't running from a fire."

"Wasn't she!" Mr. Campion laughed. "Listen, Charles. If the postman called, he reached the house at 7:25. I think he did call and delivered an ordinary plain business envelope which was too commonplace for him to remember. It would be the plainest of plain envelopes. Well then: who was due at 7:30?"

"Bert Heskith. I told you."

"Exactly. So there were five minutes in which to escape. Five minutes for a determined, resourceful man like Peter McGill to act promptly. His wife was generous and easy-going, remember, and so, thanks to that decisiveness which you yourself noticed in his face, he rose to the occasion.

"He had only five minutes, Charles, to escape all those powerful personalities with their jolly, avid faces whom we saw in the wedding group. They were all living remarkably close to him—ringing him round as it were—so that it was a ticklish business to elude them. He went out the front way so that the kindly watchful eyes would see him as usual and not be alarmed.

"There wasn't time to take anything at all and it was only because Maureen, flying through the garden to escape the back way, saw the sheets in the basket and couldn't resist her treasures that she salvaged them. She wasn't quite so ruthless as Peter. She had to take something from the old life, however glistening were the prospects for . . ."

Campion broke off abruptly. Chief-Inspector Luke, with dawning comprehension in his eyes, was already halfway to the gate on the way to the nearest police telephone box.

Mr. Campion was in his own sitting room in Bottle Street, Picca-
dilly, later that evening when Luke called. The Chief-Inspector
came in jauntily, his black eyes dancing with amusement.

"It wasn't the Football Pool but the Irish Sweep," he said. "I
got the details out of the Promoters. They've been wondering
what to do ever since the story broke. They're in touch with the
McGills, of course, but Peter has taken every precaution to insure
secrecy and he's insisting on his rights. He must have known his
wife's tender heart and have made up his mind what he'd do if
ever a really big win came off. The moment he got the letter telling
him of his luck he put the plan into action."

Luke paused and shook his head admiringly. "I have to hand
it to him," he said. "Seventy-five thousand pounds is like a nice
fat chicken—plenty and more for two but only a taste for a very
big family."

"What will you do?"

"Us? The police? Oh, officially we're baffled. We shall retire
gracefully. It's not our business—strictly a family affair."

He sat down and raised the glass his host had handed to him.
"Here's to the mystery of the Villa Mary Celeste," he said. "I had
a blind spot for it. It foxed me completely. Good luck to them,
though. You know, Campion, you had a point when you said that
the really insoluble mystery is the one which no one can bring
himself to spoil. What put you on to it?"

"I suspect the charm of relatives who call at seven-thirty in the
morning," said Mr. Campion.

Hal Ellson

The Back Stairway

An unusual story, deliberately written in a hard, clear, simple style . . .

His last fifteen cents. Gordon looked at the coins on his palm, went to the stand, and bought a frankfurter. He ate it quickly and walked on. A few minutes later he found himself in Times Square.

A moving ribbon of lights flashed the news high up on the Times Building. A gaping crowd stood in the street.

MARTIAL LAW PROCLAIMED IN CONGO.

So what? thought Gordon, and noticed a man in the crowd watching him. He was struck by his face, by the look in his eyes. Finally he turned and looked directly at him.

The man walked away. Five minutes later he returned. Gordon was still there. The man asked him for a cigarette.

"Haven't got any," Gordon answered. "In fact, I'm broke."

"No job?"

"No job."

"Then how about a cup of coffee?"

Gordon hesitated, then nodded his head. They went to the Automat, had coffee, and came out.

The man glanced at the crowd on the sidewalk. "Plenty of people."

"Yes."

"My name's Tony."

"Mine's Gordon."

"Doing anything special?"

"No."

"Care to take a ride uptown a way? I've got to pick up something at my room."

"All right."

They boarded a bus and rode uptown.

"What business are you in?" Tony asked.

"None. I'm on the loose," Gordon answered, and produced a big switch-blade he was carrying.

"What's that for?"

"I always carry it, and I know how to use it."

Tony nodded. Gordon casually put the knife back in his pocket. He wasn't afraid, but he wanted to make sure Tony knew he had it.

They left the bus and went to a cheap rooming house in the Fifties, between Eighth and Ninth Avenues. Tony went up and came down and they returned to Times Square. They had another coffee and some pie in a restaurant and walked around, talking of fighters.

At eleven they knew as much of each other as they cared to tell, and they were back at the rooming house.

"Where're you sleeping tonight?" Tony asked.

"I don't know."

"Want to come up to my place?"

Gordon hesitated, but he didn't know where else he could go and nodded his head.

Tony took the elevator. Gordon walked up the back stairs— four flights.

Tony was waiting at the door to his room. He laughed when he saw Gordon panting.

"Another flight and I wouldn't have made it," Gordon said.

"Well, it's done. Come on in."

They entered the room and Gordon looked around. It was a real dive, with a single bed, faded yellow walls, and no pictures.

Tony was watching him. Their eyes finally met.

"Not so nice, but it could be worse," Tony remarked and sat down on the bed.

Gordon took a chair. They talked some more. Finally Tony said, "I guess you're wondering what I do for a living."

"That's none of my business."

"Well, I'm a crap-game hustler."

"You make a living at it?"

"I manage to get by."

Gordon nodded. His face showed doubt.

"You don't believe I hustle, do you?" Tony said. "Well, I don't blame you. I guess both of us have doubts about each other."

"You were wondering about me?"

"About the knife."

"What about it?"

Tony grinned. "I had an idea you were a character. Some kind of clip artist."

"No, the knife is just for protection."

Tony nodded and yawned. "Getting late," he said. "I'm going to turn in. What about you?"

"I could use some sleep."

"Good."

Tony stood up. Gordon did too, and they both prepared for bed. Tony hid his wallet in the bottom drawer of the bureau.

Gordon noticed and thought, That's how much he trusts me, but I can't blame him—he's probably thinking about the knife.

They slept in the same bed that night.

Gordon awoke the next afternoon. Tony was gone. He didn't return until evening.

It went on like that: Tony hustled for money while Gordon remained in the room most of the time, waiting for evening. No demands were made on him. He could leave when he wished, or stay. It was up to him.

"When you find a job, we'll split the expenses." That was all Tony had said.

He's a nice guy, Gordon thought, but he still had doubts about him. Besides, this was too good to last. As for finding a job, daily he promised himself he'd look for one, but he never did. All day he stayed in the room, sleeping and reading. At night, when he went out to eat with Tony, he always used the back stairway so the rooming house proprietor wouldn't see him.

Two weeks passed, then he and Tony had a minor argument. Tony left in a huff. Gordon heard his steps fade away on the stairs.

The quiet of the house came back, a deep silence. Suddenly the room seemed too small.

He finished his cigarette, undressed, and doused the light. Darkness filled the room. Immediately those four dingy walls, already so close, seemed to be moving in on him.

Quietly he went to the window and lifted the shade. The window was closed. Tony's work. He flung it open and felt the night air moving into the room.

There was nothing to see outside but a single, tiny bathroom light that was no more than a slit in a blank wall. The sky was dark and aloof.

He went back to bed, but he couldn't sleep. Woven into the cool air drifting through the window were fragmented sounds and the soft, sonorous purring of the city—a nocturnal eddying that seemed like the very life-breath of the vast network of life outside. It was a quiet yet morbid sound.

He closed his eyes. Quick and soft, then, footsteps echoed in the hall, passed, and someone whispered, "Hurry!" The whisper was so close he sat bolt-upright.

A door closed down the hall. Then there was nothing but silence.

The footsteps didn't bother him. He was used to them. People came and went anonymously here. He expected them, as he used to expect the attendants in the institution which he'd left—men making the rounds at night, a flashlight spraying the dormitory walls, footsteps all through the night. Voices.

But the whispered "Hurry!" that had been so close to him moments ago turned his body cold. Now he felt the speaker was in the room and standing beside him. It was someone he knew, and his flesh turned to ice.

But no one was there.

His heart slowed its beat again. He waited, then looked about the room.

A nebulous whiteness swirled like smoke in the dark. It's the mirror, he told himself. But he was still frightened and half expected someone to appear before him.

No one did. He waited for the footsteps to pass through the hall once more. They didn't, and the door which had closed didn't open.

This wasn't an unreasonable sequence. Doors opened, closed, or were left ajar here. Footsteps came and went, fragments of conversation threaded the narrow corridor, and no one in all the world could decipher the comings and goings, or guess what was happening within this rat nest.

The thought was heartening, but it didn't help for long. He couldn't shake off the fear. Once more his heart began to pound.

The walls of the room were closing in again. He couldn't breathe, couldn't do anything but wait to be crushed. His nails sank into the flesh of his palms.

Suddenly he remembered the Blue Room—so called for the single bulb that lit its bleak interior. The patients in the hospital never said much about it, and none wanted to be sent there. Gordon had told himself he'd never be.

He went there for fighting with another patient. Vividly now he remembered the two attendants who met him—the one who spoke, and the one with the glove.

He saw the glove too late. It exploded in his face and he fell to the floor.

A week later he returned to his regular ward, tame as a fly, remembering nothing but the feeling of walls that threatened to crush him.

Now he understood why this room bothered him, why all the rooms he'd stayed in did. This knowledge released him from the fear he'd hidden from himself and he was able to lie back on the cot again.

But immediately his thoughts returned to the Blue Room. He saw the blue light, the gloved hand; he saw himself sprawled on the floor and the attendant standing over him.

Suddenly he began to shiver. With immense effort he brought himself under control.

That's the past. They'll never get me back there. But why am I afraid? he asked himself; and he had his answer in the question —fear of being brought back to the hospital.

I'm not insane, he told himself; but who believes it of himself if he is?

It was better not to think like this and he rolled over. Oddly, he heard no footsteps, but the door of the room opened and closed so quietly that he thought he was dreaming. A chill set him trembling. Someone was in the room.

If it were Tony, he thought, he'd have switched on the light.

The light didn't go on. He held his breath and waited. The one who'd entered moved across the room. He wanted to scream.

"Tony?"

"You awake?"

"Yes."

The switch clicked on the wall, the light blazed. Gordon looked up, blinking his eyes.

"What's wrong with you?" Tony said.

"Nothing. Why didn't you put the light on before?"

"I thought you were sleeping."

"Couldn't," Gordon answered. He sat up and looked at the brown paper bag Tony was holding.

"Coffee? I brought back two containers."

Gordon nodded. "You came back early."

"I had to make it fast tonight."

He took the containers from the bag, then met Gordon's eyes. There was an expression in them that Gordon had never seen before. He looked away. Tony handed him a container.

It was bitter coffee. He drank it anyhow. That way he didn't have to speak. The two of them sat like strangers till they emptied the containers.

Then Tony stretched out on the bed. Gordon knew he was watching him.

Waiting for me to speak, he thought. It's my move.

"You hustled up a game?" he said.

Tony nodded, a faint smile on his face.

"That was real fast."

"Real fast, but too close for comfort."

"What's that mean?"

Tony smiled unpleasantly. A long scar on the side of his face seemed unnaturally white.

"Too close for comfort," he said again.

"What was?"

"Getting the money."

He couldn't have got it running a floating dice game tonight. He'd been gone too short a while.

"What happened?" Gordon asked.

"I rolled a guy."

"You're kidding."

"Not at all. It looked easy. The guy was drunk. I followed and got him in a side-street next to a theater alley," Tony went on. "A real tough baby. I belted him and he wouldn't go down. I almost busted my hand on him."

He lifted his right hand. It was swollen. "So I had to get tough," he said calmly as he examined his hand.

"How tough?"

"I mugged him." Tony raised his eyes. "It was him or me. I had to do it."

Gordon was stunned, but his face showed nothing. A moment later the real shock came.

"I think I killed the guy."

"You're joking."

"No. The guy finally went down in a lump, but he started to yell. I had to give him an extra squeeze. Something cracked. It felt like his windpipe."

The coffee came burning up in Gordon's throat. He didn't want to believe this.

"How could you be sure?" he asked.

"Because I happen to know. I killed a man like that in the war," Tony said almost casually, as if the experience hadn't touched him at all.

Perhaps it hadn't. Gordon wasn't sure. Oddly now, he no longer felt shocked and couldn't explain this to himself.

At any rate, nothing had changed. Tony was still the same person. He didn't look like a murderer. Gordon thought of several attendants he'd known at the hospital. Their faces were inhuman. Tony's was only hard and knowing.

"Anyway," he said at last, "I've got the money for the room, so we don't have to sleep in the gutter."

This, too, was put casually, and its full meaning didn't hit Gordon for several moments. Then he felt sick. For he realized he was at least partly responsible for what had happened.

He looked at Tony and saw no sign that he felt anything. It had been merely an accident. Anyway, he'd killed before, in the war. Tonight it had probably been much simpler.

Tony was undressing now. Gordon kept watching him, and he didn't seem worried. At last he lay down on the bed. He glanced at the light, then at Gordon.

"Going to sit up all night?" he asked.

"No."

"What's the trouble?"

"Suppose the cops find out what happened?"

"Don't worry about it. They won't. Nobody saw me, and I didn't leave anything behind."

"They still might find out."

"How?"

"I don't know. Sometimes they do."

"What's the matter? Scared?"

"No."

"You don't have to be. It's my concern."

"Maybe we ought to blow out of here."

Tony smiled. "You are scared. Want to leave?"

Gordon didn't answer; but he wasn't afraid—at least, not for himself.

"We're good for another week in this dump," Tony went on.

"And I'm starting to like the place. Not that it's anything like home."

The last words stung Gordon. Home? He'd never had one, never would now. It would go on like this forever—a succession of cheap rooming houses and hotels.

Oh, God, he thought, and stood up. Tony was still smoking. That kept him from switching off the light. But Tony understood why he was waiting.

"Put it out," he said.

The light went off. The eye of the cigarette glowed in the dark.

"Pretty cool after the rain," Tony said.

"Is that why you closed the window?"

Tony laughed. A moment later the glowing end of the cigarette made an arc and vanished, snuffed out in a tray. The springs of the bed complained. Silence followed. Within a minute Tony was fast asleep.

He always went off like that, and Gordon envied him. Apparently the mugging meant nothing at all to him.

It couldn't have, thought Gordon, remembering the coffee. After killing a man, he'd picked up the containers on his way back to the room.

The silence was deadly now. Gordon waited, hoping to hear a sound outside, or in the hall. Nothing broke the quiet. The whole city had gone down in a cloud of dust.

For Gordon the city returned sometime beyond noon and in the same cell-like room. Tony had left. The house leaked sounds. The city's daytime clamor rose drowsily toward the pale summer sky.

Another day of heat and emptiness. It was better to sleep . . .

It was always gray in the room. When he opened his eyes again, the gray was deeper. A wavering figure stood in it and finally came into focus.

A policeman. Another stepped through the door. Then the man who owned the rooming house. His thick-lensed glasses gleamed dully.

"What's wrong?" Gordon asked, jumping out of bed.

The first policeman said, "Get your clothes on. You'll find out soon enough."

The second policeman went to the bureau, picked up a wallet, and examined it.

"This is it," he said, and pulled open the top drawer of the bureau. His hand went in. He lifted a big switch-blade knife and held it up.

"And this clinches it," he said.

Gordon's heart dropped. "Wait," he said. "There's been a mistake."

"And you made it," said the first policeman. "Get dressed."

"But the knife . . ."

"It's not yours?"

"It is, but . . ."

"It killed a man. That's his wallet."

Gordon was stunned, but he understood now—the argument last night with Tony.

Tony had used his knife on the man he'd killed and left the wallet behind to put the guilt on him. It was all clear now.

"Tony," he shouted. "He did it."

"Who's Tony?"

"We roomed together here. He's the one. Last night . . ."

The policeman turned to the old man who owned the rooming house.

"Know anybody named Tony?" he asked.

The old man stared through his thick-lensed glasses, shook his head slowly, and pointed at Gordon. "I only rent one to a room, and that's the fellow," he said.

"No, that's not true," Gordon cried out. "You've never seen me before. You couldn't have."

"Couldn't have? You think I'm blind because of these glasses?"

"It's not your eyes. But you never saw me because I always used the back stairway."

The old man's jaw fell slack. "The back stairway?"

Gordon nodded and smiled. "So you wouldn't know there were two of us in the same room," he said, and turned to the policeman.

The policeman cleared his throat and frowned at the old man whose mouth was agape again. "What about that?" the policeman asked him.

The old man hesitated, as if uncertain of himself; then he raised his voice. "I live here twenty years. I should know," he said, and paused.

"Know what?" said the policeman.

"There is no back stairway in this house."

John Reese

The Symbolic Logic of Murder

*Meet Darwin Carlisle, young space scientist and genius,
as he applies simple algebra to a not-so-simple murder
here on good old earth. Elementary, my dear reader—
and yet fascinatingly ingenious!*

"I dread talking to him again," said Detective Rich Hinkle. "This
genius, I mean—this young space scientist, Darwin Carlisle—this
brain!"

"Him?" said Detective Jack Kunz. "How come?"

"This whole space exploration deal gives me the creeps, and so
do these young eggheads," Hinkle said moodily. "It's contrary to
the laws of nature to shoot at the moon!"

"Oh, Carlisle's all right," said Kunz.

"He is? Listen, any guy of twenty-four that sits around with
a pretty girl and works equations—Jack, he's got to be *slightly*
abnormal!"

Kunz thought it over. "I don't react that way. I kind of like
the kid. It's old McKinstry that gives me the creeps."

"The preacher?" said Hinkle. "What's wrong with him?"

"Nothing," Kunz replied slowly, with a shiver, "but all preachers give me the creeps. It must be a subconscious guilt left over from something that happened when I was a kid. I guess where you are afraid of science, I'm afraid of religion, or something."

"Well," said Hinkle after a moment, "this whole case gives me the creeps. Especially Darwin Carlisle."

As a rule, homicide men are immune to moods, and these two were veterans, above average in intelligence. Both were college graduates; both were big, dark, neat men in their forties. They had been partners on the night watch for so long that, like old married people, they now looked alike, and had grown heavy, deliberate, thoughtful, and slow-moving together.

It was 1:35 A.M. They had worked all night on what should have been an easy case. A petty thug who had made his living extorting money from bookies on the North Side of Los Angeles had been murdered last evening. Hinkle and Kunz had interviewed three witnesses, and had caused the arrests of four cheap racketeers.

All four had been associates of the dead man, all were capable of murder, and each had ample reason to desire the victim's death. Hinkle and Kunz were sure that they had the killers in jail, but they were just as sure that they would never be able to prove it. The four suspects had refused to talk—a stupid tactic but an effective one since there was really nothing to connect them with the crime.

It was an unimportant killing, but like all men, policemen are depressed by defeat. To be so close to success and still to be humiliated by the four miserable specimens now languishing in jail was a peculiarly painful form of frustration.

Hinkle and Kunz even thought alike, so that when one had the creeps, the other had them too. Between them they filled the room to overflowing with eerie gloom. It was a small room, furnished only with a table and six chairs. They had pulled the records of the four suspects, but there was little in them that they did not already know. Other details had been supplied by robbery and vice squad stoolies. Few men know as much about their own wives as Hinkle and Kunz knew about their suspects. Yet the homicide men were at a dead end.

"May as well get it over with," Hinkle sighed. "We can't keep three honest witnesses waiting all night."

Kunz went to the door, opened it, and said, "If you people will come in, we'd like to talk to you once more, please."

First to enter was Shelley Parkinson, a small, vividly dark girl with such a look of innocence that it was like turning on more lights in the room. Some of the gloom melted from it. Both detectives had to smile at the mere sight of her pretty, cheerful face and trim, girlish figure. Hinkle stood up and pulled out a chair.

"Here, Miss Parkinson," he said. "It's certainly good of you people to wait so long for us."

"Oh, we didn't wait all this time. We went out for coffee. Was that all right?" the girl said. Her huge, brown eyes grew enormous as it occurred to her, too late, that they might have done something wrong.

"Of course it was all right!" Kunz said enthusiastically, before his surprised partner could open his mouth.

The girl was followed by a well-dressed man with a heavy shock of white hair and a lined but ruggedly handsome face. This was the Reverend Doctor G. Bart McKinstry, the minister who gave the obscurely sinful Kunz the creeps. He sat down opposite the girl, with the exhausted sigh of an old man who should have been in bed hours ago.

Lastly came a blond youth with a crew-cut, with horn-rimmed glasses and a halfback's physique. Much of his muscular grace, however, seemed to have been oddly eroded away, as if by the drain of condensation from the pleasant intellectual fog in which he lived. His pockets were stuffed with crumpled papers, sharp pencils, and the inevitable slide rule; his blue eyes beheld without really seeing; and he walked with the dreamy shuffle of one whose motor nerves were better attuned to the orbit of Venus than to his own feet.

Darwin Carlisle sprang from a long line of university forebears. His father taught physics, his mother geology, at Columbia. Darwin was a graduate student at California Institute of Technology, where he was earning his doctorate by designing guidance systems for space probes, and then describing them in monographs that not more than a dozen people in the whole world could understand. There are such people, and they differ from most mortals in that foggy, dreamy, star-smitten expression. Otherwise they look as normal and wholesome as shoe clerks, faucet manufacturers, and first basemen.

"This is a nice room," Darwin said, looking around at the naked walls, the gaunt furniture, and the bare ceiling with its one stark light. "Nothing to distract you here, is there? A room for thinking!"

Hinkle flinched. Dr. McKinstry angrily looked the other way. These three witnesses had been together for more than four hours—plenty of time for the young man's neo-functional, interplanetary personality to have collided violently with the old preacher's stern fundamentalism. It was plain that Hinkle was not the only man who got the creeps from Carlisle.

Darwin sat down beside Shelley. She put her hand on his arm, a gesture both trusting and proprietary. It showed that while she relied on him to protect her from tigers, bandits, and traveling salesmen, she also was ready to wipe his nose for him whenever necessary.

"Sorry we made you wait so long," said Kunz, "but we hoped you would remember something that had slipped your mind when we first talked to you."

"We're badly in need of help," said Hinkle.

"Oh, dear!" Shelley wailed. "Didn't you catch the four men you wanted so badly?"

"Yes," Kunz said grimly. "They were picked up by various units of the department within one hour of the murder. They were scattered all over the city, but not so far that they could not have been together at the scene of the murder at the time it took place."

"But if you have the murderers, how can we help?"

Hinkle said, "All four of them have alibis, miss. Not unimpeachable alibis, I'm sure, but all four have dummied up and won't even admit what time it is. This is not the only thing this department has to do, and it will take more time and manpower than the chief can spare to prove that two or more of our suspects, plus two or more of their alibi witnesses, are lying."

"I see," the girl said.

"What do you mean by 'prove'? The term is subject to narrower definition," said Darwin.

Hinkle glared at him. "Oh? In what way?"

"Well, I can 'prove' the speed of light to you with analogic instruments, because you accept their rationality. But how can I 'prove' it to a jungle cannibal? Conversely, I can 'prove' to the cannibal that he owes me a debt, by merely hitting him over the head. He accepts the logic of brute force, while you, I'm sure would demand invoices."

There was a moment of deep silence. Shelley looked proud, Kunz looked worried, and Hinkle and Dr. McKinstry seemed to be counting silently from one to ten.

"I'm familiar with that point of view," Dr. McKinstry said. "The exact quotation is, *And Pilate said, What is truth?* The time comes, young man, when all we get by splitting hairs is smaller fragments of hair!"

"I didn't mean to be argumentative, sir," said Darwin.

"Then why not just listen?" the minister snapped. "I can 'prove' that the firmament is not merely a shooting gallery for you young squirts over there at Cal Tech, but at this moment these officers have requested our help in solving a murder."

"We have to 'prove' it to a jury beyond a reasonable doubt, Darwin," Kunz explained. "Let's go over it again, and see if one of you can remember *something* that will help us connect these men with the job."

The detectives were skilled interrogators and the witnesses were eager to help. Unfortunately, there were excellent reasons why they could not.

It had been raining hard at 7:54 P.M., the moment of death for Rudy Lambert, alias Walter Lane, alias Rudolf Walters, but better known as Needle Nose the Fink. According to the stoolies, Needle Nose had, by his own code, earned execution. Two weeks ago he had extorted $100 from one Albine Wooten, a girl bookie, by threatening to pour acid in her ears. Albine later had calmed her nerves with a fifth of vodka, and then strolled in front of a five-ton truck. Four men had attended her funeral.

One was her brother, Mickey Boyce, a strong-arm robber with a psychopathic record. One was her "lay-off man," Red Pearson, the North Side's boss bookie. A third was her boy friend, Stanley Manlo, a pinsetter in a bowling alley and a pathological coward who slept with a switch-blade knife under his pillow. The fourth was Sid Filette, whose North Figueroa Street newsstand also handled a little cut-price marijuana. Sid's grief had perhaps been most poignant of all, since Albine had expired owing him money.

Four more unappetizing individuals than Boyce, Pearson, Manlo, and Filette do not exist; but charming people rarely commit premeditated murder, and when they do, they employ elaborately ingenious devices that always go wrong. Then the homicide men, who have seen everything, easily whisk them in. There had been no such defect in the brilliantly stupid simplicity of this murder.

Needle Nose had ducked vengeance by the unlikely ruse of working as a handyman in the last house on Frenchick Way, a dead-end street one block long. Rain or shine, Dr. McKinstry, who lived at 4772 Frenchick, always took an evening walk. He was on his way home in the heavy rain when he saw, across the street, another pedestrian whom he recognized as his neighbor's new employee.

He was sure no one else was afoot on the street. The handyman hurried on. Dr. McKinstry turned into his own sidewalk. He had taken two steps when several gunshots—he was not sure if there were two or three—boomed out.

There was no outcry of accusation or pain—no sound at all but those shots and the violent beating of the rain. Dr. McKinstry knew instantly that something terrible had happened. He stopped, half paralyzed by horror.

Then the starter of an automobile began grinding. The engine started, and the dark mass of the car hurtled past him.

"It must have been parked at the end of the street. Its lights did not go on until after it turned the corner. It passed within ten feet of me, but I don't know how many men were in it. I have a feeling, though, that I saw more than one shadow," said the tired old preacher. "I made an effort to control myself, and I remember thinking that I had to memorize the license number. I felt it would be important to the authorities, but it was too dark, or perhaps I was just not alert enough."

"You can't give us any idea of that license number—even one digit or one letter?" Kunz asked hopefully.

"No. I remember only the terrible roar of the engine. I recall the thought that went through my mind—*'Their roaring shall be like a lion, they shall roar like young lions.'* Then I'm afraid my mind simply went blank."

Hinkle sighed. "We can't blame you, sir. You have no idea what make of car it was?"

"Officer, I don't really know one car from another."

Kunz looked at Shelley. "You got a look at it—do you think you might be able to identify it now, after thinking it over?"

She looked troubled. "No, sir—only that it was an old-model sedan. You know, before they started putting on those tail fins. And I seem to recall that it was a grubby blue in color. You know what happens to blue when you don't take care of it."

"Oxidization," Darwin Carlisle murmured.

"I'll make a note of that," Hinkle said coldly. "Now, you two were on Miss Parkinson's porch, at 4770 Frenchick Way, next door to Dr. McKinstry—right?"

"Yes, sir. I was facing the street and Darwin was facing the house. That's why he didn't see as much as I did," said Shelley.

"But he knows it was oxidized," said Hinkle. "May I ask why you were facing the street, and why he was not?"

"He—he was kissing me good night," she said, "but do you have to put that in the papers?"

"Of course not!" said Kunz. "Have you remembered how many shots you heard?"

"No, sir. It could have been two or three or four."

"Have you been able to recall how many people were in the car you saw?"

"No, sir, only that I have a distinct impression of more than one."

"You and the Reverend both have that impression, and several quick shots don't sound like a one-man job," Hinkle said. "In other words, none of you can add anything to what you told us earlier tonight?"

All three witnesses shook their head. Darwin Carlisle said, "What about your prisoners' cars? If one of them is an old-model sedan—"

"They don't own any cars, any of them," Hinkle snapped. "Oxidized or otherwise. They've got us whipped and they know it. That's what burns me up!"

They sat there in dispirited silence a moment, five sincere people whose best was not good enough. Then Dr. McKinstry murmured apologetically, "I'm sorry. I guess we didn't give you very good clues, did we?"

"It's not your fault, Reverend," said Hinkle. "At least we're sure of one thing—it wasn't a one-man job. But were there two, three, or four of them in on it? That's what we don't know!"

"And none of them will talk?" said Darwin.

Kunz grinned. "Well, we did get one squeal out of Red Pearson when we started to leave him alone with Sid Filette and Mick Boyce, right here in this very room. Red is not what you'd call a trusting soul, not even here."

"Not with those two," said Hinkle. "Sid and Mick are bad medicine. Red's not taking a chance on one of them getting behind him with a shiv, while he's watching the other one. That's how he has run the North Side bookies so long—by not ever letting Boyce and Filette get him between them."

"Oh, they sound horrid!" Shelley cried. "I had no idea there were such people in the world."

"You're giving these guys the benefit of the doubt, miss," Hinkle said. "You see, ganging up on this job doesn't make them pals. We're dealing with thieves that hate everybody, especially one another. All that could possibly bring them together is mutual hatred."

She shuddered. "I can't imagine human beings living like that. I can't!" she said in a low voice.

Kunz gritted, "Miss, guys like that are why my partner and I have careers. Let me tell you about them—Mickey Boyce, for instance. The fun you get from television, Mickey gets from breaking somebody's arm. Why, I've seen little Stanley Manlo run like a rabbit on an open street in broad daylight just to avoid meeting Mick. Stanley lives in terror of that goon. Mick is one of those guys that enjoys torturing people. The only man on earth he's afraid of is Red Pearson."

"Red threatened to kill him one day," Hinkle explained, "and some day he'll do it, and Mick knows it."

"This Red Pearson seems to have a strong, dominating personality," Dr. McKinstry observed.

"Yes," said Hinkle, "but he couldn't dominate Albine Wooten. She told me once that Red warned her to cut loose from Stan Manlo because she couldn't depend on a coward. But she loved the guy. Well, Red was right! Stan sure wasn't around when Needle Nose put the old arm on her."

Again a small shudder ran through the girl's shapely body, and her brown eyes reflected shocked admiration as they darted from one detective to the other. Kunz saw the impression they were making, and after this frustrating night's work he needed admiration. He warmed to his subject.

"Or you take the noble small businessman, Sid Filette. Now there's a way to live! Sid has been held up and shaken down and rousted around so often in that crummy newsstand of his—and by his own friends!—that he has a standing rule never to be alone with any one of them. His nickname is Witness, because he's a guy who wants a witness around at all times. Even when we want to talk to him, we have to be sure that two officers go in. How do you like that?"

"It's unbelievable!" the girl gasped.

"To you, maybe," said Hinkle, "or to a jury. But not to anyone who knows these guys. These aren't big-time hoodlums, miss. These are the scum of the underworld. But that doesn't mean that they haven't made us look like jackasses."

"If only we had that license number!" said Kunz.

"Why," said Darwin Carlisle, "do you need that?"

He blinked genially through his horn-rimmed glasses. Both detectives were discouraged and tired. Even Kunz grew slightly red-faced, and Hinkle winced with the effort of holding his temper. It was Hinkle who said, with excessive politeness, "Just how else do we connect these guys with the job, kid?"

"It seems to me you already have," said Darwin.

"Oh, we have, have we?" said Kunz.

"Yes. Look, I'll show you—"

Darwin took a pencil from one pocket, a piece of paper from another, and scribbled rapidly for a minute. He handed the paper to Hinkle. Kunz got up quickly and came around to read over Hinkle's shoulder. The two detectives found themselves staring at this:

$$BP + BM + BF + PM + PF + MF + BPM + BMF + BPF + PMF + BPMF \neq 0.$$
$$\overline{B}P = 0.$$
$$BM + BF + PM + PF + MF + BPM + BMF + BPF + PMF + BPMF \neq 0.$$
$$\overline{P}M + B\overline{P}M + \overline{P}MF + B\overline{P}MF = 0.$$
$$BM + BF + PF + MF + BMF + BPF \neq 0.$$
$$B\overline{P}F = 0.$$
$$BM + BF + PF + MF + BMF \neq 0.$$
$$B\overline{M} = 0.$$
$$BF + PF + MF + BMF \neq 0.$$
$$B\overline{F} + P\overline{F} + M\overline{F} + = 0.$$
$$BMF \neq 0.$$

Kunz so far forgot himself as to blurt out, "What the hell is this a—prescription?"

"A set of equations in symbolic logic," said Darwin, "or inequations, rather, this being the simplest attack on so simple a problem."

"And what," said Hinkle hoarsely, "is symbolic logic?"

"A method of solving logical problems by algebra."

"Do you do this when you shoot rockets at the moon?" said Hinkle. There was a dangerous glint in his eye.

"It is used in designing all complex circuitry, and that includes rocket guidance systems."

"Now wait a minute, Rich. Let him work this out!" Kunz pleaded as Hinkle stumbled to his feet. "What have we got to lose?"

Hinkle sat down. Darwin reached across and took back the paper. Shelley beamed proudly. Kunz and Hinkle leaned across the table to watch. Even Dr. McKinstry showed interest, if not approval.

"We know that with four factors, sixteen combinations are possible, including 'one' and 'none,' " said Darwin. "We can eliminate the four 'ones,' since both Shelley and Dr. McKinstry are quite sure there were more than one man in the car. We can, of course, also eliminate 'none,' since somebody had to be there to commit the murder. That leaves us with only eleven combinations. Now, using letters to represent your men—B for Boyce, P for Pearson, M for Manlo, and F for Filette—we write our eleven combinations in our first equations, as follows:

$$BP + BM + BF + PM + PF + MF + BPM + BMF + BPF + PMF + BPMF \neq 0.$$

"Only one combination can be guilty. The others aren't; so our equation is not balanced. That's why we draw a line through the 'equal' sign—to make it mean 'not equal,' or rather, 'not true.' Now we'll consider these men one at a time. You say Boyce was so afraid of Pearson that he would never be alone with him. In the Boyce-Pearson combination, Boyce therefore becomes a negative quantity. We draw a line over him to indicate the negative, writing that as a separate equation, as follows:

$$\overline{B}P = 0.$$

"Here we use the 'equal' sign, because this combination is true. Having eliminated that combination, we have left this equation:

$$BM + BF + PM + PF + MF + BPM + BMF + BPF + PMF + BPMF \neq 0.$$

"Now let's consider Pearson. He distrusted the coward, Manlo, so profoundly that it's hard to believe he would ever participate in a murder with him. So in all combinations where both P and M appear, P must be negative. Let's write those combinations that way—using, as you will note, the 'equal' sign to indicate truth:

$$\overline{P}M + B\overline{P}M + \overline{P}MF + B\overline{P}MF = 0.$$

"Now we have only this left of our first equations:

$$BM + BF + PF + MF + BMF + BPF \neq 0.$$

"But you say Pearson never lets himself be caught between Boyce and Filette—that he objected when you tried to leave him alone with them here. Would he go out on a murder job with them?—and with them armed? Hardly! So we must write the Boyce-Pearson-Filette combination as true, with a negative P and the 'equal' sign:

$$B\overline{P}F = 0.$$

"Which leaves us only this of our original equation:

$$BM + BF + PF + MF + BMF \neq 0.$$

"But Manlo, you say, ran like a rabbit at the very sight of Boyce. Certainly he'd never help him on a murder, unless someone was alone to protect him. So we write the Boyce-Manlo combination with a negative M and the 'equal' sign:

$$B\overline{M} = 0.$$

"Which leaves us only these combinations:

$$BF + PF + MF + BMF \neq 0.$$

"But you say that Filette is so afraid of his friends that he has a rule never to be alone with any one of them. In all two-man combinations where Filette appears, we must therefore use a negative F and the 'equal' sign, as follows:

$$B\overline{F} + P\overline{F} + M\overline{F} = 0.$$

"Which leaves us, of our eleven original combinations, only BMF. This part of the equation *is* true, and it is the *only one* that can be true. It proves that Boyce, Manlo, and Filette *together* were the murderers. If any sum is equal to zero, then all of its parts are equal to zero too, and in a binomial system the opposite is also true. In short, not one of the three can possibly deny his guilt!"

Darwin pushed the paper across to Hinkle who gave it one quick, creepy look and refused to touch it. "Is that what you call *proof?*" he said in a choking voice. "What'll you guys at Cal Tech dream up next?"

"We didn't dream it up. Symbolic logic was invented, if we may use that term, in 1847 by an English mathematician, George Boole, who is probably doing handsprings in his grave over the way I have oversimplified his system. It's often called Boolean algebra, and it has been used by logicians and mathematicians for over a century," said Darwin.

"But what is a century in the story of mankind?" Dr. McKinstry said indignantly. "Men aren't numbers or letters! That's the trouble with you scientists—you try to reduce human beings to mere quantitative symbols."

"Not quantitative, sir—relational," said Darwin. "The letters, B, P, M, and F do not represent men, but only the narrow characteristics that make it possible or impossible for them to be at a certain place at a certain time for the certain purpose of committing murder."

"I cannot believe it!" The old man shook his white head. "Human beings are far too complex for such—such abracadabra!"

Kunz picked up the paper. "I'm not so sure, sir," he said thoughtfully. "These are pretty primitive specimens of mankind. I don't understand all these hieroglyphics, but I give you my word I understand those four crooks."

Shelley did not understand either, but her faith never wavered. "They're always trying to trip Darwin up on the electronic computer at Cal Tech, but they never can," she said. "Why don't you ask them to check this out? I bet you find out that Darwin is right again!"

"Unfortunately, miss, there are no electronic computers on a jury," Hinkle said gloomily. He hit the table with his fist. "No, we've got to find that car!"

"If the information you gave me about the suspects is accurate, then my symbols are valid, my equations correct, and my conclusion inescapable," said Darwin. "However, I have an idea about the car, too."

He wrote something on another piece of paper which he handed across the table to Dr. McKinstry. "Please take a look at that, sir. At the same time, try to recall when you heard those shots and saw that car, and see if anything comes back to you."

Kunz and Hinkle craned their necks to read what looked to them like a list of California automobile license numbers:

LOV 538; HLE 886; JIK 213; ISA 529; SRP 471; MOI 398; DCH 935.

The old preacher took the paper reluctantly. Kunz and Hinkle saw him run his eyes over the list, lay the paper aside with an impatient frown, then snatch it up again. They saw him stare at it and then turn pale, as he remembered 7:54 P.M. in all its shock and horror.

"That's it—the license number of that car!" he shouted. "It's the fourth number on the list. Why, I can see it as plainly as though it were—"

But Hinkle and Kunz had already snatched the paper from him and were running from the room. They were back in three minutes—it takes no more than that to check a license number with the California Department of Motor Vehicles. And now both men had a creepy look.

"It's a 1952 blue sedan, registered to Sid Filette's landlord's sister," said Kunz. "This ties him in, and I'll bet we tie the other two in, too!"

Hinkle looked at Carlisle with an expression almost of fear. "But don't you dare show us your equations on this one!" he muttered. "If I have to see any more symbolic logic tonight, I'll go nuts."

"This wasn't symbolic logic, sir," said Darwin. "Dr. McKinstry twice quoted Scripture tonight. The verse about Pilate was pointedly apropos to our discussion of the exact meaning of words, but I'll have to ask him to pardon me for saying that his other quotation did not make the same kind of sense. This was when he said that the automobile made him think of the roaring of lions. Unfortunately, here we must again use the most precise definitions.

"It *did* roar, but not like a lion. The two sounds have nothing in common, and the one could not suggest the other. Why, then, did Dr. McKinstry recall so irrelevant a passage? Could it be that, for some reason, he had made an effort to remember that exact verse? If so, why?"

"Most of us, when we must remember something like a phone number or an address, associate it with something already familiar. When I first met Shelley, for a long time I had to remind myself of silver and ytterbium, these being the forty-seventh and seventieth in the periodic table of the elements. It was the only way I could remember that she lived at 4770 Frenchick Way. Do you follow me?"

"Oh, yes, sure!" said Hinkle, swallowing hard. "Silver what was it? Sure, anybody would do it that way!"

"I think," said Darwin, "that Dr. McKinstry, being an intelligent, conscientious man, tried to associate the license number with something familiar—in this case, the fifth chapter and the twenty-ninth verse of the book of Isaiah. Somehow, the human mind being the marvelously complex thing it is, he afterward associated the verse through its context, rather than its number, which would be written ISA 529."

"How do you know so much about the Bible?" said Dr. McKinstry.

"My grandfather, who teaches philosophy at Harvard, gave me a hundred dollars for memorizing the book of Isaiah when I was sixteen. It's a very helpful reference for a scientist. For instance, in the sixty-fifth chapter—"

"Go home," said Kunz. "All of you go home!"

He had just remembered why preachers gave him the creeps. It had to do with the dishonest way he had won a camera as a Sunday School prize—by writing Bible verses on his cuff, instead of memorizing them.

To the end of his life Kunz would feel like a crook, just as Hinkle would feel stupid. But a little humility is good for all of us, and it probably helped the two men when they sat down to reason with Red Pearson.

Once Red realized that they were not trying to frame him for a murder he had not committed, he cooperated willingly, even enthusiastically. After that it was easy to break down the cowardly Manlo.

It was 3:29 A.M. when they left the police building, with their case all wrapped up. The rain was over and the stars were out. So was the moon—a bloodshot crescent that was just about ready to set. It looked weak and helpless to Hinkle, hanging there above the mountains as though half of its supports had been shot away. He looked up at it with a sigh.

"I still wish they'd leave it alone!" he said.

Norman Daniels

The Town That Will Never Forget

An unusual story of cumulative power and increasing impact—and with a climax that will stick fast in your memory . . .

It was the kind of hearse not even a small and isolated town like Pierceport ever saw any more, and hadn't for many years. Old Man Hart handled most of the local funerals and if his hearse wasn't a shiny Cadillac, it was still reasonably new. This one was at least thirty years old.

It was high, with running boards below the driver's door. The glass panels on the side had black wreaths painted on them. Much of the decoration had peeled or faded, but enough remained so there was no mistaking what had originally been placed there. The headlights were brass and raised above the old fenders on three-inch mountings.

In the front seat were two people—a man at the wheel, a woman at his side. They were both over middle age. That much could be seen. As the vehicle made its way slowly up the street this cloudy morning, people might have been inclined to laugh and ask what Mack Sennett movie the hearse had come out of; but in back was a plain wooden shipping box that filled the whole space and was obviously meant to contain a casket.

People were coming out of the neat white-painted church with its tall steeple. Nearly everybody in Pierceport went to church on Sunday; the few who didn't were mostly young men who would rather lounge in front and ogle the girls as they came out, and try to impress them by smoking cigarettes that dangled from their lips.

The hearse engine gave a rumbling, loose sort of sound, as if it weren't much longer for this world; but it kept going out of sheer respect for its cargo. The vehicle rolled to a stop directly in front of the church and the driver got out. Now he could be seen as a heavily built man. There was no fat on him, just huge layers of muscle rarely seen in this backwater town.

He opened the door and helped the woman get out. Compared to the man she looked puny, yet she wasn't really a small woman. She just seemed to be, as she stood beside her husband.

The lean, kindly-looking clergyman was watching the newcomers as he shook hands with members of his congregation. Naturally, he felt there was something he could do, so he walked down to the sidewalk and greeted the man and the woman.

"This is quite unusual," he said. "Perhaps I can be of assistance?"

The man spoke. He had a deep bass voice that went with his size, but it was a cultured voice and respectful.

"I am Edward Granger. This is my wife, Yvonne. We ask your permission for a funeral service."

"But I don't quite understand," the minister said. "It isn't that I'd refuse you, but . . . well, it just isn't done this way. No undertaker, no cortege. You are strangers who want to bury someone in this town. Why this town?"

"Because we have purchased a grave in your cemetery," the man explained, as if that settled it completely. "As for the undertaker . . . the body is prepared for burial and we have a permit. Everything is quite in order, I assure you."

"Ah, yes. Well, in that case, naturally I shall do all I can." The clergyman still sounded doubtful.

It was Tom Keeley who pushed his way through the gathering

crowd. Tom Keeley was a tall young man with a surly face and moody dark eyes. He moved close to Granger, gently shouldering the clergyman to one side.

"Wait a minute," he said. "What did you say your name is?"

Granger offended Keeley by totally disregarding him. Then Tom Keeley made a mistake. He walked to the back of the hearse, yanked open the rear door, grasped one of the handles on the outer box, and hauled it out so the end of it tipped down and rested on the road. That was as far as he got. A hand with a powerful grip closed around his wrist. He was suddenly twisted about and sent crashing to the ground. He lay there stunned—and then the pain came, and a kind of unholy fear, as he stared at his hand dangling like a useless appendage from his wrist.

"He busted my arm!" Keeley cried out. "He busted it!"

Granger said, "Please, everyone. I am very sorry about this, but what this foolish man did—well, it made me lose my temper."

The woman spoke for the first time. Later, much later, when it was all over, someone remembered her voice. They said it sounded like a small silvery bell.

"My husband is an uncommonly strong man and he has a short temper. I too am sorry."

Steve Hollister, built something like Granger but on a slightly smaller scale, was the man who had nerve enough to step out to the tilted box and read the shipping permit tacked to its top. He said nothing, just lifted the end of the box and pushed it back inside savagely—like a man with a sudden hate, but with a certain grudging respect for the dead.

Granger waited for him to come up on the sidewalk and then he said, "So now you know who the dead man is. He was my son. Mike he called himself—Mike Granger. He killed three men in this town seven months ago and last night they killed him in the electric chair. Yes, it is that Mike in the box—with his head shaven. It is your murderer."

"Take him out of here," Steve Hollister said curtly. "We don't want any trouble, but take him out of here. Dead or alive, we don't want that guy in this town."

Yvonne said, "What is it you object to, please?"

"He was a damned killer. Three friends of mine are buried in the cemetery because of him and believe me, there ain't nobody can plant this murderer in the same ground with them."

"Be quiet," the clergyman warned.

"You keep out of it," Steve said sharply. "This don't concern you."

"It does concern me, Stephen. It concerns all of us. A dead man is no longer a murderer or a sinner. An executed man has paid for his crime and is entitled to respect and to the dignity of a Christian burial. And he shall have it."

"Thank you," Yvonne said quietly.

Steve didn't bulge. "This guy leaves town. You heard me. And I ain't saying it again."

It was then that Edward Granger moved up to face Steve. "You are a well built man," he said quietly. "I have no doubt you can fight very well. But I am stronger, and I can fight better, and I shall break your arm too. If you stand in my way, I shall break your arm or worse."

Another voice—this one the shrill voice of Barney Frommer who clerked in the General Store—came from the crowd. "Somebody get the Mayor. Somebody get Mayor Harris. This guy has gotta be arrested and Mayor Harris is the only one who can do it."

Yvonne walked up half a dozen of the steps to the church.

"I would like to say something, if you please. I would like to say that we have a plot in your cemetery—a plot we paid for. We can bury whom we choose there. We are arranging for a rather elaborate tomb to be built—or should I say, a monument. I'm not very sure of those things. But it will be the tallest and largest grave marker in the cemetery. We wish to keep alive the memory of our son. And we do not wish this town to forget."

"Is there a law against what we want to do?" Granger asked. "That the graveyard is banned to an executed person?"

"You're damned right there is," Steve Hollister shouted, "and you won't get away with it. I'm warning you, Granger, take your son's body out of here. If you head that hearse to the cemetery, I swear I'll stop you!"

Granger made no reply. He waited until Yvonne joined him

and they both climbed into the front of the hearse and drove off. A few in the crowd ventured the opinion that the old crate would never even reach the town limits under its own power.

The minister said, "I doubt they are leaving. There is a persistency in that man which will not be denied, and I dread what may happen. It might be that black day all over again, when three young men were killed."

The crowd began to break up. After all, it was Sunday morning and time to go home and put the roast in the oven, or get out the family car. As quickly as the old hearse disappeared down the road, the quiet returned and the street emptied.

But the hearse did not go far. It stopped in front of the only hotel in town and Edward and Yvonne Granger went inside, registered, and paid for the room before the hotel clerk found out who they were and why they were in town.

Yvonne said, "I noticed a florist was open, Edward. I think a wreath—some small token . . ."

"Yes," he said. "We'll arrange for it now."

They had their one suitcase sent up to the room, then went out and passed the hearse without a glance in its direction. Down the street was Lombard's Flower Shop. It wasn't much of a place because there weren't many funerals in this small town and most of the weddings were held in Loganport, ten miles away, because the facilities were better there.

Mr. Lombard came forward eagerly—until he found out they wanted a funeral wreath.

"You two are that crazy kid's folks, ain't you? Yes, you don't have to answer. No other funerals are scheduled, if you can call this one scheduled. Now I ain't selling you no flowers. I don't want your business and all I ask is you leave here peaceably before I have you thrown out."

The laugh was low and deep in Granger's throat as he merely grabbed Lombard by the front of his shirt, lifted him while he kicked and struggled, and set him firmly on top of his counter. Then he walked casually out of the shop behind his wife.

In the hotel room—which they hadn't been ordered out of yet, because the news still hadn't reached the clerk—they took stock of things. Granger stood at the window looking down at the small crowd beginning to gather around the hearse. Yvonne wet a towel with cold water and applied it to her forehead.

"Do you really believe what we are doing is right, Edward?"

"Yes," he said. "It's absolutely right. We owe it to Mike."

"Very well. But, Edward, the trouble may be greater than you anticipate."

"I can handle it," he said, and turned to look at her. "Have you ever known any trouble I couldn't handle? Except my son who was blessed with an ambition to roam and look out for himself, and cursed with a temper like mine. I can handle it—don't worry, my dear."

"When shall we get on with it?"

"Let the crowd assemble first. Let them spread the word so everyone will be there."

Yvonne sighed and sat down on the edge of the bed. She kicked off her shoes and rubbed her feet. "I wish that we were back in the North Country. I'm afraid I've become almost unwilling to look at good people make fools of themselves." She lifted her legs onto the bed. "At first, when we went to live in the preserve with all the animals you are paid to guard, I thought I could never bear it—but now I miss the peace and quiet, and I wish we were back."

"We'll be back," he said. "Soon now. Rest, Yvonne. The afternoon may be—difficult."

But Yvonne had no time to rest. Mayor Harris used his fist on the door and came in like a bill collector. When he had a good look at Granger, he ceased snorting and wondered why those idiots hadn't told him Granger was such a big man.

"I'm Harris," he said. "Mayor of this town. We have no police department and enforcement of the law is up to me. That's why I'm here."

Yvonne squeezed her feet into the shoes again. "How do you do, Mr. Mayor," she said and offered her hand. Harris took it because Yvonne was the kind of woman no man would dare offend in any way. "I'm delighted you came to see us. There is so much to be straightened out."

"Please sit down," Granger said.

"No, thank you." Harris put up his hackles again. "The fact is, I have something to say and I will not listen to any argument about it. I should put you in jail, Mr. Granger, for assaulting one of our young men."

"I am sorry for that," Granger said.

"Then there's the florist."

Granger laughed. "His dignity is slightly damaged, that's all, and he shouldn't mind because he hasn't much dignity to lose. You wish us to take our hearse and our dead son and get out of town? Is that what you came to say?"

"Yes," Harris said loudly, just in case some townspeople were listening in the hall.

"If you will show us any state law or town ordinance which directs that an executed man cannot be buried in a graveyard in this town, then we shall leave, just as you suggest."

"Who'd ever think to write such a law?" Harris scoffed.

"Then we shall stay, bury our son, arrange for the monument, and then leave very quietly. That's all there is to it, Mr. Mayor."

"It's not quite as simple as that," the Mayor said nervously. "They won't let you bury him here."

"Who won't?"

"Friends of the three young men your son killed. Friends, relatives—they'll stop you."

"Why? Is there any great and compelling reason why?"

"They don't want that—that murderer buried here! They don't want to be reminded . . ."

"Ah," Yvonne murmured, "now you have come to the core of the problem, Mr. Mayor. They don't wish to be reminded. Yes, I think that's true. And yet, if our son deserved to be electrocuted, and if this town and its people are completely convinced he should have been, they would hardly care if the presence of his grave did remind them. But if, by chance, their consciences are not clear, then a reminder of what they fear to remember would be anathema to them, wouldn't it?"

"No matter what it is," Harris said, not precisely certain of her meaning, "there'll be big trouble if you persist in this terrible foolishness."

"Yes," Granger said, "big trouble. Seven months ago there was big trouble. My son killed three young men. A frightful thing. A thing I could hardly make myself believe. Yet I do not doubt one word of the testimony against him. I do not doubt his guilt and I cannot condone his actions—but that has nothing to do with burying him, and he shall be buried here."

Harris sat down and mopped his face. "Look, Mr. Granger . . . Mrs. Granger, you talk and act like two sensible people. I'll tell you what I'm afraid of. It might wind up with somebody else dead. We've had enough of that in our town. We've had all we want for all time to come. But it will happen—I swear it will—if you don't leave!"

Yvonne shook her head. "We will promise you this. After the burial we'll go away at once, instead of staying the night as we intended."

"But there won't be any burial," Harris persisted. "That's what I'm trying to make you understand."

Granger looked down at the street. There was a large crowd around the hearse now, but nobody was opening the rear door. They were milling a bit and he could hear the murmur of their voices. He sat down and began to shine his shoes with one of those treated cloths which hotels provide. He was thinking more of the past than of what he was doing.

"Seven months ago our son told the authorities he had no relatives. But just before the end he had to see us once more, so he had them wire. Therefore, we don't know all the facts. We did not wish to embarrass him by asking too many questions at such a time. Perhaps you would be kind enough to give us your version of what happened that day."

"It was a drunken brawl," Harris said.

"No," Yvonne countered quickly. "Our son did not drink."

"Well, maybe that's true—I guess it is—but the others were drunk. Nobody knows exactly how it started, but it wound up with your boy defying the whole crowd—you know how kids are —and they piled into him and he used a knife. Maybe, if he didn't have a knife . . . if he hadn't bought the blasted thing that very day and said he'd use it if they pestered him any more . . . I don't know—but he did use it. And we don't want him here. Not even dead."

Granger flicked the shoe cloth and examined the high polish. "We shall bury him soon now. Perhaps right away, if you're ready, Yvonne."

"Yes," she said, "I'm ready. I think I would like to leave this town as quickly as possible. I don't like it here."

Harris lost his patience—besides, he thought he'd better do some more shouting. Election came next year and he liked the job even if there wasn't any money in it. So he raised his voice in anger.

"I'm warning you, Granger, if anything happens, I'll hold you responsible. You *and* your wife! Remember that! Take my advice and get out of town with your son's body. Just—just get out—all three of you!"

He stormed out and found the corridor so well populated that he was glad he'd had the last loud word.

Inside the room Yvonne said deeply. "It is going to be bad, Edward—worse than I feared."

"Still we must do what we must do," Granger said. "Are you ready?"

The halls were empty when they left. There was nobody in the lobby and the crowd had left the hearse.

Granger looked through the time-yellowed side windows at the outer box and saw that it had not been disturbed. Then he helped Yvonne into the front and went around to cram his great bulk behind the wheel. The motor caught and wheezed and groaned, but the vehicle started to move and he headed it toward the long street at the end of which was the town graveyard.

As they passed the church, they saw the minister standing on the steps and then hurry to a car parked at the curb. The clergyman soon caught up and fell into line behind the hearse. It wasn't much of a funeral procession. Yvonne, looking back, smiled gratefully to the clergyman.

Granger grunted and fussed with the brake pedal. He turned a faint smile toward his wife. "This hearse is just about ready to fall apart."

"I hope it will last as far as the cemetery," Yvonne said.

He shook his head. "It is not necessary for it to go all the way. In fact, I'm sure it won't. There—near the gates—do you see them?"

She peered ahead in the grayness of the afternoon and made out the crowd gathered at the cemetery entrance. It seemed that everyone in town must be there, and both sides of the road were now lined with cars.

Suddenly the minister speeded up, cut in front of the hearse, reached the gates ahead of the Grangers, and got out. He waved his arms for attention, but the townspeople ignored him. They were all watching and waiting as the hearse rumbled up.

"The one whose wrist you broke," Yvonne said. "He is among the leaders. And that big man—the one who first ordered us away . . ."

"And the loud-talking one," Granger said. "I heard someone call him Frommer. I think he is the one we have to fear most. However, I am not afraid."

"No," she said, "you never have been, and I've become like you. I'm finally convinced this thing must be done."

He patted her hand and started to slow down. The crowd closed in, blocking the road in a solid mass of humanity. He brought the hearse to a halt and set the handbrake before he climbed down.

Steve Hollister, the biggest man of the group, stepped out. "All right, Granger," he said, "now you know we meant it when we warned you to take that body and get out."

"You warned me," Granger admitted. "But I also warned you that I'll fight any man—one at a time, or all of you together. For my broken head I promise you there will be ten broken arms. So we might as well begin, my friend, because I'm going through if I can keep on my feet."

The minister elbowed a path and took up a position between the two men. "We've had quite enough of this," he said. "It is Sunday, the Lord's day, and no day for quarreling or challenging one another to a fight. Mr. Granger, I am on your side, please believe me, but I beg you not to go on with this. Let us try to find another way, or at least give us a little more time to find a sensible solution."

"No," Granger said. "I am not a wealthy man. I cannot afford to waste time. It shall be now."

"Out of the way," Hollister said to the minister. "You heard him. He don't care if it's Sunday or anything else. All he wants to do is make us feel sorry his kid got electrocuted. Well, we don't care if he did. In fact, we're glad he did, because he had it coming and he ain't going to be buried here."

"Then try and stop me," Granger said, and took two steps forward before Hollister hit him. It was a solid, well delivered blow that rocked Granger almost off his feet—but not quite. Hollister, in getting set to fight, didn't move quite fast enough and Granger's two great arms suddenly wrapped around his middle, and squeezed. The pressure was exerted about twenty seconds, and when Granger let go, Hollister simply fell in a heap and didn't move.

"I was gentle with him," Granger said. "I shall not be as gentle with the next man." He looked around. "Who will be next?"

It was inevitable that they'd come at him all together. There was simply no other way to handle a man like Edward Granger, for two or even three men would stand no chance against him. As it was, Granger resisted less than they thought he would, and they soon had him down and seized and held.

Frommer, the smaller man, took command. "Okay, now we do what we gotta do. I guess there ain't gonna be any shirkers. Let's get it over with."

They moved toward the hearse. Granger struggled just once, not using all his strength. "If you harm my wife, what happened here before will be as nothing. Do you hear me?"

The minister reached the hearse first. "I'm sorry," he said to Yvonne. "I can't stop them. Not now. It's gone too far, but I assure you they will not harm you—or your husband, unless he turns on them again."

He extended his hand and helped her down. She smiled wanly.

There were women in the crowd, a lot of them, and some men who were taking no active part. They made way for Yvonne and she went over to where the minister's car was parked and stood there.

The men in the angry group went to work then. First, they yanked open the back door of the hearse, lifted out the wooden box, and set it down on the road. Frommer walked up to Granger.

"We'll give you one last chance. If you give us your word to take that out of here and never come back, we'll let you go."

Granger tried weakly to shake himself free. "I intend to do exactly what I said I'd do."

"All right," Frommer said. "You named it, mister. Boys, get on with it."

They tipped the hearse over and began to smash it with axes until it was reduced to a heap of broken glass, wood, and rusted metal that could be dragged off the road and into the vacant lot opposite the cemetery. They piled up most of it, then someone cut the gas tank free and they axed a hole in it and sloshed the gasoline around the remnants of the old hearse; but they saved half of the fuel. Four of them carried the wooden box over and set it on top of the gasoline-soaked debris.

Granger called out, in an oddly calm voice, "Open the box. Open it—and then the casket—and see what you are doing. Are you afraid? Can't you even look at the man you intend to burn? Does death shock you so much you cannot do this? Open it!"

Somebody smashed at the pine box with an ax and they threw the splintered top onto the funeral pyre. Then they lifted the cheap plain casket out and began to swing it so it would land on top of the rubble now ready to be burned. Somebody remembered the extra gasoline and poured it on the coffin.

"I'm sorry," the minister said to Yvonne.

"You did all you could," she said calmly.

Then Granger suddenly sprang forward, burst through the crowd, and ran to where the men were holding the casket. They let go and backed up quickly. Granger hunched his shoulders and seemed to pull his head down into them.

"Now," he said, *"now* it is time to fight. Now it is time to break you. Come on. Come on—one or all. Come on!"

Frommer brought up the first gun, an old nickel-plated thing that was still an effective death-dealer. A rifle and a shotgun appeared. The armed men moved forward.

Granger said, "You would kill me to do this thing? Yes . . . yes, you would! But I thought killing was to be barred—barred forever in this town where my son killed three young men."

"Stand aside," Frommer warned, "or, so help me, we'll kill you."

Granger straightened up. "So. So I have goaded you into an admission that you will kill. I have taunted a whole town into a position where murder seems to be *the only way out.*"

Granger sighed. "Listen to me: I am custodian of a forest preserve where animals are allowed to thrive and breed—so I know animals, my friends. I know that any animal can be driven to defend itself. I also know that any man can be so goaded that he will lose his sense of reason—like my son was goaded seven months ago. Like my son was taunted and tantalized and tortured until he couldn't take any more—until he turned on you, and men died. *Now you have turned on me in exactly the same manner*—and it is time for me to die."

They stared at him. The voices which flowed in small waves over the crowd were suddenly hushed. Granger eyed them, moving his head back and forth slowly.

"My son stood with his back to the wall and he fought. Now you have your backs to the wall. I've threatened to build a tomb over my son's body—so you will always remember what you would like to forget. It rests heavily on your minds—so heavily that it was easy for me to make you use violence to destroy the corpse you were ashamed of. That is what we had to do—my wife and I—to make you understand."

Yvonne came to his side and took his hand and faced the crowd too. "We sent our son home—to our own town far from here. We did not purchase a burial plot in your cemetery. I do not believe my son would have wished to be buried here. The casket is empty —only weighted to fool you."

"Our son killed," Granger went on, quietly now. "But he was not a wanton murderer, and this you people had to be taught. He did no more than most of you would have done right now. And he was as sorry for his act as most of you would have been."

Frommer opened the casket, closed it again, and walked away. Nobody else doubted Granger's word. They left, singly and in small groups, their lips pressed tight.

The minister held open the door of his car. "I can at least be of some slight service, my friends, in taking you to the bus stop. Thank you for showing all these people how wrong they would have been. They aren't bad people—not really bad."

Granger stood looking at the retreating backs of the townspeople. "No," he said, in an oddly flat voice. "No, they aren't really bad."

"We can go home now," Yvonne said.

He helped her into the minister's car. "Yes. It's all right for us to go home now because the memory of our son isn't as black as it was, and these people here need no tall tomb to remind them of that."

Arthur C. Clarke

Crime on Mars

*The Martian equivalent of stealing the Mona Lisa from
the Louvre! Crime plus detection plus science fiction
by one of the leading science fiction writers of our
time . . .*

"We don't have much crime on Mars," said Detective-Inspector
Rawlings, a little sadly. "In fact, that's the chief reason I'm going
back to the Yard. If I stayed here much longer, I'd get completely
out of practice."

We were sitting in the main observation lounge of the Phobos
Spaceport, looking out across the jagged sun-drenched crags of the
tiny moon. The ferry rocket that had brought us up from Mars
had left ten minutes ago and was now beginning the long fall back
to the ochre-tinted globe hanging there against the stars. In half an
hour we would be boarding the liner for Earth—a world on which
most of the passengers had never set foot, but which they still
called "home."

"At the same time," continued the Inspector, "now and then
there's a case that makes life interesting. You're an art dealer,
Mr. Maccar; I'm sure you heard about that spot of bother at Meridian City a couple of months ago."

"I don't think so," replied the plump, olive-skinned little man

I'd taken for just another returning tourist. Presumably the Inspector had already checked through the passenger list; I wondered how much he knew about me, and tried to reassure myself that my conscience was—well, reasonably clear. After all, everybody took *something* out through Martian Customs—

"It's been rather well hushed up," said the Inspector, "but you can't keep these things quiet for long. Anyway, a jewel thief from Earth tried to steal Meridian Museum's greatest treasure—the Siren Goddess."

"But that's absurd!" I objected. "It's priceless, of course—but it's only a lump of sandstone. You couldn't sell it to anyone— you might just as well steal the Mona Lisa."

The Inspector grinned, rather mirthlessly. *"That's* happened too," he said. "Maybe the motive was the same. There are collectors who would give a fortune for such an object, even if they could only look at it themselves. Don't you agree, Mr. Maccar?"

"That's perfectly true," said the art dealer. "In my business you meet all sorts of crazy people."

"Well, this chappie—name's Danny Weaver—had been well paid by one of them. And if it hadn't been for a piece of fantastically bad luck, he might have brought it off."

The Spaceport P.A. system apologized for a further slight delay owing to final fuel checks, and asked a number of passengers to report to Information. While we were waiting for the announcement to finish, I recalled what little I knew about the Siren Goddess. Although I'd never seen the original, like most other departing tourists I had a replica in my baggage. It bore the certificate of the Mars Bureau of Antiquities, guaranteeing that "this full-scale reproduction is an exact copy of the so-called Siren Goddess, discovered in the Mare Sirenium by the Third Expedition, A.D. 2012 (A.M. 23)."

It's quite a tiny thing to have caused so much controversy, only eight or nine inches high—you wouldn't look at it twice if you saw it in a museum on Earth. The head of a young woman, with slightly oriental features, elongated ear-lobes, hair curled in tight ringlets close to the scalp, lips half parted in an expression of pleasure or surprise—and that's all.

But it's an enigma so baffling that it has inspired a hundred religious sects, and driven quite a few archeologists out of their minds. For a perfectly human head has no right whatsoever to be found on Mars, whose only intelligent inhabitants were crustaceans—"educated lobsters," as the newspapers are fond of calling them. The aboriginal Martians never came near to achieving space-flight, and in any event their civilization died before men existed on Earth.

No wonder the Goddess is the Solar System's Number One mystery. I don't suppose we'll find the answer in my lifetime—if we ever do.

"Danny's plan was beautifully simple," continued the Inspector. "You know how absolutely dead a Martian city gets on Sunday, when everything closes down and the colonists stay home to watch the TV from Earth. Danny was counting on this when he checked into the hotel in Meridian West, late Friday afternoon. He'd have Saturday for reconnoitering the Museum, an undisturbed Sunday for the job itself, and on Monday morning he'd be just another tourist leaving town . . .

"Early Saturday he strolled through the little park and crossed over into Meridian East, where the Museum stands. In case you don't know, the city gets its name because it's exactly on longitude 180 degrees; there's a big stone slab in the park with the Prime Meridian engraved on it, so that visitors can get themselves photographed standing in two hemispheres at once. Amazing what simple things amuse some people.

"Danny spent the day going over the Museum, exactly like any other tourist determined to get his money's worth. But at closing time he didn't leave; he'd holed up in one of the galleries not open to the public, where the museum had been arranging a Late Canal Period reconstruction but had run out of money before the job could be finished. He stayed there until about midnight, just in case there were any enthusiastic researchers still in the building. Then he emerged and got to work."

"Just a minute," I interrupted. "What about the night watchman?"

"My dear chap! They don't have such luxuries on Mars. There

weren't even any burglar alarms, for who would bother to steal lumps of stone? True, the Goddess was sealed up neatly in a strong glass and metal cabinet, just in case some souvenir hunter took a fancy to her. But even if she were stolen, there was nowhere the thief could hide, and of course all outgoing traffic would be searched as soon as the statue was missed."

That was true enough. I'd been thinking in terms of Earth, forgetting that every city on Mars is a closed little world of its own beneath the force-field that protects it from the freezing near-vacuum. Beyond those electronic shields is the utterly hostile emptiness of the Martian Outback, where a man will die in seconds without protection. That makes law enforcement very easy; no wonder there's so little crime on Mars . . .

"Danny had a beautiful set of tools, as specialized as a watchmaker's. The main item was a microsaw no bigger than a soldering iron; it had a wafer-thin blade, driven at a million cycles a second by an ultrasonic power-pack. It would go through glass or metal like butter—and leave a cut only about as thick as a hair. Which was very important for Danny, as he could not leave any traces of his handiwork.

"I suppose you've guessed how he intended to operate. He was going to cut through the base of the cabinet and substitute one of those souvenir replicas for the genuine Goddess. It might be a couple of years before some inquisitive expert discovered the awful truth, and long before then the original would have been taken to Earth, perfectly disguised as a copy of itself, with a genuine certificate of authenticity. Pretty neat, eh?

"It must have been a weird business, working in that darkened gallery with all those million-year-old carvings and unexplainable artifacts around him. A museum on Earth is bad enough at night, but at least it's—well, *human*. And Gallery Three, which houses the Goddess, is particularly unsettling. It's full of bas-reliefs showing quite incredible animals fighting each other; they look rather like giant beetles, and most paleontologists flatly deny that they could ever have existed. But imaginary or not, they belonged to this world, and they didn't disturb Danny as much as the Goddess, staring at him across the ages and defying him to explain her presence here. She gave him the creeps. How do I know? He told me.

"Danny set to work on that cabinet as carefully as any diamond-cutter preparing to cleave a gem. It took most of the night to slice out the trap door, and it was nearly dawn when he relaxed and put down the saw. There was still a lot of work to do, but the hardest part was over. Putting the replica into the case, checking its appearance against the photos he'd thoughtfully brought with him, and covering up his traces might take a good part of Sunday, but that didn't worry him in the least. He had another twenty-four hours, and would positively welcome Monday's first visitors so that he could mingle with them and make his inconspicuous exit.

"It was a perfectly horrible shock to his nervous system, therefore, when the main doors were noisily unbarred at eight-thirty and the museum staff—all six of them—started to open up for the day. Danny bolted for the emergency exit, leaving everything behind—tools, Goddesses, the lot.

"He had another big surprise when he found himself in the street: it should have been completely deserted at this time of day, with everyone at home reading the Sunday papers. But here were the citizens of Meridian East, as large as life, heading for plant or office on what was obviously a normal working day.

"By the time poor Danny got back to his hotel we were waiting for him. We couldn't claim much credit for deducing that only a visitor from Earth—and a very recent one at that—could have overlooked Meridian City's chief claim to fame. And I presume you know what *that* is."

"Frankly, I don't," I answered. "You can't see much of Mars in six weeks, and I never went east of the Syrtis Major."

"Well, it's absurdly simple, but we shouldn't be too hard on Danny—even the locals occasionally fall into the same trap. It's something that doesn't bother us on Earth, where we've been able to dump the problem in the Pacific Ocean, But Mars, of course, is all dry land; and that means that *somebody* is forced to live with the International Date Line . . .

"Danny, you see, had planned the job from Meridian West. It was Sunday over there all right—and it was still Sunday there when we picked him up at the hotel. But over in Meridian East, half a mile away, it was only Saturday. That little trip across the park had made all the difference! I told you it was rotten luck."

There was a long moment of silent sympathy, then I asked, "What did he get?"

"Three years," said Inspector Rawlings.

"That doesn't seem very much."

"Mars years—that makes it almost six of ours. And a whopping fine which, by an odd coincidence, came to exactly the refund value of his return ticket to Earth. He isn't in jail, of course— Mars can't afford that kind of nonproductive luxury. Danny has to work for a living, under discreet surveillance. I told you that the Meridian Museum couldn't afford a night watchman. Well, it has one now. Guess who?"

"All passengers prepare to board in ten minutes! Please collect your hand-baggage!" ordered the loudspeakers.

As we started to move toward the airlock, I couldn't help asking one more question.

"What about the people who put Danny up to it? There must have been a lot of money behind him. Did you get them?"

"Not yet; they'd covered their tracks pretty thoroughly, and I believe Danny was telling the truth when he said he couldn't give us a lead. Still, it's not my case. As I told you, I'm going back to my old job at the Yard. But a policeman always keeps his eyes open —like an art dealer, eh, Mr. Maccar? Why, you look a bit green about the gills. Have one of my space-sickness tablets."

"No, thank you," answered Mr. Maccar, "I'm quite all right."

His tone was distinctly unfriendly; the social temperature seemed to have dropped below zero in the last few minutes. I looked at Mr. Maccar, and I looked at the Inspector. And suddenly I realized that we were going to have a very interesting trip.

Esther Wagner

Miss Weird-O

*Esther Wagner is the name of a relatively new author—
and a name to be reckoned with not only now but, more
importantly, in the future. We wish that we had the
honor of "discovering" Mrs. Wagner. But she sent her
"first story" to "Atlantic" monthly and it won the
Atlantic "First" Award of 1958. Since then Mrs.
Wagner's stories have appeared in "The New Yorker,"
"Harper's," and again in "Atlantic," and at the time of
this writing, other stories by Mrs. Wagner are scheduled
to be published by "Seventeen" and "The Saturday
Evening Post." A novel titled* THE GIFT OF ROME, *
written in collaboration with her husband, appeared in
1961; it is an historical novel about the Roman republic
and specifically about a great Roman murder trial of the
first century* B.C. *in which Cicero acted as "Perry
Mason" for the defense.*

*Mrs. Wagner was born in Chicago, educated there
and at Bryn Mawr, and also at the Universities of Paris
and Poitiers. At present she is teaching English at the
College of Puget Sound in Tacoma, Washington.*

*The author's original title for the story you are about
to read was "Contemporary Gothic"—and that,
surprisingly, is all we are going to say of the story
itself . . .*

Michael Harker had had an old-fashioned education and upbringing, of which he was often made to feel ashamed. When his wife died and he moved with his small son David to another town, he was impelled in his loneliness to seek the sort of house and household he had always longed for—with a longing he was now unable to fight. So he bought a huge old house on a lot so large it was almost a park.

The house was one of the last of its kind in the town—indeed in the country, thought Harker—and his mind filled with a savory blend of shame and pleasure whenever he walked through its long halls, glanced into its big rooms and up at its high ceilings, sensed its dark corner, roomy attic, and many-chambered basement.

Harker had never been poor, and was now almost rich. But his adult life had been lived in houses very different from this. His wife had liked breakfast nooks, dining areas, bedrooms on the same floor as the living room, half basements, patios. Largeness in a house was for her a matter of windows. Harker's houses had all looked out on the world. The inward-looking, closing-out houses of his boyhood had become identified in his mind with backwardness and unenlightenment.

He hired the most old-fashioned of household help, a plump, kindly woman named Mrs. Poole, who lived on the third floor. Harker, who in his married life had known only cleaning women, cateresses, and baby-sitters, felt guilty about this comfort, too. It was altogether too reminiscent of his mother's and grandmother's establishments. He felt he was backsliding, and backsliding with a voluptuous sense of sin.

When an opportunity for reparation presented itself, he was only too glad to take advantage of it. He hired a baby-sitter, who had never done anything in her life but baby-sit. Harker felt familiar with her; she was like the help hired by his late wife in that she didn't do very much. But by paying her the small weekly sum which she asked for as "pocket-money," and allowing her to occupy a little basement room, formerly the gardener's apartment, he could tell himself that he was not only helping the girl get a college education but that he was doing an expected thing—hiring a baby-sitter.

Moreover, the girl did not violate the beloved spirit of his house. She seemed much at home amid the non-Philippine mahogany paneling and blue grasspaper of the dining room; she had *wanted* the spooky little basement room, rather than anything upstairs. In some secret way she responded to the old house, and Harker valued this.

The girl was so young that it was hard to imagine her ever, outside real childhood, looking any younger; but then, Harker realized slowly, it was hard to imagine her, outside real middle-age, looking any older either. She was extremely pale, with a kind of luminous pallor which Harker easily recognzied as the prevailing fashion in make-up. She was lean and tall, also in the prevailing mode, and so spare that you thought "She's been sick!"—until you remembered how today's models look.

But there was the strange youthful glow of that pale skin, triumphing over livid make-up; the victorious deep red of her lips, the rich red-brown of her eyes, the sheen on her black straight hair, and the careless-power in her swift walk. Harker knew they were all beyond the gift of any cosmetic house or modeling school. She had, too, the glorious confident mindlessness which helped him feel she was the contemporary feature he needed in his household. She knew nothing about anything. She could only make peanut butter sandwiches and Instant chocolate milk for David; Mrs. Poole found this unsatisfactory, and insisted on her own menus for the boy.

Harker knew that this was quite standard, and that it was Mrs. Poole who really needed re-education. Yet he had to admit that the sitter made him obscurely uncomfortable. He disliked seeing her bend over David. The long body, the long neck, the long black hair . . . well, Harker knew he was being absurd, and he knew too, guiltily, that he was something his last wife had called "over-read." His mind was haunted by images derived from his book-loving youth and his rather obsessive taste for old books, a taste which he felt was a sign of arrested development. He knew that after college it was expected you would forget all that. But he couldn't. And the girl reminded him of the bloodstained mouths of Borgia legend, of the deadly graces and phosphorescent beauties emanating from the victims and initiates of great Count Dracula.

Harker had always thought these old romances very pleasant, and had even thought warmly of the Count when he bought the old house, and imagined as a visitor to those tall rooms the lord of the dark Castle. But he gradually found these associations unpleasant in connection with the baby-sitter. He avoided the girl; after all, it wasn't *her* fault. She did not get home from college till early evening, and he never saw her leave in the morning. She was easy to avoid.

But one evening she appeared in the front hallway, coming in from a little-used entrance that led to the pantries, just as he was preparing to leave for an evening of work at his office. Nervous as always in her presence, he asked if she had enjoyed her dinner. She stared at him.

"Dinner?" she said. "Oh. That. Well, I haven't had it yet. But I wanted to ask you a favor."

Harker welcomed this.

"I saw this little kiln in your workshop down there," she said in her sweet, small, stupid voice, so thin and silvery for one so tall and striking. "I *like* those things. I had one of my own, but I wrecked it experimenting. It got all burned out and stinky. But if you'd let me use that little one I know I wouldn't wreck it. I see nobody else uses it."

"David doesn't care for it," said Harker quickly. "Please have it."

She gave him her little blank-eyed smile—not really a smile since she never opened her lips for it; she just curved her mouth a bit.

"Thanks," she said, and started to move swiftly away.

"Wait!" said Harker, wanting to show intelligent interest. "Experiments? Are you in science?"

"What?" she asked, drawing her thin brows together. "Oh, science! You mean at college? No. I'm in Home Ec."

"Oh, yes," said Harker. Trapped in his limited academic experience, unable to make the smallest remark about Home Ec, he could only come up with "I guess that's what in my day the girls took in high school and called Domestic Science."

"I guess," she echoed in the sweet blank voice.

"Well," he said, "let Mrs. Poole know if you dream up any revolutionary new foodstuffs," and immediately feared she would take this for sarcasm about her lack of effort in the kitchen. But she smiled the almost-smile again, blinked in the hall light, and vanished soundlessly through her door.

She was beginning to bother him. He even thought about her at the office. Was it a sign of his general out-of-touchness and old-fashionedness that he felt so odd about this very unsingular girl? Or *was* there something fishy about her?

He had a good friend in the town, a social worker who had been a college friend of his wife's. Hilda Grose had done a lot of work among "difficult" young people. Harker called her up, and was soon comfortably settled in her little apartment, confiding in her while he swirled and rattled ice in his fat glass.

"Well, did you check?" said Miss Grose in her most common-sensical way, sounding exactly like his wife when she had been faced with a domestic problem: bored, but ready to come to grips. "References?"

"Of course I called the college. They said she was okay; never been a resident there, but she gets some money from a relative abroad—sort of Continental background. But she was born in this country, and makes the rest with these part-time jobs. Grades okay. Really no trouble of any sort."

"Well, Mike!" said Miss Grose. "Anyway, it's nice you stopped by." She grinned at him in friendly scorn. Then she felt sorry.

"Look," she said, "can't you be a little more down-to-earth about what bothers you with the girl? All you've told me is that there's no boy friend trouble, no klepto trouble, no noise trouble, no trouble with David you can put your finger on. She looks weird —what girl doesn't, if she goes in for the business, the clothes and posture and hair and make-up now? What exactly—"

"Well," he said, shamefaced but stubborn, "why does a girl like that *want* to live in our house? You saw it before I bought it and *you* thought I was crazy. Remember the basement, that little gardener's room? That's the room she wanted! And *she* came to me for the job, you know. What if she lets somebody through one of those basement doors? What if she goes out and stays all night and I don't know anything about it? What if she's *hiding* somebody down there?"

"Oh, Lord! You've been watching too many midnight television shows. But look: why don't you just get rid of her?"

"I can't do that!" Harker meant it.

"Okay, okay! So if anything happens—I mean really happens —call me. You wonder if there's something funny about the kid; brother, with the ones I see every day, you wouldn't have to do any wondering. Betcha one thing: your little Miss Weird-O isn't going to have any surprises for *this* old girl."

Harker lost a dog, and a neighbor lost a dog. David had some bad nightmares, about which he was very close-mouthed. Mrs. Poole complained just a bit about a smell coming up through the registers. Harker found a dead cat in the garbage can.

On an obscure impulse, wishing to "check" once more, he called up the college again. The Dean of Women allowed him to perceive that she was used to these vague, troublesome calls from fussy people who didn't quite know what they were calling about. He tried hard to expel the question of the sitter from his conscious mind. Then once he saw her gliding down the main staircase, looking incredibly vital and dead-pale. He spoke quite sharply to her.

"Miss Graves!" he said. She did indeed look gravely at him as she came down.

"Aren't you going anywhere? I, uh, I rather thought someone your age would be going—do you have friends at the college?" He felt, like an object inside his ears, the heavy weight of his own mean inquisitiveness.

"Why, sure," she told him calmly. "I'm going to a dance right now."

"The dress is very nice," said Harker lamely, and indeed it was a striking affair of black silk, with a broad band of red going diagonally across the front like some knightly order. Perhaps *nice* wasn't the word, but . . .

"Thank you, Mr. Harker," said the Graves girl demurely, and passed him.

Harker read late that night, determined to gather a few facts, make some concrete observations, rid his mind. He left enough doors open, including the door to the basement stairs, so that he could keep reasonable track. She came in fairly late, but not very; she did come in from the garden, though—through one of the basement doors to which he had not known she had a key.

Suddenly he heard a wild scream from the upper floor. David cried with his nightmares, but this scream was new. Yet, with a curious steady impulse, Harker went not upstairs but down. As he ran to the basement he heard Mrs. Poole pattering along the upper hall to David's room.

Miss Graves was not in her little bedroom. The door was open; he could see her chenille bedspread, her writing table with the kiln in the middle of it, a bunch of shiny glass jars; but she was in the little basement bathroom just down the passageway.

To Harker's stark amazement he found himself pounding on the bathroom door. He heard an ordinary splashing from within, of faucet water running in a basin, but there was no answer to his knock. He ground his teeth, swore, thrust open the unlocked door.

Miss Graves was bent over, brushing her teeth. She straightened and reached with a darting gesture for a towel, which she applied immediately to her face. Harker stared. She buried her face in the towel, wiped and blotted. When she raised her head to look at him, her red-brown eyes were more red than brown.

Had he made her cry? But he stared in gaping horror at the reddening towel with which she had wiped away the pink froth he had seen all over her mouth; at the stained toothbrush still in her other hand, at the thin streak and blotches of red on the washstand, escaped from the water's cleansing tide.

Miss Graves herself had to break the silence.

"What is it?" she asked, and turned away to put up her toothbrush, wipe the basin top, and turn off the water. Harker was still speechless. When she turned back to him, her mouth dropped at its soft curling corners and her face was full of a strange, dark woe.

"Mr. Harker!" she said, her thin little voice rising. Harker gesticulated toward the towel.

"I *know,*" she said mournfully, and her head hung. "It's terrible, It's always been so *terrible,* ever since I was a kid! Nobody can do anything about it, no matter what the ads say, Mr. Harker, I've just *got* pink toothbrush, sensitive gums. They bleed and bleed. I wish you—" Her voice trailed away.

Harker felt with a cruel, glad pang of self-castigation that he had done an enormous thing. He knew how these minor defects could damage a girl's idea of herself, break her confidence, haunt her with humiliation.

"These things go away," he muttered awkwardly. "I'm terribly sorry . . . shouldn't, wouldn't ever crash in like this, but I had to ask you about David. We're having trouble with him. I couldn't make you hear—" And he felt himself blushing, heard himself stammering.

"The nightmares?" she spoke again in her small crystal voice. "I heard him yell, down the register. I went in there once when he woke up and he nearly had a fit yelling. Mrs. Poole said I'd better not go in to him again. Didn't she tell you?"

"Well, I thought you—do you know about any stories he's heard, programs he's seen—anything that could be behind this?"

She shook her head. Harker backed away, muttering his apologies. But as he turned, he tensed up again, for there in the basement passageway, bare feet on his linoleum, stood a girl he had never seen, wearing a flannel bathrobe. He shouted at her, "Who are *you?*" taken aback, outraged by her pale thick-skinned thick-featured face, her stolid expression. Miss Graves moved quickly to his side. The stranger was silent.

"Oh, that's Celia," said Miss Graves. "Celia Graves. My cousin. She's at the college too. I thought you wouldn't mind, Mr. Harker. She was at the party with me. I know I should have asked, but it was so late, I didn't think you'd—" The other pale girl gave nothing but a numb half-smile.

"It's all right," said Harker confusedly. He brushed past and went up to David and Mrs. Poole.

But the next day he called up Miss Grose and made a date with her for dinner.

"Well, something *did* happen."

"You mean the kid's got pyorrhea?" said Hilda Grose. Harker enjoyed her smile; he'd not seen a real smile for some time.

"I only told you that because I thought the laugh on me was coming to you. I mean the other girl. This Celia. So I was right, there's been somebody else in and out. She looks queer, too, queerer than my Miss Graves, if you want to know."

"How could that *be?*"

"Okay! I called up the college. That damned dean. She tells me there's no other Graves at the college—just mine, Cynthia Graves. So mine was lying."

Miss Grose had to admit she was getting interested.

"All right, Mike," she said. "Funny family goings-on some-where—it's usually that. Look: send your Cynthia over to me to-morrow afternoon on some errand. I can talk to these kids. I'll bet you another dinner I can tell you a lot about this Celia after I'm through."

When he got home that night he had no trouble finding Miss Graves. She was in the kitchen, boiling water. Harker asked what she was making.

"Instant," she said tranquilly.

"Did Mrs. Poole order it for you?" he asked in a fussy, hosty tone. Mrs. Poole never served it and had always seemed to him completely ignorant of the product. He had not missed it.

"What? Oh! No, I don't drink coffee. I make this other stuff, sort of soup, like, in that kiln you gave me. I just come up for the water."

He told her of the favor he wished to ask her. When she heard of the call on Miss Grose, a little wary look crossed her face.

"What time?"

"Late afternoon. I know you have some late classes. Just go when you can." She nodded. Apparently the wary look had come simply from the thought of having to alter her schedule. Harker, a man of schedules not lightly rearranged, felt this reassuring.

"What'd I tell you?" said Miss Grose over the dinner he had to buy her the next day. "It's usually family. That poor kid! Both of them come from broken homes. Cynthia feels more like a sister than a cousin to Celia. Looks out for her. Gets her invited to college parties; pretends she's a student, but she works somewhere downtown. Only relative they have is some terrible old uncle in some weird part of Europe. He sends Cynthia a little money every year, but ignores Celia. Cynthia helps Celia, and it's clear they're sort of mutually dependent. The lie was just a reflex. Ignore the whole thing, Mike! Those kids have had tough times. Let her have Celia there whenever she wants! What skin is it off you? Don't give her reason to lie and evade, then the lies and evasions stop. Rudiments! Come on, I'll buy you a drink at home and play you some new records. You'll still get home early.

"That kid loves your house, Mike. You've done a good thing for her. They can't ever come out with their gratitude, but *I'm* grateful to you, Mike, on the kid's account." He responded warmly to her kind smile.

But he didn't get home early, after all. Mrs. Poole called him at Miss Grose's to tell him that a terrible thing had happened and the house was full of police. A police officer spoke to him and told him a girl's body had turned up in his alley. The officer didn't want to ask the housekeeper to take a look; she was too old. Shock. A neighbor had found the body. The police ambulance was there; would he meet them at the morgue?

Hilda Grose went with him, for she honestly feared that he was going to have an attack of some sort. Remorse and terror drained the blood from Harker's ruddy face. Knowing him, she was sure he'd find some way to blame himself.

In the car he began to mutter.

"Poor kid, poor kid! You just don't *know,* Hilda! You don't know how I . . . Why, I used to *amuse* myself, pretending that what I saw about her was that she was a vampire or werewolf or something! Why, I used to sit there for hours handing myself a laugh, thinking the Instant she brewed for herself was instant blood, that her sort didn't need to suck any more because of modern science . . . glass jars . . . cats and dogs, raw blood for the Instant . . . Why, I used to think, well, she can't really be a vampire—she goes to classes all day and everybody knows they can't get around by day . . . The *dean* knows her, she's there all day . . . So I'd hand myself a laugh: I'd think, well, she's the new type vampire; she's not interested in David anyway, more interested in just staying in the house, wouldn't risk her place . . . after all, they have their housing problems; they've learned to adapt . . . Then I'd laugh, I'd *laugh* . . . that poor kid, with her broken-home background and her pink toothbrush . . . and me, *laughing!*"

Miss Grose was at a loss. She couldn't even believe he had laughed as he said he had; he was too emotional now. Somehow she realized that she was, after all, surprised. She really hadn't known that Michael was like this.

She stuck with him when they went in for the identification, for she was now seriously worried about Harker's condition. She had gathered that something pretty gruesome was involved. But when the sheet was pulled down, neither she nor Harker even shrank from the sight of torn throat and lacerated young shoulders; they were too stunned by the face, unmarked, pale, drained in death.

"That's not her!" said Miss Grose.

"No," said Harker, who had only half his voice, and whose face was drained too. "It's Celia."

The officer was considerate. He took in without effort the shift in the case. He assured Harker an alarm would be sent out. He didn't dare be too encouraging, he said, but after all, there was not even any indication that the dead girl had been with her cousin at the time of the happening. It was possible Cynthia was perfectly safe somewhere.

"We've got to get back to the house," said Harker, dry-lipped.

"I left a patrolman there, Mrs. Harker," said the officer.

"Hilda," said Harker hoarsely.

"Of course I'll come with you, Michael," she said.

She was unable to control her sudden fascination with Harker's unsuspectedly complex mental processes. Alone in his car with him, she started to probe.

"Now Mike! This sort of thing does happen. There's been some rise lately in our figures on juvenile delinquency in this supposedly wholesome town. This case will turn out to be one of those statistics. Though I must say I prefer, like you, the Teenage Vampire stuff."

Harker said nothing.

"Just to pass the time, tell me how you'd have fitted this development in with your private joke."

Harker shot her a look, dull-eyed, obscurely panicky.

"The girl Celia wouldn't be her cousin at all," he muttered, "just some poor, near-half-wit she picked up. Too dumb. But not too dumb to go to college, of course, enroll, sit there, take care of there being someone there who was thought of as Cynthia Graves. The dean's going to say I'm wrong and it *is* Cynthia Graves, and you and I and Mrs. Poole are going to have to say different. That girl kept mine from having to go out by day. Also she was a sort of, uh, reservoir . . ."

Miss Grose giggled helplessly.

"What an imagination, Mike! But if she used cats and dogs for her Instant, why did she need Celia?"

"You can't live on Instant alone," said Harker in a deep sad voice. Miss Grose felt really quite excited. There was certainly more to Michael's case than she'd ever suspected. His wife Helen had always told her he had been insecure as a child, living in those large old-fashioned households full of servants and shifting generation-patterns. And all that reading . . . well, everybody knew how that studious type of boy is likely to turn out. His instability had been settled for a while by marriage to Helen; but Helen's death had knocked out more props than he had realized, and now . . .

"Hilda," he said. "I'd better tell you something. After this, even if the girl comes back, I can't have her in the house."

"Of course," she soothed him, though she privately thought that Michael would never get anywhere that way, always evading, always refusing to face up to things.

"I can help you, Mike. I'm a wheel, after all, at the Home, you know, the hostel for young people from broken homes. It's a good place, comfortable, lots of group activities, expert counseling."

"If she comes tonight, will you take her to this Home right away?"

"Of *course,* Mike."

The policeman met them at the door. No Miss Graves, nor any

word. Mrs. Poole had taken David to bed, and was sleeping in the little boy's room.

"Hilda," said Harker, "would you do something for me? I'm going to sit up tonight. Don't argue, please! I want you to take David back with you. He's fond of you. I'd feel more comfortable if he were with you until we get this thing more nearly cleared up. Let me go up now and get him and drive you both back. I'll come for him in the morning before you have to leave."

Miss Grose was quite pleased to do this, for she liked David and got on well with him.

Harker went up to get his son from the bedroom. He found the boy's small nightlight on, as always since the nightmares. He could see the orderly features of the old housekeeper, relaxed in deep sleep, her breath coming evenly, her hair neatly confined in a fine gray net, a net which suddenly moved Harker, for it reminded him of others he had seen, made of real hair, in the days before synthetics. He determined not to wake Mrs. Poole, to let her have her slumber unbroken for once. He lifted the sleeping boy from his cot.

David barely woke at all and was installed at Miss Grose's with a minimum of fuss. Harker drove back slowly.

On the second floor of his house he heard a slight stirring, and moved toward the door of David's room, feeling that since Mrs. Poole had been waked up after all, she must be informed of David's absence. The room was dark, though. As he walked down the hall toward it, there suddenly appeared in the doorway the tall beautiful form of Miss Cynthia Graves.

Harker banished from his mind, with discipline, every morbid thought that was there.

"There you are," he said. "You've heard about your cousin. But I have some good news for you." He drew closer to her, looking past her at the door-paneling, the wallpaper, anything but at her face. "I've made a much better arrangement for you. Miss Grose whom you met this afternoon is going to get you into the young people's home where she does much of her work. This will be better for you, now that your cousin is gone."

"Celia's not gone."

"She's dead, Miss Graves."

"I know. But she'll be around. Death is a prelude."

Harker was moved by this most unexpected revelation of Miss Graves' calm faith. Still, his regressive self was stubborn.

"Miss Grose will be coming for you in the morning."

"The morning," said Miss Graves quietly. "I'll have to get ready. And I'll need some more."

"Mrs. Poole—" began Harker, without paying attention to this last remark. But he fell silent, looking past Miss Graves into the dark room, and seeing in the pale hall-light a large dark pool on the floor.

He shifted his gaze, slowly bringing his eyes to rest at last on the face of the baby-sitter.

His whole being was invaded ruthlessly by a sudden deep sensuous delight in the girl's astonishing beauty. Her thin lids drooped over her eyes as she swayed in the doorway.

Harker's eyes passed over her body, and a forgotten heat spread slowly through him.

"You killed her," said part of him.

"I *had* to have more," the thin silvery voice assured him. "Please. I had to."

He put his hands on her shoulders.

"Mr. Harker! I'm sick. I didn't tell Miss Grose everything. After our home broke up, my mother—she was so sick, Mr. Harker." The light voice deepened and went on, rhythmically, in a slow and lyrical incantation. "Her mind was sick, her mind and mine, so sick, so very, very, very . . ."

Harker crushed her to him, just as they say in the old novels. He closed his eyes, so did not see the long-fanged gleaming smile, full and wide for the first time since he had known Miss Graves. But he knew, for he saw it in his mind's eye; knew it in his secret, educated heart; and in a great swoon of voluptuous awareness he surrendered, made ready in the last bone of his body and the last recess of his spirit for the piercing, ultimate kiss.

Don Knowlton

For Sale—Silence

How J. Pennington Smythe, meticulous man of affairs,
faced a crisis in his life—a clever and immensely
readable story.

"Miss Ford," said J. Pennington Smythe, "as I have repeatedly told you, I want three sharpened pencils ready on my desk. I see only two."

Miss Ford repaired the omission in venomous silence.

"When Mr. Cruikshank calls," Smythe continued, "tell him that I will see him at two o'clock sharp. I want two carbons of the letter to Talbot, one for the office file and one for my personal file. And you had better start a separate folder for the Hargraves correspondence, with a cross-reference under B for Bolton, Hargraves' president. And I would appreciate it, Miss Ford, if you could complete each day's filing before leaving the office, instead of letting it ride over until the next morning, which is a most untidy habit. I shall be in the sales conference in Mr. Jacobs' office until noon—"

The phone buzzed. He picked up the receiver.

"J. Pennington Smythe speaking."

"Mr. Smythe," said a voice, a dead-toned and disagreeable

voice, "I think you will wish to see me at my office at two o'clock this afternoon."

"Who is this?" asked Smythe.

"Never mind who I am," said the voice. "My office is in Room 713 at the Tower Hotel. I shall expect you at two."

"Is this a joke of some sort?" Smythe demanded, somewhat nettled.

"No joke."

"Then you will please tell me who you are and the nature of your business with me."

"You will learn all that," said the voice, "when you see me at two o'clock."

"This conversation may as well be concluded right now," snapped Smythe. "Of course I'm not going to—"

"Oh, yes, you are," broke in the voice. "You'll be here. Just recall where and under what circumstances you spent the night of June 17th."

There was a silence.

"Room 713, Tower Hotel," said the voice—and hung up.

For some moments J. Pennington Smythe sat very still.

"Miss Ford," he said finally, "when Mr. Cruikshank calls, tell him that unfortunately I will not be able to see him this afternoon."

Save for a desk, a typewriter, and a steel filing cabinet, Room 713 was an ordinary hotel room. Behind the desk sat a large bald-headed man with a slightly bent nose and insolent gray eyes.

"Come in, Mr. Smythe," he said. He did not get up or offer to shake hands. "Sit down. This office is not as imposing as yours, but it is sufficient for my business. Now may I introduce myself: my name is Hamilton Briggs."

Smythe took a chair across the desk. He was a slim, trim figure —accurately clipped mustache, knife-creased trousers.

"I assume," said Smythe, "that Briggs is not your real name."

The eyebrows of the gentleman behind the desk raised slightly.

"Your assumption is correct," he said, "but immaterial. I operate under the name of Hamilton Briggs, and as such am known at my bank and in all my financial transactions. And as you have no doubt already gathered, we are concerned here with a financial transaction."

"How much do you want?" asked Smythe, with disconcerting directness.

"Oh, come now," replied Briggs, "don't rush things. In order to set a fair price we must appraise the value of the merchandise. As you have already deduced, and it took no great perspicacity to do so, the merchandise I have for sale is silence. So it would seem pertinent to acquaint you with the extent of my knowledge."

"Go ahead," said Smythe.

"You are forty-seven years old," continued Briggs, "you are married, you have no children, you are reasonably fond of your wife but, to put it delicately, you are not enamoured of her. She has been of great value to you because her family are heavy stockholders in the company which employs you, and they have pushed you forward. You are now vice-president in charge of finance, and in view of pending retirements you are slated, within a matter of weeks, to become the next president of the company. Am I correct?"

"Correct," confirmed Smythe.

"On the afternoon of June 17th last," Briggs went on, "you and a female whose name it is unnecessary to mention registered as man and wife at a hotel which it is needless to name, and there spent the night. I have some substantiating photographs. Would you care to see them?"

"I would not," answered Smythe. "I can recall the incident without benefit of visual aids. I am, however, curious as to how you learned we were there."

"I do not reveal trade secrets," answered Briggs. "To continue. It is my assumption that if your wife, and the directors of your company, discovered the facts which I have so briefly summarized—and saw the pictures—you would not have a snowball's chance in hell of becoming president of the company."

"Your assumption is right," answered Smythe. "That was why I said at the outset—how much do you want?"

Hamilton Briggs smiled coldly.

"It is a pleasure," he said, "to do business with a man like you. I want ten thousand dollars."

J. Pennington Smythe lit a cigarette.

"I do not have ten thousand dollars," he stated.

"That is the usual opening gambit," commented Briggs. "It probably is a lie. If it is not a lie, it is just too bad. Because if I don't get the ten thousand dollars—"

"Let me save you some breath," broke in Smythe. "You are about to say that if I am unable or unwilling to cough up that amount, you will approach my wife and/or my company and sell the information to them—which would of course mean ruin to me. You are about to urge me, therefore, to squeeze my assets to the utmost, promising that if I come through with ten thousand you will give me the photographs, and that your lips will then be sealed forever. Whereas I know, of course, that if you say that, you are a liar. You would simply keep the negatives of the photographs, and you would try to bleed me for the rest of my life. Look here, Briggs, why can't we be realistic about this thing?"

Hamilton Briggs seemed actually somewhat taken aback.

"What do you mean?" he asked.

"I don't have ten thousand dollars," said Smythe, "but if I get the presidency of my company I shall have a substantial earning capacity over, I hope, quite a period of years. Why don't we put our deal on a time basis? In that way you can realize a lot more than ten thousand dollars, and I can carry the freight. Let's call it blackmail on the installment plan."

Briggs shot a quick suspicious glance at Smythe—but Smythe's imperturbable blue eyes were expressionless.

"I don't like your choice of words," Briggs observed, "but your proposition interests me. Would you mind going into details?"

"It's very simple," replied Smythe. "If and when I become president of the company, my salary will be such that I should be able to pay you four hundred a month, over a reasonable period of time, without undue financial embarrassment. Furthermore, the amount per month would not be so large as to attract attention."

"It is a new approach," commented Hamilton Briggs, "but certainly worth exploring. What would you consider to be a reasonable period of time?"

"I have given considerable thought to that question," answered Smythe. "The first consideration has to do with life expectancy, the second with job duration. Bearing in mind the vicissitudes of health and of business, I do not think it would be reasonable to extend the arrangement for more than seven years. Besides, by that time, assuming that under my direction the company has grown and prospered, if my one-night peccadillo of seven years previous were to be revealed to the directors and to my wife, I doubt very much that it would unseat me with either. So I will say, arbitrarily, seven years. Four hundred a month, forty-eight hundred a year—over seven years that comes to $33,600. That is considerably more than $10,000."

For some time Briggs was silent.

"I know what you're thinking," Smythe went on. "You think there's a catch somewhere. There isn't. It's as simple as ABC. As things stand today, I can't pay you anything at all. It has taken every cent I've earned to keep up appearances. If I become president of the company, and I will unless you interfere, I *can* and *will* pay you. Four hundred a month for seven years."

"And if for some reason you are *not* made president?" asked Briggs.

"In that case," answered Smythe, "publish the pictures on the front page of the Sunday paper and to hell with you. I'm offering you a proposition. Take it or leave it."

"I'll take it," said Hamilton Briggs.

"Okay," returned Smythe. "Now all we have to do is to draw up the contract."

"How's that?" asked Briggs.

"I said," repeated Smythe, "that now we have to draw up the contract."

"Contract?"

"Of course," said Smythe. "You wouldn't go into a deal of this importance, would you, without a contract?"

"Well, I must say," observed Briggs after a pause, "that I don't know of any precedent—"

"Mr. Briggs," Smythe stated, "I am very meticulous in my methods of doing business. In fact, my secretary, Miss Ford, thinks that I am overmeticulous. But it is for that very reason that I have succeeded as financial vice-president; and I believe it is that quality in my personality that makes me the obvious choice for the presidency. I do not like loose ends. I insist on being precise. You, Mr. Briggs, have something to sell. I am buying. The amount involved runs into a good many thousands of dollars. In the ordinary course of business no prudent man would enter into a deal of this size without a written agreement. Let's get this down in black and white, for your protection as well as mine, so that there can be no possible misunderstanding between us."

"Somehow," said Briggs slowly, "I don't like the idea of a written document—"

"Why not?" asked Smythe. "It pins us both down, doesn't it? You say you won't talk, I say I'll pay for seven years, and how much. Let me sit down at your typewriter—if you'll be good enough to hand me a couple of sheets of paper and a carbon—"

While Smythe typed, Briggs lit the wrong end of a cigarette and swore.

"Here we are," said Smythe, a few minutes later, rolling the paper out of the machine. "Duplicate copies. It's dated today, with places for both our signatures. Each of us keeps a copy signed by both. Here is what it says:

" 'The undersigned Hamilton Briggs hereby agrees to reveal to no one the whereabouts and the identity of the overnight female companion of the undersigned J. Pennington Smythe on the afternoon and night of June 17th of this year, and to hold concealed and undisclosed the photographs of Smythe and companion taken on that occasion.

" 'In consideration of and in payment for such silence and concealment, J. Pennington Smythe agrees to pay Hamilton Briggs the sum of $400 per month for seven years, payments starting as of the date of this instrument.

" 'Provided, however, that if the facts hereby sought to be concealed become known to the employer and/or the wife of J. Pennington Smythe, this agreement is null and void and of no effect.' "

"What's that last paragraph for?" demanded Briggs.

"It's merely a statement of fact," explained Smythe. "Obviously, if my company and my wife should learn about my little affair from some source other than yourself—and we cannot rule that out as a possibility—you would no longer have any grounds for blackmail."

"I wish you would not keep using that word," Briggs complained. "What you are buying is protection against the possible results of your own folly. It is really a form of insurance."

"That's right," agreed Smythe. "And did you ever hear of a *verbal* insurance contract? I say we should button this up properly. Let's both sign, and get it over with."

"Now just wait a minute," Briggs objected. "Isn't there some danger to having this in written form?"

Smythe laughed.

"Isn't there some danger," he said, "in having a file, as you have, filled with photos and written records of various people's misbehavior which, if discovered, would disclose your profession? Does it increase your risk to add this paper, with our signatures, to what you already have in your steel cabinet?"

"I didn't mean that," Briggs explained. "I was thinking about you, not me. What are you going to do with your copy of agreement?"

Smythe stared at Briggs with wide eyes.

"What do you think I'm going to do with it?" he asked sarcastically. "Show it to my wife? Present it to the Board of Directors? Put it in my safe deposit box, where it would be found if I died? Do you think I'm going to take any chances on this document being found as the result of my own carelessness? Believe me, Briggs, my copy of the agreement will be put away where J. Edgar Hoover himself couldn't find it. I'm no fool."

"But I still don't see," Briggs insisted, "why you want a written contract."

Smythe sighed.

"I have told you," he said. "It's my way of doing business. And I'll tell you something else. An honorable man does not welsh on a contract. Once we sign this, each one of us can depend on the other living up to its terms."

"I still don't like the idea," grumbled Briggs.

Smythe stood up.

"On second thought," he said, "maybe seven years is too long. Perhaps we'd better have just a verbal agreement, and then I won't feel bound by contract and I might be able to squeeze out of it somehow. And besides, you wouldn't have my signature on a document which is tantamount to a confession by me of the truth regarding my reprehensible behavior."

"Oh, sit down!" barked Briggs. "I can't figure you out, but I'll go along."

There was silence while both men signed both copies of the agreement. Briggs put his copy in the steel file behind his desk; Smythe folded his copy and put it in his pocketbook.

"Well, that's that," observed Smythe, looking at his watch. "If you'll excuse me, I must get back to the office. You'll be hearing from me."

"I certainly expect to—every month," returned Briggs, with a grim smile.

A week later Hamilton Briggs sat at his desk, opening his morning mail.

The phone rang. He picked up the receiver.

"Hello?"

"This is J. Pennington Smythe speaking. I think you will wish to see me at my office at two o'clock this afternoon."

"What's the idea?" demanded Briggs.

"You will learn that," returned Smythe, "when you see me."

"Look here, Smythe," Briggs said indignantly, "our business has been concluded. I'm not going to—"

"Oh, yes, you are," broke in Smythe. "You'll be here. Unless you prefer a visit from the police."

There was a silence.

"Twelfth floor, Peabody Building," said Smythe, and hung up.

"Sit down, Briggs," said Smythe. He did not get up or offer to shake hands. "Miss Ford, we shall excuse you for a few moments. Mr. Briggs and I wish to have a private conversation."

Miss Ford closed the door with slightly more than her usual emphasis.

"Will you please tell me," Briggs began, "what the devil—"

"Please!" said Smythe. "It will save time if you let me do the talking. There are certain facts of which you should be apprised."

He leaned back in his desk chair and put his fingertips together.

"First," he went on, "you should know that my wife, at the time it happened, was fully informed of the June 17th incident at the Tower Hotel. I told her myself. In fact, it seemed simpler —and tidier, if I may say so—to provide as corespondent in my wife's divorce suit, soon to be instituted, the woman I shall marry as soon as the divorce is granted."

Hamilton Briggs stared.

"Second," continued Smythe, "the directors of my company are confidentially aware of my marital situation, and furthermore, I never had any intention of accepting the presidency of the company even if they offered it to me. I am resigning, and going into business for myself. This is my last day in this office."

"You damned liar!" shouted Briggs.

"Quiet!" cautioned Smythe. "I do not think you wish this conversation to be overheard. Third: under the circumstances our mutual agreement is, of course, null and void, as provided under the terms of its final paragraph."

Briggs rose hastily.

"I wouldn't start anything if I were you," Smythe observed quietly. "There are plenty of people just outside this door. Now to my fourth point, which has to do with the police."

Briggs sank back into his chair. No longer did he wear an air of insolent assurance. Smythe reached into his desk.

"I have here," he said, "a photostatic copy of our agreement, plus a photostatic copy of my check to you for $400, endorsed and cashed by yourself. That evidence alone, if handed to the proper authorities, would be sufficient, if I felt so inclined, to keep you out of circulation for a long time."

"What do you mean if you felt so inclined?" asked Briggs slowly.

"I would *not* be inclined to make any disclosure to the police," explained Smythe, "if you and I can come to an understanding."

Briggs unleashed a string of profane invective.

"How much do you want?" he asked.

"I believe we have previously reviewed a matter of this sort," Smythe replied. "I do not wish to inflict any hardship on you. I assume, however, that a man of your talents has a substantial income, and that without undue embarrassment you will be able to pay me the sum of $400 per month for seven years, starting today."

Briggs glanced toward the door.

"I wouldn't try to make a break for it," advised Smythe. "A phone call from me would bring the officers to your hotel before you could get back to it to destroy your records. I doubt if you would enjoy being a fugitive from justice."

"Okay," said Briggs bleakly. "I suppose you want to get this down in black and white—"

"Good try, Briggs," said Smythe, grinning. "No, my passion for reducing a contract to precise written form seems somehow to have evaporated. This is strictly a gentleman's agreement. There will be no record of it. I shall repeat this conversation to nobody, and if you repeat it I shall deny it under oath. But of course you will not repeat it, because in so doing you would be incriminating yourself. I shall place the vital documents—the negatives and the photostats—in a place known only to myself, and at the end of seven years I shall destroy them. You will mail the $400 to me monthly in cash, and as I suggested a moment ago, the first payment is due today. I presume that a man of your calling usually carries with him what is known in the trade as a roll?"

Silently Briggs took out his pocketbook and handed Smythe eight fifty-dollar bills.

"Pardon me if I do not give you a receipt," said Smythe. "Miss Ford! You can come back in now."

As Miss Ford took her place at her typewriter, Smythe politely showed Hamilton Briggs to the door.

"Goodbye, Briggs," he said. "As you remarked the other day, it is a pleasure to do business with a man like you."

Henry Slesar

The Man in the Next Cell

When Gorwald was arrested for speeding, he thought it was just a nuisance—delay, small-town jail, at worst a heavy fine. But then the unexpected happened . . .

Gorwald's foot stayed heavy on the gas pedal, even after he heard the imperative wail of the siren behind him. He had no hope of outracing the gray-and-white patrol car that was looming in his rear-view mirror, but his foot wasn't taking any notice. The State Trooper was nudging his bumper before Gorwald lightened the pressure and slowed to a halt.

He kept his eyes straight ahead, listening to the officer's boot soles scraping on the country highway, and didn't look up until the State Trooper said, "You take a lot of stopping, mister. Didn't you hear my siren?"

Gorwald sighed. "Let's get it over with, huh? I'm in a hurry." He fished for license and registration, with an air that indicated experience. The State Trooper examined the documents, then pulled a small, fat book out of his hip pocket.

"Leon Gorwald, Philadelphia. You're a long way from home, Mr. Gorwald. You weren't leaving our state, were you?"

"Fast as I can make the line."

"You'll have to wait a while. I'm giving you a ticket, payable within five days. My speedometer says you were doing seventy."

"Look, I'm a businessman," Gorwald said, touching the brief case on the seat beside him. "I've got important things to do. Maybe we can handle this another way." He took out his wallet. There was a twenty-dollar bill peeking out of a pigskin fold. He removed it, and said, "Suppose I pay *you* the fine, how would that be?" He winked awkwardly.

The Trooper slammed the book shut and stepped away from Gorwald's car. "All right, step out," he said.

"Wait a minute—"

"Step out, mister, I'm taking you in."

Gorwald cursed his mistake, and climbed out. On the road, he was a foot shorter than the officer, and next to the Trooper's lean, muscular body he looked pudgy and ineffectual. "I was only trying to save myself some trouble," he said.

"You just bought yourself some more trouble. I don't like bribes, mister." He jerked his thumb toward the patrol car. "Get in there. I'll put a chain on your car and we'll all take a ride into Perryville."

"Perryville? Where the hell is that?"

"You passed through it five minutes ago. At the speed you were making, it was probably just a blur. It's not a big town, but it's got one important thing. A jail."

Perryville had a jail, all right, and when Gorwald saw it his expression alternated between contempt and dismay. The prison building was a whitewashed stucco cheesebox, by all odds the cleanest exterior in the town. But that was all you could say for it. Inside, the Perryville jail was dank and sunless, with sweaty green walls, a battered monster of a desk, a dented wooden filing cabinet, and two heavily barred cells running the length of the outer room.

There was no one in attendance when the Trooper brought Gorwald in, so he did the honors himself. He took the key ring from the dripping wall, opened one of the cell doors, and nodded in Gorwald's direction. The businessman, grumbling, walked in.

"When do I see a magistrate?" he said. "I'm entitled to a hearing."

"You'll see the Judge when I can find him. It's Sunday, mister. Things are quiet around here on Sunday." He walked to a back door and opened it. "Hey, Montague!" he shouted. "Sandy! Anybody here?" Then, getting no response, he shrugged. "Guess they're all out to supper or something. I'll go over to Judge Webster's house and tell him you're here. Sit tight."

When he reached the front door Gorwald protested. "Hey! You can't just leave me here!"

"You'll keep, mister." He looked at the rear door again, his face puzzled. "Can't understand where they all went to. Unless—"

He was cut short by the inward explosion of the front door. The man who had burst into the room was old and white-haired, but excitement had transformed his wrinkled, grizzled face into something resembling youthful exuberance.

"Carlie!" he cried. "Man, am I glad to see you! Minute I spotted that car of yours outside, I said thank the Lord. This fella's a rough one—"

"What in Sam Hill you talking about, Montague?"

"For God's sake, Carlie, we got the worse crime in Perryville in fifty years happen this morning—didn't you even hear about it?" He coughed asthmatically, and slapped the gun holster that was loosely buckled around his waist. "Only we got the fella that did it—me and Sandy, that is—so don't try and take credit. All you got to do is help us drag him in here, so we can lock him up." He stopped, and gawked at Gorwald. "For the love of Pete, Carlie, what's *he* doin' in there?"

"Prisoner," the Trooper said curtly. "Now will you please make some sense, Sheriff? Who you aiming to lock up? And what's he supposed to have done?"

The old man walked to the desk, sat on the edge, and mopped his forehead with his palm. "Worse thing I ever saw, Carlie," he whispered. "Lord knows, I seen lots in France that time, but nothing as bad as this. All cut up she was . . . " He paled noticeably. "It was the Fremont girl. You know her? The one called Susie?"

"No, I don't know her."

"Folks run a poultry farm. Her kid brother found her in the woods, about a quarter of a mile behind their house. She was out looking for kindling, or wildflowers, or something. Wasn't exactly a pretty girl, but not so bad. But what a sight she is now, Carlie! God forgive that crazy man."

"Who's the man?"

"Must have been hitchhiking his way through town—none of us ever saw him before. He was trying to pick up a ride, not thirty yards where we found the body, but we stopped him. He ran like hell, but we caught up. I mean Sandy did—I don't run so good any more. Put up a fight, too, so Sandy pistol-whipped him a little. He's a tramp, all right, but he must have been a mechanic once. Still wearing an old pair of white coveralls—name on front and back says Seneca Garage, if you can make it out."

"Where is he now?"

"Outside, in Sandy's car. He came to about ten minutes ago and started giving us a hard time, but he's quiet now. You want to help fetch him in?"

"All right. Then I better get a report into headquarters—maybe they'll want me to go out there. Body still where you found it?"

"Course, Carlie—I know my business. Left two deputies." He looked again at Gorwald. "But what about that one? What's he done?"

"Speeding and attempted bribery," the Trooper snapped. "He'll be okay. We'll just put your mechanic in the other cell."

Gorwald, who had been listening intently to their conversation, now broke out with a wail.

"I want a judge! Let me pay the fine and get out of here!"

The old man looked worried. "Look, Carlie, under the circumstances . . . I mean, what the heck, a traffic violator. Don't you think—"

"What's the matter, Sheriff?" the Trooper said irritably. "Two prisoners too much for you to handle?"

"It's not that—"

"No dice, Montague—a prisoner's a prisoner. I'll go see Judge Webster and get him a hearing, and then we'll see."

The old man grunted. "You always were the damnedest stickler, Carlie. Just like your Pop." He sighed, went to the desk, and dropped into the creaking swivel chair. "All right, you and

Sandy bring in the mechanic and I'll try to reach the Judge by phone. And watch out for that fella, Carlie, he's a tough one."

The Trooper went to the door. Gorwald kicked the bars of his cell and the old man glared at him like an angered turkey. "Now you cut that out, mister," he said.

The Sheriff's telephone call produced nothing. Gorwald could hear the ring on the other end, but there was no reply. Three minutes later, the door opened again. The businessman's mouth twitched when he saw the hulking form that was being supported on the arms of the Trooper and a sandy-haired stout man.

The prisoner's hair was matted, and hung over his beetling brows without diminishing the glare in his eyes. He was big in the shoulders, but not tall, and the filthy, once-white mechanic's uniform that he wore sagged on his frame. He strained against his captors' grip, but with nothing more than token resistance.

Then the old man was unlocking the adjacent cell, and Gorwald found himself no longer the sole resident of the Perryville jail.

"Don't think he'll give us any more trouble," the sandy-haired deputy panted, with a hint of pride. "Think I knocked some of the fight out of him, back on the road."

The Trooper looked through the bars at the new occupant, and said, "What's your name, mister?"

"You go to hell!" the man snarled.

Gorwald, staring through side bars that separated the iron cages, cleared his throat nervously. It made the mechanic's head spin around, and there was so much animal fury in his eyes that Gorwald instinctively backed away.

"You won't get anywhere that way," the Trooper said quietly. "A little cooperation might help you out."

The mechanic spat expertly, and the stout, sandy-haired deputy shot a thick arm through the bars and struck the man's dusty shoulders with a hard, flat palm. The prisoner staggered backward, then flung himself at the door of the cell until the steel rang. He cursed unintelligibly, then stopped in mid-sentence, turned, and shuffled to the bunk. He sat down, put his shaggy head into his hands, and grew quiet, like a man accustomed to jail cells.

Gorwald, round-eyed, watched him.

"What about the Judge?" the Trooper said. "You try and reach him?"

"You won't reach him," Sandy drawled. "Him and his missus went to Blanton to visit her folks—they go there about every other Sunday. He ought to be back around eight-thirty. Course you could try calling him there."

"Heck," Montague said, "it'll take almost three hours for him to get back—that'll be eight o'clock. Might as well let him have his dinner." He looked toward Gorwald apologetically. "Sorry, mister, we're doing the best we can."

The Trooper grimaced. "He can wait—I don't think he's in such a hurry any more. Sandy, how about going out with me to this Fremont place?"

"Sure, if it's all right with Monty."

"It's all right with me."

"I'll make my report to headquarters from there," the Trooper said. "You sure you can handle things all right?"

"Don't worry about that," the Sheriff said confidently. "I'll get along fine."

It was almost half an hour before another word was spoken in the Perryville jail. The mechanic, his head buried in his arms, remained on the bunk. Gorwald, unnerved by the presence of his dangerous neighbor, remained at the farthest corner of his cell. The old Sheriff, now the solitary guardian of the small prison, sat at the battered desk and seemed to be composing a lengthy letter.

The mechanic stirred only once. He uncovered his face and stared at Gorwald for such a long, agonizing moment that the businessman whimpered aloud. Then the mechanic, with a snort of contempt, swung his legs off the floor and stretched out on the bunk, turning his face to the wall. The light was too dim to be certain, but Gorwald thought he detected caked blood on the matted hair.

When the mechanic stopped moving, Gorwald stepped cautiously to the door of his cell, and whispered, "You. Please."

The old man looked up blankly.

"I want to talk to you. Please."

The Sheriff sighed and got up from the creaking chair. "What do you want, mister?"

"Look, it's been hours—"

"Not even an hour."

"I'm *entitled* to a hearing, damn it. That's the law!"

The old man scratched his chin. "I know you're entitled to one phone call, that's for sure. Anybody you want to call?"

"No," Gorwald grated. "Nobody I want to call." He gestured despairingly. "Look, all I did was speed through your rotten little town. You understand that? I was just *speeding.*"

"Is that all you have to say?"

"No, wait." Gorwald dug for his wallet. "Listen, how would it be—"

The Sheriff gaped at him, in genuine astonishment. Immediately, Gorwald knew it was another mistake. He stuck the wallet back in his pocket, cursing the dumb honesty that had put him in this plight. He was just starting to curse the Sheriff, too, when the front door opened and the stout deputy came in, looking flushed and bursting with news.

"You back?" the old man said. "Thought you went with Carlie to the Fremont place?"

"I didn't go with Carlie—he went out alone. He thought I ought to hang around here, when he saw that bunch over at McMurtrie's—"

He pulled the Sheriff's arm and drew him aside, but Gorwald, pushing against the bars, had no trouble eavesdropping. "I tell you something's goin' on, Monty. When we come outside we see this big gang hanging around outside McMurtrie's, talking it up—you know how they get. Mac, happy as a jaybird, he's selling drinks like it's New Year's Eve. Carlie thought maybe there might be some trouble, so he told me to hang around and keep an eye on them."

"What kind of trouble?" the old man said stupidly. "What are you actin' so mysterious for?"

"Quiet!" Sandy whispered. He jerked his thick thumb toward the mechanic's cell, meaningfully. "Look, Monty, you know some of the guys in this town—you know how mean they can get when they're likkered up. Well, don't think they don't know about the Fremont girl and everything—you can't keep that kind of thing a secret. That's what they're all talking about. You understand?"

"So what's so damned strange about that? It's the biggest thing happened around here since Teddy Roosevelt went through town. What do you think they're gonna talk about now—fishing?"

"Monty, you been Sheriff a long time, but you never saw any real trouble around here."

"Get to the point." The old man scowled.

"Those guys in there are putting away a lot of drinks, and they're talking real crazy. You know what I mean? About *him*." Again the thumb hooked toward the prison cell. Gorwald, at his own cell door, gasped.

"You're crazy," the Sheriff snapped. "You telling me they're working up a lynch mob out there?" He clucked. "Sam Dugan and Vince Merritt and *those* jokers? You're out of your head, Sandy."

"I was there," Sandy said grimly, tightening his grip on the old man's reedy arm. "I was at the bar. Most of those guys been out of work so long, ever since the flood, they're ready to bust loose at anything. You don't know how fast these things can happen. I saw it once, at Riverhead, back in 1937. I mean it, Monty—we got a problem."

The old man shook loose from the deputy's grip and went to the small window near the door. He peered out into the oncoming darkness, but saw nothing that gave him cause for concern. He returned to the desk and put his hand on the telephone. "Maybe if I called Mac—"

"Take my word for it, Monty, I heard those guys. We've got to do something, and we've got to do it now."

"What can I do? Call the Staties? They could be here in half an hour."

"Too long. Maybe if we got Carlie back in town—"

"Sandy, I just don't believe all this!"

Sandy snorted. "When you see him at the end of a rope—will you believe it then?"

His words were loud, so loud that they snapped the mechanic

out of his trance. He sat up on the bunk, his matted hair fanning out wildly, his eyes and mouth opening in an expression of sudden terror.

"Rope?" he muttered. "Who said rope?"

He stood up, and went to the cell door.

"Who said rope?" he yelled, grasping the thick iron bars.

"You quiet down," the Sheriff said calmly. "This is nothing to do with you."

The telephone on the Sheriff's desk jangled off-key. Sandy grabbed the receiver, listened for one second, and covered the mouthpiece.

"It's McMurtrie," he said. "Yeah, Mac, what's up?"

He listened for another ten seconds, then slammed the phone down.

"If you're gonna do something, Monty, do it now. Mac says a bunch of 'em are coming over here. They got three rifles between 'em, and the way they been drinking and working themselves up, I wouldn't be surprised if they used them."

"For the love of Pete," the old man said.

"Let me out!" the mechanic yelled, trying to shake the bars of his cell. "Let me outa here!"

The old man was at the window again. "Don't see nothing. They're not coming from this side, if they're coming. Sandy, you better get that shotgun in back." He unstrapped his holster and began to count the bullets in his revolver.

Sandy went at a trot to the back room and came out a moment later with a heavy-gauge shotgun and a box of shells. He loaded up, and said, "Look, Monty, if you're thinking of holding off that bunch, just you and me—"

"What the hell do you expect me to do?"

"Get me out of here!" the prisoner screamed. "Get me out! They're not lynching me! Nobody's lynching me!"

The old man looked at him, frowned, and said. "Maybe he's got the right idea. Maybe we ought to get him out of here before we shoot some of our old friends, savin' his worthless neck—"

"What about me?" Gorwald cut in. "You can't leave me in here!"

They ignored him—there was too much else on their minds. Sandy said, "Let me get out there and see if I can slow 'em down a bit. Then you take the prisoner out the back, get in the Ford, and head for the Fremont place. You can pick up Carlie there—he'll know what to do."

"All right." The old man nodded. "We'll try it. Sure you can handle them, Sandy?"

The deputy slapped the butt of the shotgun. "Not too long," he said tightly. "So you better move fast."

The mechanic was panting against the bars, his eyes darting between the two men. Then, when Sandy left through the front door, he began rattling the bars again.

"Okay, okay," the old man grumbled. "You'll get your wish, bud—just take it easy and no funny stuff."

He took the key off the wall, drew his pistol, and unlocked the cell door. As he opened it, the mechanic moved with the striking surprise of a serpent. He put his palms together in an attitude of prayer, raised his hands over his head, and then brought them down sharply, cracking the sides of his palms against the old man's neck. Without a moan the Sheriff slumped to the concrete floor and lay still, keys and pistol clattering.

It happened so swiftly that Gorwald was more baffled than surprised. He looked dumbly at the old man on the floor, then at the prisoner. The mechanic stooped down, picked up pistol and keys, and came toward Gorwald's cell door.

Gorwald stepped back, watching the mechanic insert the key in the lock and swing the door open. Gorwald thought he was being liberated, in some inexplicable act of generosity on the mechanic's part; but then he saw the gun muzzle trained on the middle button of his business suit.

"Take it off," the mechanic rasped.

"What?"

"Take it off, buddy. Suit, pants, shirt. Off!"

"What are you talking about?" Gorwald said. "I won't do it!"

The mechanic cocked the pistol: it was like the crack of a whip.

"All right!" Gorwald said. "All right!"

Fumbling, he took off his jacket and placed it on the prison bunk. Then he stepped out of his trousers, reaching down instinctively to preserve the crease, but the mechanic snatched them from his hands. Gorwald, trembling in his underwear, started to remove his shirt and tie.

"Hurry!" the mechanic said. "Hurry, damn you!"

When the clothes were removed, the mechanic switched the pistol from his right to his left hand, and began taking off his grimy coveralls. It took the mechanic's next command to make Gorwald understand the meaning of the act.

"Put these on!" he said, tossing the coveralls at him.

"Why?" Gorwald said, fearful because he knew. "Why should I?"

"Because I'll kill you if you don't!"

Gorwald put them on.

When the transformation was complete, the mechanic waved Gorwald out of his cell and into the adjoining cage. Then he slammed the door shut, locked it, and tossed the keys and gun beside the fallen Sheriff.

"No," Gorwald said pleadingly. "Don't—"

But now the mechanic was in Gorwald's cell, pulling the door shut, without locking it. His timing was good. A moment later the jailhouse door was shattered open by the blow of a rifle butt.

The room quickly filled with howling men, and Gorwald screamed at the sight of them, screamed an explanation that they couldn't hear. He screamed when the keys went back into the lock and a dozen arms reached for him, clutched at him, then moved him along on a tide of purposeful anger toward the doorway.

He tried to tell them who he was, tell them the mistake they were making, and then speech and sight failed him as his head hit the hard, cold earth outside the Perryville jail . . .

"Don't talk," the Trooper said.

He pressed Gorwald's mouth gently with the damp cloth in his hand, as if to emphasize the order. Then he smiled, with the first hint of good humor Gorwald had seen in him since they met on the highway.

The back half of Gorwald's head felt twice its normal size. But the pain was bearable. He looked past the Trooper's khaki shoulder, and saw that he was back in his jail cell, but that the door was open. His hand felt the rough texture of the prison blanket beneath him.

"What happened?" he said feebly.

"You can thank Sandy for saving you," the Trooper said. "He fired some shots over the heads of the crowd and that scared them off for a while. I was just driving into town, and when they saw the patrol car they sobered up in a hurry."

Gorwald struggled to sit up. The Trooper told him to take it easy, but Gorwald got up anyway. He looked around the room, and then at the Trooper, who frowned.

"Yeah, we lost our pigeon, all right. He got away in all the fuss. But we'll catch up with him, don't you worry about that." He stood up and hooked a thumb in his belt. "I think we've given you enough of a hard time, Mr. Gorwald. You can forget about that speeding ticket, and I'll forget about that—loan you offered me." He grinned. "But when you leave this town, don't let me catch you hot-rodding again."

"I won't," Gorwald said fervently. "You can bet on that."

Gorwald made an early start the next morning. There was a bandage on his head, and the suit donated by the town fitted him too snugly under the arms and at his waist.

When he saw the young woman on the side of the road, with her imploring thumb, her tight blue sweater, her dusty suitcases, he slowed instinctively, and then shot past her. He didn't want any more trouble—he'd had enough.

But when he was a hundred yards in front of her, her trim, forlorn figure growing smaller in the rear-view mirror, he stopped the car and threw it into reverse.

He backed up slowly, and saw her thickly made-up face break into a smile. She wasn't beautiful, but he could have done worse. He was glad now that he had left the knife in the glove compartment.

Harold R. Daniels

The Master Stroke

Harry the Jackal had an almost foolproof scheme. In the beginning he succeeded every fifth time. Then he discovered the master stroke, the psychological clincher.

It isn't easy to find fault with a scheme like Harry the Jackal's. It worked successfully for ten years, although this is as much a tribute to the care Harry took with his preparations as to the basic scheme itself. And to the fact that he wasn't greedy.

Harry's needs were not great—twelve thousand dollars a year was his planned income. Of course, it was tax free. The scheme never did actually fail but Harry the Jackal was never quite the same man after the incident in New Haven. He never was able to work up the sinister arrogance that was so vital an ingredient in his *modus operandi*. He could no longer believe in people, and so he could no longer make them believe in him.

Harry arrived in New Haven on a Greyhound bus at nine-thirty on a rain-washed April evening—a purposely nondescript little man in his fifties. The ride had been a long one—all the way from Philadelphia—and he looked a shade travelworn.

The girl at the bus terminal newsstand who sold him the early edition of the Sunday paper smiled at him in sympathy and thought he looked quite a bit like her own father, tired with the years of straining to bring up a large family. She handed him a dry paper from the middle of the stack that the porter had just brought in. She would, she decided, save the wet ones for Yale students. Harry returned the girl's smile, picked up his bag, and walked out into the street. Across from the terminal a big hotel turned the sky rosy with neon. Farther down the street another hotel announced its rates less shamelessly.

Harry registered in the cheaper hotel, was given Room 304, borrowed a city directory, and went upstairs.

Room 304 was small, with faded wallpaper, a narrow bed, and a mismated desk and chair. Harry sat at the desk and peeled the comics, the women's pages, and the sporting section from his newspaper like limp leaves of lettuce. He glanced briefly at the front page which carried a banner headline. "Assailant of Broad Street Woman Still at Large." The story began: "Police reported no progress today in their efforts to apprehend the brutal assailant of Mrs. Henry Mitchell who was viciously slugged and beaten when she apparently surprised an intruder in her home late Saturday afternoon."

He was searching for the classified ads. When he found them he turned at once to the section marked Loans. There were at least two dozen insertions. From long experience Harry had learned to avoid the real sharks whose ads gave only telephone numbers.

He marked the chain loan agencies carefully with a pencil. Some of them had taken regular ads on the classified pages—on the outside positions of the page. They featured halftones of smiling, philanthropic men. "Come in and see me," the ads invited. "Ask for Mr. Benedetto (or Mr. Stone or Mr. Weiss). $50 to $500 on your signature alone."

Harry studied one of the pictures carefully. It was that of Mr. Oakley of Seacoast Brokers, Inc. Mr. Oakley had a long narrow face with hooded eyes. Even in the blurry halftone his smile looked forced. A very mean-natured man, Harry decided. He rather hoped that he would be doing business with Mr. Oakley.

He took a notebook from his breast pocket and opened it. The pages were filled with neat entries. One of them read: Seacoast Brokers, Trenton, N. J., August 1957—$3000. Harry sighed. Too near and too soon.

He studied the ads again. Commerce Discount House featured a Mr. Snavely whose photograph revealed a balding man of about thirty-five, with a worried frown and a rabbitty chin and mouth. A likely candidate, since there were no entries in his notebook for Commerce Discount House.

Harry reached for the city directory and looked up Mr. Snavely. He lived at 1004 Woodlawn Street. Harry noted this down carefully. It was, of course, far too early to tell—these were only the preliminaries.

Harry then showered in the chipped bathtub and went to bed. Before he did so, he sprayed his throat with antiseptic. A man couldn't be too careful with one of his basic assets.

In the morning he took out the city directory again. Commerce Discount House was located on Langwell Avenue in a congested semi-industrial area. Good. Woodlawn Street, where Mr. Snavely made his home, was approximately three miles away from Langwell Avenue at its nearest point. Good again.

He breakfasted daintily on Danish and coffee before he caught a Langwell bus, watching street numbers as the bus growled and butted its way through the morning traffic. He got off at a stop a few blocks away from Commerce Discount House and started walking. He couldn't have missed the place. It had a large neon sign that must have cost the interest on many a small loan. A smaller sign, on the stairway between a drug store and a men's haberdashery, added that Commerce Discount House was on the second floor.

Harry inspected the hallway carefully, then walked up the stairs and into the loan office.

The office was split in two by a partition that contained stalls designed to give borrowers privacy. Outside the partition were several benches and a table containing literature about loan plans. He picked up a flyer and pretended to read it while he studied the private side of the office. Three girls were operating typewriters and bookkeeping machines. One male clerk was in head-to-head conversation with a loan applicant in one of the stalls.

Mr. Snavely, recognizable from his picture in the newspaper, sat at a desk near a window. Through this window Harry could see the bulk of a large red-brick office building across Langwell Avenue.

He by no means intended to overstay his welcome. Still carrying the folder and with an air that said, "I'm going to look this over. I'll be back if I like what I read," he drifted out. The folder said that office hours were from nine to five on Mondays. At five he would come back.

He did. Timing it nicely, he came abreast to Commerce Discount just as a gaggle of office girls emerged, followed by Mr. Snavely. Harry, in turn, followed Mr. Snavely and watched him, at a nearby parking lot, get into a dingy-looking coupé.

Harry had not wasted his time between the two trips to Commerce Discount. When he left the office in the morning, he had crossed the street to the red-brick office building he had seen through Mr. Snavely's window. The building superintendent had shown him a small office on the second floor. Harry, looking timid and uncertain, had asked how much it was. "I'm going to start a little magazine subscription business," he had said, and taken out his wallet. "I thought maybe sixty a month—"

From long experience Harry had calculated the actual rental at forty-five dollars, tops. Practically stealing an extra ten or fifteen dollars made most building supers hasty deal-closers, and not apt to ask for references or credentials. If the building had been a rooming house, Harry could have saved money. A room, in this type of neighborhood, went for maybe twenty a month. But Harry was philosophical about it, shrugging it off as unavoidable overhead. By afternoon he had arranged for a telephone and had had a second-hand desk and chair sent in. These cost fifty dollars. In none of his transactions did he use his own name.

At seven that evening he picked out a restaurant from the city directory that was not far from the Snavely home on Woodlawn Street and found a bus that would take him there. A taxi would have been more comfortable but taxi drivers had better memories than bus drivers, as Harry well knew. Before he dined, he walked past the Snavely home—a shoebox Cape Cod with a fragment of yard. Mr. Snavely's car was parked in the driveway. This visit was not vital to his plans but Harry the Jackal had a paternal interest in his clients. In the living room he could see the Snavelys, husband and wife, cozily watching TV. A nice couple, probably no children. Harry approved.

His last act that evening was to buy an early edition of the morning paper. He noted with satisfaction that the assailant of the young housewife had not yet been caught. Not that it made too much difference. The crime had already had its psychological effect.

He was on the sidewalk outside the parking lot when Snavely brought his car in the following morning. There was always the chance that Mrs. Snavely might have wanted the car, in which case Harry would have had to postpone things temporarily. He was grateful. Harry didn't like to postpone the business in hand once it was under way.

As soon as Snavely was safely into his office. Harry caught a bus back to Woodlawn Street. He walked up the sidewalk to the Snavely home, taking a magazine subscription pad from his pocket as he rang the bell.

Mrs. Snavely was a dumpy little woman in her late thirties. Harry studied her briefly as she opened the door. A blue dress. Brown hair, done up in curlers.

He said tentatively, letting her see the pad, "Madam, I'm—"

She said, "I'm sorry. I already take—"

He listened while she recited the list of magazines that she already subscribed to. Sometimes he wondered, in a situation like this, just what he would do if a woman did want to take a subscription. When she had finished he turned away, making it easy for her to finish brushing him off.

He made three other calls on the Snavely block—just in case she was watching. Then he hurried back to the office he had rented the previous day. Through the window he could see into the office of Commerce Discount House across the street. Snavely was at his desk. Two or three clients were waiting. Not enough. Harry settled back with a magazine to wait until noon when there would undoubtedly be a queue of people waiting to make new loans or to make payments on old ones.

From time to time he glanced over to Snavely, across the street. Nice little guy. Nice little wife. After a time he began rehearsing. Not in The Voice. Just softly under his breath. The words he had been saying for ten years. "Hello, Snavely," he would say. (Or Smith or Jones or whatever.) "Listen to me now. Listen careful. I'm calling from your home. I've got your wife here. She looks nice in her blue dress (or red or brown), doesn't she, Snavely?" Scores of times, making his calls, he had watched shoulders stiffen at this personal touch. "Don't hang up, Snavely. Don't make a move. I've got a man right there in the room with you. Now here's what you'll do, Snavely, if you ever want to see your wife in one piece. Remember what happened to that other dame the day before yesterday. Take three thousand dollars from the safe. Walk slow, move easy. Put the money in an envelope and tell the girl at the switchboard that you'll be right back. You hear me, Snavely? Don't forget, you're being watched." And scores of times Harry had seen his man nod involuntarily at the order. "Now you take the envelope and a piece of scotch tape. You walk down the stairs with it and you stick it behind the radiator at the foot of the stairs when no one is looking." (The fire extinguisher or the trash bin or whatever Harry had decided on during his first inspection trip.) "Easy now, Snavely. Remember, you're being watched." There would always be that frightened look at the harmless people waiting to be served, one of them suddenly taking on the appearance of a vicious criminal. "Now leave the money like I said and then go out the door and keep walking. Get in your car at the parking lot and don't talk to anyone. Drive around for ten minutes and then come on home here. My partner will call me two minutes after you leave the money—call me right here at your house. If he says you behaved yourself, your wife will be all right."

In the early days of his career Harry collected from twenty per cent of his calls. The other eighty per cent of the time, the finance company manager would hang up the phone and quickly call his wife and the police in that order. No harm done. A crank call that was impossible to trace and was soon forgotten.

Then Harry had discovered the master stroke—watching the newspapers until he found a city where a housewife had been the victim of an assault or a murder. Harry deplored violence, of course. But he had found that his collections went up to eighty per cent in cities shocked by such a current crime. The psychological effect. The master stroke.

He had not failed, he recollected, in his last seven tries. A perfect score. In half an hour now, he would make the call to Snavely. Harry would watch him leave the office, hide the money, get in his car, and drive off. Then Harry would slip over, pick up the money, and vanish.

If the building superintendent ever wondered what had happened to his tenant and called the police—which was highly doubtful since the super could sell the desk and chair after the month was up and pocket some more graft—the police were not likely to connect the super's story with the extortion across the street. Snavely would rush home to find that his wife had not been intruded on— "No, dear. Nobody was here but the mailman and a poor old man selling magazines." Snavely would be reprimanded by his superior, maybe have to pay the money back. In due time the company's headquarters would send a flyer around to all its branches describing Harry's method. This did not bother Harry. He estimated that he could last another three or four years without hitting the same company twice—and by that time the flyers would have been forgotten.

Harry glanced across at Snavely again. He was still at his desk. There were a dozen people waiting now, a couple of them roughly dressed workmen. This was the psychological moment.

He picked up the telephone and dialed a number. When the girl said, "Commerce Discount," he said, "Let me talk to Mr. Snavely."

Only now did he use The Voice—a deep, corrugated basso with a sinister edge. "Snavely," he said, "Listen to me and listen carefully. I'm calling from your home."

Snavely said, "What's that?"

"Shut up and listen. I'm calling from your home. I've got your wife here. She looks nice in her blue dress, Snavely."

As expected, Snavely stiffened. "What do you mean?" he demanded.

"Don't hang up, Snavely. Don't make a move. I've got a man right there in the room with you." Through the window he saw Snavely look warily at the waiting men.

"Now here's what you'll do, Snavely, if you ever want to see your wife in one piece again. Don't forget what happened to that other dame the other day. If her old man had listened, she'd be alive right now. Take three thousand dollars out of the safe—"

Snavely said, "Three thousand dollars?"

"Three thousand dollars." Harry added just a little more vibrato to his basso.

"Wait a minute," Snavely said. Harry watched him carefully to make sure he wasn't giving any sort of signal to the office help. He wasn't. Snavely's voice rose a little. "You mean, if I don't take three thousand dollars out of the safe and do whatever it is you want me to do you'll—"

"That's what I said."

Snavely sighed. Very softly he said, "Wonderful. Wonderful."

From across the street, Harry the Jackal could see him lean back in his chair with a gentle smile as he carefully hung up the phone.

Harry the Jackal left New Haven that very night. He was, as previously mentioned, never quite the same man again.

Jacob Hay

The Exploit of the Embalmed Whale

*A delightful tale of espionage behind the Iron Curtain
. . . Meet an irresistible secret service agent, Alfred
Henry Nail, otherwise known as Colonel Valerian
Twentypenny.*

Hawker was in trouble, and furious thrice over. He was first furious at himself for permitting himself to be furious—for an agitated mind is not the mind one wishes to take into the assault on an impossible problem.

He was secondly furious at his superiors for wishing the problem on him in the first place. Leave it to good old Hawker, they'd told one another, and had all gone off to tea, complacently certain that good old Hawker would wangle it somehow.

Most of all he was furious at Twentypenny, who sat superbly at ease across the cluttered desk, peering at him genially, his monocle twinkling, a Turkish cigarette wisping fragrance aloft.

"The trouble with you intelligence people is your basic dishonesty," Twentypenny observed. "Given the simplest problem, you feel duty-bound to complicate it. Why, for example, do you call yourself the Tropical Rations Evaluation Board when, in point of fact, no one would be the wiser if you called yourself M.I. 5½? The truth is, my dear old Hawker, that yours is a case of nature imitating art; you've been reading too many spy novels."

This, coming from the deepest-dyed fraud he'd ever encountered in his career, was almost too much, Hawker thought. He glared fiercely from beneath the most fearsome pair of eyebrows in the War Office, and a small vein in his temple began to throb visibly.

It served him, he decided, bloody well right for ever having allowed himself to become involved with this insufferable little man. Colonel Valerian Twentypenny, forsooth! Born Alfred Henry Nail, sometime draper's clerk, lately Second Lieutenant (Hostilities Only), Royal Army Supply Corps, more recently unlicensed purveyor of dainties, by appointment to the more elegant black markets, and rogue errant. And still more recently involuntary consultant to the Tropical Rations Evaluation Board, whose precise function it is unwise to describe at any length, in view of the provisions of the Official Secrets Act.

"The man is a scoundrel," Hawker later had occasion to remark to his opposite number in the Admiralty, "but not a blackguard. More important, he gets results, although I'd rather not know just how he manages it. How he got Bultanyi out of Budapest passes the imagination. And that incident in Istanbul—amazing." And Hawker had chuckled with satisfaction.

Now, however, he felt far from that smug satisfaction.

"Spare me your lectures," he rasped, "and for Heaven's sake, do take that ruddy monocle out of your eye. What I want to know is whether you have any suggestions as to how we are to remove from a warehouse in Pilsen, Czechoslovakia, one ton of some new type of rocket propellant? Not an ounce of the stuff, mind you, nor a pound, but one bloody ton, and right out from under the Czechs' noses."

Valerian Twentypenny folded his fingers across his superlatively tailored waistcoat and pursed his lips beneath his enormous black Guards mustache. "That does seem rather a lot," he murmured. "May one inquire why so much?"

"Because our rocket people are desperately eager to put a fast one over on our American cousins, that's why. According to the reports, this new staff is pretty sensational—makes anything the Yanks have look feeble. So our boffins want more than enough for analysis; they want enough to put into one of their own playthings. Then they can send it up and cry triumphantly, 'See, we knew how to do it all along.' "

"Absurd," Twentypenny said decisively.

"Not so much as you might think. The Americans are getting a bit restive about our research programs, militarily speaking. And the Russkies are getting more and more convinced that we're letting the whole business go by default to the Yanks. In any event, ours not to reason why; ours but to produce."

"How much time have we?"

"As usual, none."

"In that case, I'd best be off," Twentypenny said, rising from the depths of the battered leather armchair which was Hawker's furthest concession to office luxury.

"Where the devil to?" Hawker asked, taken aback. "You can't quietly walk away from this, confound it!"

"You *are* edgy, old boy," Valerian Twentypenny reproached, resuming his monocle and settling his splendid jacket on his shoulders. "I'm going to Prague. When one intends to steal something from the Czechs, one should start at the top. And by the way, there's something you can be doing for me meanwhile."

"Name it."

"Set your people to finding me an embalmed whale," Twentypenny replied pleasantly. Hawker turned a curious shade of purple. "No, really, I'm quite serious."

"Now see here, dammit!" Hawker exploded.

"I should prefer a largish whale," Twentypenny said at the door. His smile was sunny, his manner serene. "I have always wanted a whale of my own."

And he was gone from the seedy chamber which housed the Tropical Rations Evaluation Board, the grimy windows of which rattled in their ancient frames as Hawker's fist slammed down on his desk.

Much restored by an excellent lunch served by a courteous attendant, Twentypenny relaxed in his seat and gazed unseeing from the window of his Berlin-bound plane, pondering the military mind. Hawker had told him earlier of the elaborate negotiations between the junior British air attaché and the group of anticommunist Czech scientists who had carefully and cunningly contrived to secrete a hoard of their newly developed rocket fuel in the Pilsen warehouse.

There had been endless furtive meetings, the giving and taking of intricate passwords, and all manner of ponderous nonsense, each bit of which endangered the whole operation. How far simpler it would have been if Hawker had come to him in the first place!

A simple, businesslike transaction would have arranged matters beautifully. A bank account of no inconsiderable size would have been established in Switzerland; the cooperating Commissar for Rocket Propellant Production would have found good and official reason to attend a scientific congress in Zurich, and the incident would have been closed. Of course, the Commissar might later meet with an unavoidable accident; but that was his affair.

But the military were like small boys playing at hide and seek; they would insist on the devious approach. They would somehow involve a group of rank amateurs like the Czech scientists.

Twentypenny lit a cigarette and sighed.

At Berlin there was a message from Hawker. An embalmed whale had been located at Amsterdam, where it was on display for the astonishment and edification of the Dutch. The whale and the giant lorry on which it was transported had been forthwith purchased and awaited Twentypenny's pleasure, together with a certain Captain Lars Bjornsson, a Norwegian and the whale's former owner, who had been retained in an advisory capacity. "Embalmed whales require careful handling," Hawker's message noted gravely. "Urge you make fullest use Bjornsson's technical knowledge."

"Bjornsson and whale to proceed soonest to Regensburg and await further orders," Twentypenny cabled Hawker. "Many

thanks for prompt action. Do you fancy Daphne as a name, provided whale of proper gender?"

Hawker's remarks on receipt of this communication will not
bear repetition. And his fist ached until late that evening.

During the flight from Berlin south to Prague, Twentypenny
took the opportunity to brief himself on the British whaling industry with the help of an excellent pamphlet prepared by the Ministry of Trade and published by Her Majesty's Stationery Office.
This done, he rechecked the really admirable credentials prepared
for him by the Documents Branch of the Tropical Rations Evaluation Board—elegant forgeries which attested him to be the official
European representative of the British Fisheries Industrial Council.

"And I was so hoping they'd send the London Philharmonic,"
muttered Her Britannic Majesty's Ambassador to the Czecho-
slovak Republic wistfully as he finished his perusal of Twentypenny's imposing papers. "However, I suppose they know what
they're doing. I'll arrange an appointment for you with the Minister of Culture and Education in the morning. Good day to you,
Colonel." As the door closed behind Valerian Twentypenny, the
Ambassador pressed a button, picked up his telephone, and spoke
sadly to his cultural attaché. "They've sent us a whale," he said.

"Monstrous," said the cultural attaché, his tone bitter.

"Quite," said the Ambassador, his tone resigned.

"I shall take but little of your Excellency's time," Twentypenny
said briskly the following morning to the People's Minister of Culture and Education, "for I realize how busy you must be. To be
blunt, I'm selling the British whaling story. You Czechs have sent
us your outstanding athletes, your wonderful folk dancers, your
finest concert artists." The Minister of Culture and Education
beamed. "Indeed," Twentypenny continued, warming to his
theme, "our program of cultural exchanges is, I firmly believe, an
example to the world. But—and who knows it better than your
Excellency—there is more to culture than folk dancing. A nation's
industry is a part of its culture, too.

"And that is why my government has asked the industry of

which I am proud to be European representative to prepare an exhibit to be displayed in Czechoslovakia."

"And this exhibit would consist of . . . ?" the Minister of Culture and Education inquired tentatively.

"A British-caught whale," Twentypenny replied, his voice ringing with the pride instinct in the son of a maritime people. "Suitably mounted for public display and demonstrating the whale's many contributions to our modern world. If it is said that the American pork packers use all of the pig but its squeal, it may be said with equal truth that we in British whaling use all of the cetacean but its spout, as it were."

"Amazing," murmured the Minister of Culture and Education. "One has read Melville, of course, but—amazing!"

"Consider the corset industry," Twentypenny bored inexorably ahead, "which despite all the advances in the manufacture of elastic yarns still requires an annual production of twenty thousand tons of whalebone." (And whoever was responsible for updating the Ministry of Trade's pamphlets, Twentypenny decided, had slipped badly on that one. 20,000 tons! Ridiculous!)

"Naturally," the Minister of Culture and Education observed, remembering his duty to his doctrine, "your exhibit will also point out that, under your capitalist system, no provision is made for whale conservation and repopulation; that the world's whales are being exploited for the benefit of the few, rather than the general good."

"We are prepared to go that far," Twentypenny conceded gravely, "in the interests of mutual understanding between our two great nations. Indeed, Excellency, I would be grateful if your own experts prepared a number of banners on which the facts you have outlined would be fully set forth. These will be displayed as part of the exhibit. Thus we can both be assured of satisfaction."

"A second-class power," the Minister of Culture and Education sneered to his First Deputy after Twentypenny's departure. "In the old days the British would never have knuckled under like that. I remember when I was desk clerk at the Bristol back in the bad old days—the British were intolerable." He smiled complacently. "But, my dear Ploski, we can afford to be generous to them in their decline. You will arrange to have banners prepared. Be sure they state clearly that this English whale died a victim of the class struggle."

"Where will this exhibition tour begin, Excellency?" asked the faithful Ploski, opening his notebook.

"Klatovy, since I understand the exhibit itself is now at Regensburg. Thence to Pilsen, and thence here to the capital. After that, we shall see."

The way thus prepared, Twentypenny had further cemented international relations by the purchase of a Skoda sedan, and it was in this vehicle that he traveled from Prague to the border at Zelezna Ruda where, in accordance with his telegraphed orders, Captain Lars Bjornsson awaited with the giant mammal that Twentypenny had fondly determined would be named Daphne, and gender be blowed.

Lars Bjornsson's size and appearance were such as to suggest that he had captured his awesome prize barehanded, with the odds heavily against the whale. His English was so heavily accented that he might have been mistaken for a Scot, although the fashion for immense red beards has passed its zenith north of the Tweed.

"Mighty 'tam fine beast, not so?" Bjornsson asked proudly, and Valerian Twentypenny could not but agree. They were standing inside the titanic lorry which housed a truly magnificent specimen of *physeter catodon,* or sperm whale, fully 50 feet long and resembling a thoughtfully disposed armored cruiser. It was, happily for Twentypenny's hopes, a girl whale. Large and black and prodigiously ugly, her huge bulk nearly filled the lorry's body, leaving only room for narrow walkways along her gleaming flanks. Even in repose, the giant head looked brutally dangerous.

From the forward end of the enormous van came the businesslike hum of a small petrol-driven generator which powered the refrigerating machinery by means of which Daphne was preserved. "Much better than embalming," Lars Bjornsson declared, his great voice reverberating dismally off the lorry's metal sides. "Sometimes embalming yust can't do the yob."

"And what happens then?" Twentypenny asked.

Bjornsson held his prow of a nose and assumed an expression of profound distaste. "You get yourself a new whale," he replied. "Fast."

"Hmmm," Twentypenny mused, gnawing the end of his mustache. "I suppose much the same thing would happen if anything went wrong with your refrigerating gear, eh?"

"Only faster. But don't you worry while Lars Bjornsson is on the yob. That machine will run forever, by golly." The Norwegian patted Daphne's towering snout. "Once she was full of oil, now she's full of copper tubing. At that, it's better than being boiled down for fertilizer."

"Oh, infinitely," Twentypenny agreed.

They stepped out of the van and inhaled deeply. The aroma inside Daphne's traveling home, all compound of cold whale and petrol, was not invigorating.

Along the sides of the lorry, again according to telegraphed directions, Bjornsson had caused to be painted legends informing the public that this was the International Traveling Exhibit of the British Whaling Association, a member in good standing of the British Fisheries Industrial Council. Beneath this statement was the stirring legend: *When You Think of Whales, Think Big— Think British.* Twentypenny had been absurdly pleased at this fancy. It was all, he told himself, most impressive.

"Now," he said to Lars Bjornsson as they strolled toward the none-too-inviting hotel in which, according to a plaque over the door, the Zelezna Ruda Junior Chamber of Marxist Dialecticians met for luncheon every Thursday, "I think it is time you knew more of my plans. I suggest that we share a bottle of the native brandy in my room."

At the conclusion of Twentypenny's recital the bearded Norseman silently drained his glass of brandy and refilled it. "That," he said solemnly, "was to honor a gallant whale. Now I drink to our survival."

"Our survival," Twentypenny echoed.

To say that Daphne's initial appearance in the town square of Klatovy was a thundering success would be to understate the case. Even a small whale is an uncommon spectacle in Klatovy, and Daphne was, as *physeter catodon* females go, no mean *physeter catodon.* From early in the morning until late in the evening Klatovy's residents queued in scores to see the whale in their midst.

Some days later Twentypenny, his whale, and his Norseman proceeded to Pilsen where Twentypenny promptly got in touch with the local representative of the Tropical Rations Evaluation Board, a dental surgeon named Novotny, who was thin and tall, terribly nervous and badly in need of a shave.

"Which one?" Novotny asked, peering uneasily into Twentypenny's mouth and fumbling with a long, gleaming steel probe.

"Right bicuspid," Twentypenny gargled. This absurd business of passwords again; this sham of seeking an appointment and waiting in Novotny's unreasonably depressing reception room.

"The warehouse at Number Sixty, Griesecki Street," Novotny whispered hoarsely, his Adam's apple bobbing in an ecstasy of terror. He reached for his drill. "Please to scream," he whispered as he pressed a switch and the drill began to whirr.

"Have you no pride of workmanship?" Twentypenny demanded sharply. "Stop that wretched noise, and stop quivering. I shall have my truck at the warehouse tomorrow evening. See that your friends are ready to load it."

"Please," Novotny pleaded, his forehead beaded with perspiration, his eyes liquid with anxiety, "just a small scream . . ."

Hell, thought Twentypenny, taking a deep breath.

Outside in the waiting room the last patient of the day, a clerk in the State Tobacco Monopoly, leaped like a stricken doe, took one horror-stricken glance at the door to the dentist's operating chambers, and fled. It sounded as if Novotny were killing somebody in there.

"It is not beer as we understand the term in Oslo, but it is not bad," Lars Bjornsson said later that evening after a prolonged sampling of the produce of Pilsen's famed breweries. "Here's to tomorrow, and our grand openings—both of them." He winked as Twentypenny raised his glass in response to the toast.

In Pilsen no less than Klatovy, Daphne proved an immediate popular success. The immense lorry was parked in Lenin Place (formerly Adolf Hitlerplatz, once Stefanik Square), and the ancient buildings surrounding the tree-shaded square echoed and re-echoed to the recorded lecture on British whaling techniques which had been provided by the Special Effects Branch of the Tropical Rations Evaluation Board. Long queues formed as Pilsen lined up to file slowly through the lorry past Daphne's lowering glare and down her leathery sides. Twentypenny accepted with becoming modesty the congratulations of the Pilsen Regional Sub-Director of Culture and Education, who had come to make a personal inspection of the display.

At 2:30 P.M., shortly after the Regional Sub-Director had finished his tour of Daphne's remains, there occurred a breakdown in the refrigerating machinery which maintained her even temperature and, with expressions of regret courteously translated and delivered to the waiting public by the Regional Sub-Director himself, the exhibition was temporarily closed.

"But you must not trouble yourself further, Excellency," Twentypenny declared. "It is a minor matter and easily remedied, I'm sure. My driver—the big chap with the beard—tells me he has already arranged to move our lorry to a warehouse in Griesecki Street where we can effect the necessary repairs. It is advisable, you comprehend, to get our vehicle under cover, out of the sun."

"But you are most welcome to the use of the facilities of the People's Tractor Works, Comrade Colonel."

"Wouldn't dream of it, my dear chap. But I really think we'd best be getting on with the job. Warm day, and all that . . ."

Once inside the large, dimly lighted shed at 60 Griesecki Street, it was but the work of seconds for Lars Bjornsson to replace the bit of wiring he had removed from the refrigerating machinery. At the rear of the van Twentypenny and Dr. Novotny, his teeth a-chatter, concluded arrangements for the transfer of the rocket propellant with Korovnic, chief research chemist of the People's Rocket Works.

Then, atop Daphne and roughly amidships, Bjornsson strained briefly and removed a large square hatch by means of which he was enabled to descend into Daphne's hollow, rib-vaulted interior to check on the copper tubing through which flowed the coolants so vital to her preservation. The Norwegian flicked a switch inside the hatch and Daphne's innards glowed eerily. Then he vanished below decks, as it were.

"Plenty room," came his voice, much muffled.

Now from the shadows at the rear of the warehouse emerged a small band of men bearing stout wooden crates. Twentypenny mounted the ladder leaning against Daphne's side, and swiftly and efficiently the crates were passed up to him and by him lowered into the waiting arms of Lars Bjornsson.

An hour later the job was done. Daphne was loaded to what would have been the gills had she not been a mammal.

"Free Czechoslovakia will never forget this," Korovnic declared, his voice vibrant with emotion.

"I don't suppose," Dr. Novotny put in wistfully, "there's an extra bit of room inside there? I mean, there's bound to be a stench about this affair, and perhaps one would be well advised to . . ."

Twentypenny surveyed the dentist with distaste. It would, he thought, serve the man right. On the other hand, Novotny had rendered an important service to the Tropical Rations Evaluation Board.

"Climb aboard," he said brusquely. "But remember, you asked for whatever you get." He lit a cigarette and inhaled deeply. Despite its size, the warehouse was already richly redolent of cetacean. It was the first fish-flavored cigarette Twentypenny had ever tasted.

The hum of the refrigerating machinery took on an eccentric note as Lars Bjornsson climbed down from the lorry, looking shaken.

"Not even the man who invented it could fix it now," he said heavily. "I give it about six hours and then—" He shrugged.

With the lorry once more installed in Lenin Place, Twentypenny sought out the Regional Sub-Director of Culture and Education and once more apologized for the interruption to the exhibit. "We haven't quite been able to overcome a slight malfunction," he said soothingly, "but we mustn't let that interfere with our mission of bringing the whale's fascinating story to the good people of Pilsen. I feel certain that we'll have everything tickerty-boo by tomorrow, or the day after at the latest."

"I am sure you will," said the Regional Sub-Director, quietly pleased at this demonstration of the marked inferiority of British refrigerating devices. "You would not object, I trust, to hanging another banner on your van, pointing out that such failures would never happen in a Russian-made machine?"

"It will be a moral lesson to us all," Twentypenny replied.

Attendance that day, which was warm for the season of the year, dropped sharply. The following day was still warmer. Lenin Place was deserted; its windows stood closed and curtained.

Twentypenny and Lars Bjornsson stood stubbornly by their van, wreathed in great clouds of pipe smoke. The recorded lecture boomed remorselessly on. The refrigeration machinery had long since ceased even its tubercular coughing.

Daphne was going.

"Hang on, old boy, and breathe slowly," Twentypenny grated around the stem of his pipe. "They can't hold out much longer."

"I wouldn't mind so much if it didn't burn my eyes," the Norseman said grimly, exhaling a jet of smoke.

Unheard beneath the roar of the lecture came a series of thumps from Daphne's interior. Gradually they grew weaker and then ceased altogether.

A breath of air stirred the wilted leaves on the ancient trees bordering the square. Several blocks away a policeman named Josef Hrudlic paused in his dutiful pacing, sniffed and sniffed again. Then he shook his head as if to clear it. Today was not Friday. It was absurd. But there it was again. Patrolman of the Second Grade Hrudlic began to walk away from it. He increased his stride, but to no avail. It was still with him, only more powerful now, it seemed. He began to run.

How unfair it was, he thought, that he, Josef Hruldic, who had just passed his examination for promotion to Patrolman of the First Grade, should be the first to die as the Western Imperialists launched World War III in the form of a poison gas attack on the innocent city of Pilsen.

Thereafter, events moved forward with eminently satisfactory speed. Let no one declare that, given a crisis, the Czechs cannot react swiftly and decisively.

At the border crossing at Zelezna Ruda, Twentypenny crawled down from the lorry's cab and confronted the Regional Sub-Director of Culture and Education, who was nattily attired for the occasion in the gilt-braided uniform of his office and a gas mask.

"For the last time, I protest this high-handed and outrageous expulsion," Twentypenny said loudly and harshly. "I shall complain to the Minister himself that our agreement has been violated. Our whole program of international cultural exchanges is endangered by your foolhardy actions. And furthermore, what about my Skoda?"

By way of reply, the Regional Sub-Director raised his arm and pointed west. "Out!" he yelled, although the effect he had intended was somewhat marred by the gas mask.

"I demand to be permitted to telephone Prague," Twentypenny thundered. "I am a British citizen and I have my rights."

The Regional Sub-Director turned in the seat of his official limousine and raised his right arm. From the turret of the medium tank just to the rear, a lieutenant of the Second Light Armored Division nodded briskly, gas mask bobbing, and the tank's long-barreled gun swung purposefully toward Twentypenny.

"Out, out, out!" howled the Regional Sub-Director as the face-piece of his overburdened gas mask sprang a small leak.

Engine roaring, the huge lorry trundled slowly out of Czechoslovakia, gathering speed as it approached the border station of the West German Federal Republic. From its sides streamed the tattered banners proclaiming Daphne's identity. Now they were utterly redundant. Daphne's identity was unmistakable for miles around.

From the interior of his impeccably maintained check point, *Oberleutnant* Friedrich Shaffer of the Border Police stared through the eyepieces of his gas mask and grinned gleefully. *Der Englischer* was coming through exactly as planned.

Two miles down the road waited a squad of his men, suitably protected. There the Englishman's mysterious cargo was to be unloaded and transferred to another van, after which the lorry now careening past was to be doused with petrol and burned. The plan was simple and efficient, and *Oberleutnant* Shaffer's tidy Teutonic soul was soothed at its smooth functioning. As to what it all signified, a simple lieutenant of Border Police did not question the instructions he had received from Bonn.

Overcome by a sudden whim, *Oberleutnant* Shaffer slipped his gas mask off momentarily. *"Lieber Gott,"* he whispered, awed, as he hastened to resume its aroma-proof safety.

"It was, my dear old Hawker, simplicity itself," Twentypenny told his chief that evening at the hotel in Regensburg, whither he and Lars Bjornsson had repaired to refresh themselves. "Although I shall never be able to face a fish again as long as I live. Poor Novotny will live, they tell me from the hospital, but he needs a long rest and plenty of fresh air. And I suspect that Bjornsson here has rather had the whale and its finny friends."

"There are other careers yust as rewarding," said the Norwegian, taking a large sip of his brandy and wincing.

"I know," Twentypenny said hurriedly. "Everything will taste like bouillebaisse for a few days, and then things will come back to normal." He turned back to Hawker. "But the real credit is yours, old boy."

"Mine!" yipped the Chief of the Tropical Rations Evaluation Board, bristling fearsomely. "Mine! Of all the idiotic schemes I've ever heard of, this tops the wildest. And you accuse me of it! Ha!" His snort was ferocious.

"But after all, old son," murmured Colonel Valerian Twentypenny reproachfully, his eye wicked behind his gleaming monocle, "it was you who said the problem was merely one of getting the stuff out from under their noses. And that's all we've done, really. You see how simple these things become if you avoid complicating them?"

He raised his glass. "To Daphne," he said quietly. "I shall miss the old girl."

Avram Davidson

Where Do You Live, Queen Esther?

*When we asked Avram Davidson to suggest an alternate
title for "Where Do You Live, Queen Esther?" he
considered other titles, then wrote a defense,
explanation, and justification for his original choice.
Mr. Davidson's words are just too good to be passed
over—and, in a sort of minor miracle, they add depth
and dimension to his story.*

 Mr. Davidson is now speaking: Where does *Queen
Esther live? In the United States? In the West Indies?
In the Twentieth Century of electric toasters, washing
machines, and television sets? In the Eighteenth
Century of cruel Creole slaveholders, obeah, duppy?
She lives in a world composed of all these elements,
plus elements that make up a world peculiar to herself
and a few thousand other Negroes and mixed-bloods
inhabiting remote and tiny islands, a world of Biblical
Hebrew first-names and antique African-Amerindian
sorcery and archaic English . . . Where, indeed,* do
*you live, Queen Esther?—and though we can never live
there ourselves, may we not catch at least a fleeting
glimpse of it?—where old kings still reign and old gods
have never died?*

 *There is more than a little magic in this unusual
story. Savor it—we think you will find it a haunting
experience . . .*

Cold, cold, it was, in the room where she lodged, so far from her work. The young people complained of the winter, and those born to the country—icy cold, it was, to them. So how could a foreign woman bear it, and not a young one? She had tried to find another job not so far (none were near). *Oh, my, but a woman your age shouldn't be working, the ladies said. No, no, I couldn't, really.* Kindly indeed. Thank you, mistress.

There was said to be hot water sometimes in the communal bathroom down the hall—the water in the tap in her room was so cold it burned like fire: so strange: hot/cold—but it was always too late when she arrived back from work. Whither she was bound now. Bound indeed.

A long wait on the bare street corner for the bus. Icy winds and no doorway, even, to shelter from the winds. In the buses—for there were two, and another wait for the second—if not warm, then not so cold. And at the end, a walk for many blocks. But in the house it was warm. The mistress not up yet.

Mistress . . . Queen Esther thought about Mrs. Raidy, the woman of the house. At first her was startled by the word—to she it mean, a woman live with a man and no marriage lines. But then her grew to like it, Mrs. Raidy did. Like to hear, too, mention of *the Master* and *the young Master,* his brother.

Both of they at table. "That second bus," Queen Esther said, unwrapping her head. "He late again. Me think, just to fret I."

"Oh, a few minutes don't matter. Don't worry about it," the master, Mr. Raidy, said. He never called the maid by name, nor did the mistress, but the boy—

As now, looking up with a white line of milk along his upper lip, he smiled and asked, "Where do you live, Queen Esther?" It was a game they played often. His brother—quick glance at the clock, checking his watch, head half turned to pick up sounds from upstairs, said that he wasn't to bother "her" with his silly question. A pout came over the boy's face, but yielded to her quick reply.

"Me live in the Carver Rooms on Fig Street, near Burr."

His smile broadened. "Fig! That's a fun-ny name for a street . . . But where do you live at home, Queen Esther? *I* know:

Spahnish Mahn. And what you call a fig we call a bah-nah-nah. See, Freddy? *I* know."

The older one got up. "Be a goodboynow," he said, and vanished for the day.

The boy winked at her. "Queen Esther from Spanish Man, Santa Marianne, Bee-Double-You-Eye. But I really think it should be Spanish *Main,* Queen Esther." He put his head seriously to one side. "That's what they used to call the Caribbean Sea, you know."

And he fixed with his brooding ugly little face her retreating back as she went down to the cellar to hang her coat and change her shoes.

"The sea surround we on three sides at Spanish Man," she said, returning.

"You should say, 'surrounds *us,*' Queen Esther . . . You have a very funny accent, and you aren't very pretty."

Looking up from her preparations for the second breakfast, she smiled. "True *for* you, me lad."

"But then, neither am I. I look like my father. I'm *his* brother, not *hers,* you know. Do you go swimming much when you live at home, Queen Esther?"

She put up a fresh pot of coffee to drip and plugged in the toaster and set some butter to brown as she beat the eggs; and she told him of how they swim at Spanish Man on Santa Marianna, surrounded on three sides by the sea. It was the least of the Lesser Antilles . . . She lived only part of her life in the land she worked in, the rest of the time—in fact, often at the same time—she heard, in the silence and cold of the mainland days and nights, the white surf beating on the white sands and the scuttling of the crabs beneath the breadfruit trees.

"I thought I would come down before you carried that heavy tray all the way upstairs," said the mistress, rubbing her troubled puffy eyes. Her name was Mrs. Eleanor Raidy—she was the master's wife—and her hair was teased up in curlers. She sat down with a grunt, sipped coffee, sighed. "What would I ever do without you?"

She surveyed the breakfast-in-progress. "I hope I'll be able to eat. And to retain. Some mornings," she said, darkly. Her eyes made the rounds once more. "There's no pineapple, I suppose?" she asked faintly. "Grated, with just a little powdered sugar?— Don't go to any extra trouble," she added, as Queen Esther opened the icebox. "Rodney. *Rod*ney? Why do I have to shout and—"

"Yes, El. What?"

"In *that* tone of voice? If it were for my pleasure, I'd say nothing. But I see your brother doesn't care if you eat or not. Half a bowl of—"

"I'm finished."

"You are not finished. Finish now."

"I'll be *late,* El. They're waiting for me."

"Then they'll wait. Rush out of here with an empty stomach and then fill up on some rubbish? No. Finish the cereal."

"But it's *cold.*"

"Who let it get cold? I'm not too sure at all I ought to let you go. This Harvey is older than you and he pals around with girls older than he is. Or maybe they just fix themselves up to look—Eat. Did you *hear* what I say? Eat. Most disgusting sight I ever saw, lipstick, and the *clothes?* Don't let me catch you near them. They'll probably be rotten with disease in a few years." Silently, Queen Esther grated pineapple. "I don't like the idea of your going down to the Museum without adult supervision. Who knows what can happen? Last week a boy your age was crushed to death by a truck. Did you have a—*look* at me, young man, when I'm talking to you—did you have a movement?"

"Yes."

"Ugh. If looks could kill. I don't believe you. Go upstairs and —Rod*ney!*"

But Rodney had burst into tears and threw down his spoon and rushed from the room. Even as Mrs. Raidy, her mouth open with shock, tried to catch the maid's eye, he slammed the door behind him and ran down the front steps.

The morning was proceeding as usual.

"And his brother leaves it all to me," Mrs. Raidy said, pursuing a piece of pineapple with her tongue. She breathed heavily. "I have you to thank, in part, I may as well say since we are on the subject, for the fact that he wakes up screaming in the middle of the night. I warned you. Didn't I warn you?"

Queen Esther demurred, said she had never spoken of it to the young master since that one time of the warning.

"One time was enough. What was that word? That name? From the superstitious story you were telling him when I interrupted. Guppy?"

"Duppy, mistress." It was simply a tale from the old slave days, Queen Esther reflected. A cruel Creole lady who went to the fields one night to meet she lover, and met a duppy instead. The slaves all heard, but were affrighted to go out; and to this day the pile of stones near Petty Morne is called The Grave of Mistress-Serve-She-Well.—Mistress Raidy had suddenly appeared at the door, as Queen Esther finished the tale, startling Master Rodney.

"Why do you tell the child such stories?" she had demanded, very angry. "See, he's scared to death."

"*You* scared me, El—sneaking up like that."

Queen Esther hastened to try to distract them.

" 'Tis only a fancy of the old people. Me never fear no duppy—"

But she was not allowed to finish. The angry words scalded her. And she knew it was the end of any likelihood (never great) that she might be allowed to move her things into the little attic room, and save the hours of journeying through the cutting, searing cold.

Said the mistress, now, "Even the sound of it is stupid . . . He didn't eat much breakfast." She glanced casually out the window at the frost-white ground. "You noticed that, I suppose."

Over the sound of the running water Queen Esther said, "Yes." She added detergent to the water. He never did eat much breakfast—but she didn't say this out.

"No idea why, I suppose? No? Nobody's been feeding him anything—that you know of? No spicy West Indian messes, no chicken and rice with bay leaves? Yes, yes, I know: not since that one time. All right. A word to the wise is sufficient." Mrs. Raidy arose. A grimace passed over her face, "Another day. And everything is left to me. Every single thing . . . Don't take all morning with those few dishes."

Chicken and rice, with bay leaves and peppercorns. Queen Esther, thinking about it now, relished the thought. Savory, yes. Old woman in the next yard at home in Spanish Man, her cook it in an iron caldron. Gran'dame Hephsibah, who had been born a slave and still said "wittles" and "vhiskey" . . . Very sage woman. But, now, what was wrong with chicken and rice? The boy made a good meal of it, too, before he sister-in-law had come back, unexpected and early. Then shouts and tears and then a dash to the bathroom. "You've made him sick with your nasty rubbish!" But, for true, it wasn't so.

Queen Esther was preparing to vacuum the rug on the second floor when the mistress appeared at the door of the room. She dabbed at her eyes. "You know, I'm not a religious person," she observed, "but I was just thinking: It's a blessing the Good Lord didn't see fit to give me a child. You know why? Because I would've thrown away my life on it just as I'm throwing it away on my father-in-law's child. Can you imagine such a thing? A man fifty-two years old, a widower, suddenly gets it into his head to take a wife half his age—" She rattled away, winding up, "And so now they're both dead, and who has to put up with the results of his being a nasty old goat? No . . . Look. See what your fine young gentleman had hidden under the cushion of his bedroom chair."

And she riffled the pages of a magazine. Queen Esther suppressed a smile. It was only natural, she wanted to say. Young gentlemen liked young ladies. Even up in this cold and frozen land—true, the boy was young. That's why it was natural he only looked—and only at pictures.

"Oh, there's very little gets past *me,* I can assure you. Wait. When he gets back. Museum trips. Dirty pictures. Friends from who knows where. No *more!"*

Queen Esther finished the hall rugs, dusted, started to go in to vacuum the guest room. Mrs. Raidy, she half observed in the mirror, was going downstairs. Just as the mistress passed out of sight, she threw a glance upward. Queen Esther only barely caught it. She frowned. A moment later a faint jar shook the boards beneath her feet. The cellar door. Bad on its hinges. Queen Esther started the vacuum cleaner; a sudden thought made her straighten up, reach for the switch. For a moment she stood without moving. Then she propped the cleaner, still buzzing, in a corner, and flitted down the steps.

There was, off the kitchen, a large broom closet, with a crack in the wall. Queen Esther peered through the crack. Diagonally below in the cellar was an old victrola and on it the maid had draped her coat and overcoat and scarf; next to it were street shoes, not much less broken than the ones she wore around the house.

Mistress Raidy stood next to the gramophone, her head lifted, listening. The hum of the vacuum cleaner filtered through the house. With a quick nod of her head, tightlipped in concentration, the mistress began going through the pockets of the worn garments. With little grunts of pleasurable vexation she pulled out a half-pint bottle of fortified wine, some pieces of cassava cake—"That's all we need. A drunken maid. Mice. Roaches. *Oh,* yes."—a smudged hektographed postal card announcing the Grand Annual Festivity of the St. Kitts and Nevis Wesleyan Benevolent Union, a tattered copy of Lucky Tiger Dream Book, a worn envelope . . .

Here she paused to dislodge a cornerless photograph of Queen Esther's brother Samuel in his coffin and to comment, "As handsome as his sister." There were receipts for international postal orders to Samuel's daughter Ada—"Send my money to foreign countries." A change purse with little enough in it, and a flat cigarette tin. This she picked at with nervous fingers, chipping a nail. Clicking her tongue, she got it open, found, with loathing large upon her face—

—a tiny dried frog—a *frog?*—a—surely *not!*—

"Oh!" she said, in a thin, jerky, disgusted voice. "Uh. *Uh!*" She threw the tin away from her, but the thing was bound with a scarlet thread and this caught in her chipped fingernail.

"—out of this *house!*" she raged, flapping her wrist, "and never set foot in it *again,* with her *filthy-ah!*" The thread snapped, the thing flew off and landed in a far corner. She turned to go and had one unsteady foot on the first step when she heard the noise behind her.

Later on, when Queen Esther counted them, she reckoned it as twenty-five steps from the broom closet to the bottom of the cellar stairs. At that moment, though, they seemed to last forever as the screams mounted in intensity, each one seeming to overtake the one before it without time or space for breath between. But they ceased as the maid clattered down the steps, almost tripping over the woman crouched at the bottom.

Queen Esther spared she no glance, then, but faced the thing advancing. Her thrust she hand into she bosom. "Poo!" her spat. "You ugly old duppy! Me never fear no duppy, no, not me!"

And her pulled out the powerful obeah prepared for she long ago by Gran'dame Hephsibah, that sagest of old women, half Carib, half Coromantee. The duppy growled and drivvled and bared its worndown stumps of filthy teeth, but retreated step by step as her came forward, chanting the words of power; till at last it was shriveled and bound once more in the scarlet thread and stowed safely away in the cigarette tin. *Ugly old duppy . . . !*

Mr. Raidy took the sudden death of his wife with stoical calm. His young brother very seldom has nightmares now, and eats heartily of the savory West Indian messes that Queen Esther prepares for all three of them. Hers is the little room in the attic; the chimney passes through one corner of it, and Queen Esther is warm, warm, warm.

Geoffrey Household

To Die with Decency

*"There was no telling where the generosity of wine
ended and Andalusian pride began." But murder is
never far away from inordinate pride . . .
a distinguished story.*

The only murderer I ever knew was a personal friend. Yet I had
to admit that his sentence was absolutely just, legal, and merited.
Even the Military Police were kind to Valdes. They assured him
that it did not hurt at all to be executed by a firing squad. Valdes
politely agreed with them—not that he cared about pain. He was
as used to that as a retired boxer, and looked a little like one, too.

He wanted to live as eagerly as the rest of us, but he realized
that his death, like any other military ceremony, had to be performed with dignity. He was a soldier all through. He made one
understand the character of that handful of men who conquered
the Americas. Yet the luck of war had landed him in a noncombatant unit.

He was an Andalusian, sturdy, of middle height, and with the
type of face which the Spaniards call *chato*—looking as if it had
been flattened out by a steam roller and come up smiling. It
must be common in the Peninsula. I had three other toughs with
much the same lack of features.

Valdes had fought right through the Spanish Civil War and been interned in France at the end of it. In 1940 some of those internees were evacuated before the Germans could grab them and formed into a Spanish commando. A good idea on paper. What they didn't know about bloodshed wasn't worth knowing. And yet their commando was unusable—too fierce, too desperate. They hadn't the flair of the British for discreet, deadly action.

When the Spanish commando was disbanded, Valdes, with a few of his mates, was posted to the Pioneer Corps. What an outfit that was! We had plain laborers recruited from Africa or obscure islands in the Indian Ocean, and able-bodied poor of every color in need of work and regular rations, and always some Q men, as they were called—habitual army criminals who had learned by experience and low cunning to anticipate the psychiatrist's next move and to get themselves registered as psychopathics. My own company was a mixture of Arabs, Q men, and vaguely oriental beachcombers. Corporal Valdes and his section of Spaniards formed a solid island of sanity and hard work.

In 1944 the company was with the Eighth Army in Italy, cleaning up close behind the advance. My main trouble was Italian hospitality. The men were not accustomed to red wine in that quantity. Valdes and his Spaniards, who were, acted off duty as nursemaids in the cafés. The amount of murder and theft those fellows prevented was astonishing. They were proud of the reputation of the British Army—yes, proud of it, even in the Pioneer Corps. For them there was no other army in the war at all.

"My captain," Valdes said to me one night, "we cannot all be in the Guards. But we wish to assure you that we know how to die with decency."

They were going out beyond the front line with a Field Company of sappers to fill up craters in a mountain track which was going to be badly needed the next day. It was late in the evening when they volunteered for the job, and they were all, I suppose, at the third liter; but there was no telling where the generosity of wine ended and Andalusian pride began.

Pride. Perhaps murder is never very far from it. There didn't seem room for either when one morning I sent Valdes and his section down to the railhead to collect a consignment of picks and shovels. Nothing but picks and shovels—but to Valdes they were Toledo steel. I had seen him use them under shell fire with such nonchalance that even the Q men didn't find an excuse to run back to safety.

That hardware was important to my Spaniards—so important that when a young French sergeant told them to get the hell out of the way and let him load his truck with warlike stores they ignored him. Unfortunately Valdes, after two years of internment, spoke French. Unfortunately, too, he had that unreasonable Spanish contempt for his neighbor across the northern frontier. At last he told the French sergeant to pipe down and wait his turn.

The sergeant replied that he was not going to wait for any noncombatant sons-of who were not even fit to shovel—well, you can imagine the number of uses that an angry and imaginative Frenchman could find for a shovel. Valdes did not lose his temper. He rose to the occasion with dignity and developed his favorite creed—that if there were no shovels, the luckier men who had fighting to do would never get near enough to the front line to do it. The Frenchman (so much we had in evidence) remarked that all the British Army ever did was shoveling while their allies did the fighting.

Corporal Valdes quietly picked up a rifle belonging to the French detachment and shot the sergeant dead.

It was astonishing how correct and soldierly Valdes' movements then were. The only authority handy was the railway transport officer. While the startled Frenchmen were busy with their sergeant, Valdes marched up to the R.T.O., saluted smartly, gave his name and unit, handed over the rifle, and reported the incident. The R.T.O. wiped the sweat off his elderly brow—he had been naturally disconcerted by the approach of a murderer with a loaded rifle—and sent for the Military Police. The section, still an island of proud discipline, returned to camp.

There was nothing I could do. If it had been a British soldier he had shot, I think I might have got the court-martial sentence reviewed and had Valdes punished by a long term of imprisonment. But he had shot an ally, and allies were touchy. It was more essential for the war effort that Valdes should die than that the French should suffer a sense of grievance.

He admitted as much himself. He did not regret the murder at all; he only regretted that it had been unavoidable. He pointed out that he had paid no attention to personal insults, but that an insult to the British Army was not to be borne. For three years, he said, we had treated him as a friend and a gentleman. The least he could do in return was to defend our honor.

I was determined that Valdes should not be executed. Somehow I, a mere captain, reached the French G.O.C. I speak reasonable French—that and a bit of Arabic and the remains of several tropical diseases were my qualifications for the Pioneer Corps— and I nearly won him over. I insisted that there was no need to prove Valdes mad; to shoot an unknown and gallant Frenchman he must be mad.

The general was exquisitely courteous. He knew that these were mere empty words, but they pleased him. Speaking for himself, he said at last, Valdes could be reprieved; but for the sake of the suffering mothers of France and the damned politicians—he dared to couple the two together with the irony of a man who was absolutely sure of himself—he regretted that he could not interfere.

I came to a dead end.

I tried the corps psychiatrist—with whom, thanks to the curiosities among my Q men, I was on excellent terms. He told me that Valdes had the only faultlessly healthy human mind he had met in years, and that if hard scientific lying could help him, helped he would be. He did his dishonest best, but the big shots above him refused to play. About ten per cent of my company had deserved a firing squad at some time, and they were tired of finding excuses for their behavior. They refused to distinguish between Q men and emotionally primitive Spaniards.

I had no military ambition. I was just a gray-haired captain, only fit enough for the Pioneer Corps. So my plans for saving Valdes were quite uninhibited. I seriously considered every trick one reads of in fiction—down to supplying the firing squad with blanks and bribing them to say nothing. But not a single one of my ideas was practicable.

Valdes' section was equally desperate. They took it for granted that I was on their side. Their experience of impossible escapes in the chaos of civil war was to the point, but such plans in a more formal army were unworkable. Private Moreno, who was some sort of relation of Valdes from the days when they had possessed homes and wives, wanted to get inside the jail and substitute himself for the condemned man. He couldn't very well be shot instead, and a court-martial—always merciful when its collective sense of humor was aroused—was unlikely to give him more than a year.

I thought about it night after night. I even trained Moreno to imitate Valdes' voice and accent. But he was more than an inch too tall; and though he did have a similar type of squashed and wrinkled features in the same tint of deep tan, common sense insisted that one could never be mistaken for the other unless they were heavily made up or bandaged, and then only in a crowd of Arabs or Englishmen.

Valdes was in the jug at Bari. I used to drive down and see him whenever I had a spare moment and could invent a reasonable excuse. On what would have to be my last visit, two days before he was due to be executed, I ran into the corps psychiatrist being let out through the formidable gate as I was being let in.

"Another of your beauties," he said to me.

"Who is it this time?"

"Pidgegood. There's nothing wrong with him whatever except that he knows as much of our routine as I do. You can have him back when he's served his sentence."

Myself, I knew all along that there was not a trace of maladjustment in Pidgegood; he had merely been born without a sense of shame. But it had taken a long time for overconscientious psychiatrists to realize that jail was the proper place for him. He was a gipsy, or said he was. He had found in peacetime that wild eyes and dirt and a general air of rural eccentricity always intimidated housewives and farmers, and he trusted that the military were just as easy.

They were. Pidgegood couldn't read or write, but he had the cunning of the devil to make up for it. By the time he had been dismissed from his battalion as an incorrigible and cowardly rogue, he knew enough psychiatry to fool any solemn doctor. He put on an act just sufficiently unbalanced to make sure that his crimes would land him in a mental ward rather than a cell, but not enough to get him invalided out of the service. He preferred the army—what little he saw of it—to being drafted into a factory.

Courts-martial had no effect whatever on him; he always came back to me with a careful letter of advice from the psychiatrists. But my chaps found a use for the man. If there were any inquiries about missing pigs or chickens and no chance of the company's innocence being believed, they always put the blame on Pidgegood. He was perfectly willing to accept it, even on the rare occasions when he wasn't guilty, and was rewarded by privileged idleness.

I was far from fond of him, but he was a part of my company. So I asked to be escorted to his cell and went there before my visit to Valdes. It was going to be the last time I should see my corporal, and I knew I should want to be alone afterward.

Pidgegood would talk of nothing else but Valdes. He reproached me to my face with not getting him off. There wasn't a man in the company, he said, whatever his color, who wouldn't have died for Valdes, except me. I didn't attempt to explain. Pidgegood never understood the army machine.

"Have you seen him?" I asked.

"Gawd, yes! We runs round the yard together."

They did not have a condemned cell, you see. Firing squads were hardly ever used in the humane army of the last war. I suppose the proper procedure for dealing with Valdes was laid down, but it was not a matter of everyday experience and nobody wanted to be too formal.

And then, corrupted by the mere presence and criminality of Pidgegood, I suddenly saw a remote chance.

"Do you want to go back to the psychiatric ward?" I asked him.

"They won't 'ave nothing more to do with me," he said.

"Ever tried attempted murder?"

"Not worth it. Touch one of them warders and they'll 'alf kill you and swear it was done resisting constraint."

"It wasn't one of them I meant," I explained.

He got it. He got it instantly. His gipsy mind took him right to the point before I had done more than feel for it myself.

"I couldn't do 'im any 'arm with my bare 'ands," he said, "before they'd separate us."

We were alone in the cell. The warder was outside, but he didn't bother to supervise interviews between a prisoner and his long-suffering commanding officer. I took a handkerchief from the pocket of my battle-dress trousers and blew my nose, looking away from Pidgegood. When I had replaced the handkerchief and done up the button I noticed that the familiar lump against my thigh, which was my powerful pocketknife, had disappeared. I swear I felt nothing. It only occurred to me later that the unaccountable loss of several of my treasured possessions had always taken place when that scoundrel was with the company.

"The face, if possible, Pidgegood," I said, getting ready to go. "And if there is anything I can do for you at any time, you know I will."

"Thank you, sir. But I reckon I won't be coming back to the company this time."

Then I went on to see Valdes. There was a sergeant of Military Police present throughout the interview, and I couldn't drop a hint of what was brewing. When I left the cell I returned Valdes' salute with the tears running down my face. I was sure I would never see him again. Pidgegood seemed a frail ally against the imposing formality of military justice.

Not till the morning when Valdes, we all assumed, had been executed did I hear what had happened. The Spaniards of his section came babbling into the orderly room all at once and for the first time in their lives had to be reminded by a roaring and indignant sergeant-major that they were soldiers.

Did I know the news from Bari? No, I didn't. Valdes had been attacked in the exercise yard by Pidgegood and carved up with two strokes of a knife. The first had slit him from mouth to ear and taken the ear three-quarters off; the second had ripped open the artery of his left arm. Did I know that it was not the custom to execute a hospital patient? Did I know that he must be nursed back to health before he could be shot?

I showed as much pleasure as could be expected from an unemotional company commander and asked how Pidgegood had come by a knife. That did not seem to bother anybody. Pidgegood could not be imagined without a knife. They forgot the regular searches of cell and person. In fact, it was very fortunate that Valdes, Pidgegood, and their fellow criminals had been doubled out for exercise within a few hours of my visit.

Through the correct channels I asked whether it was permissible to visit Valdes in the hospital, not being quite sure whether he was officially dead or not. Nothing against it. He was very glad to see me. His head was swathed in bandages, and the pale oak color of his face had changed to yellow. He could not understand what had come over Pidgegood. He assumed that the doctors must have been right about him after all.

Military justice was now following all the rules of the game. Valdes had a guard continually at his bedside—or at least playing cards not more than three beds away. He was not even allowed to attend to the needs of nature alone, though his escort remained outside the swing door. I took a fatherly interest in all these arrangements. I also took note of the exact measurements and windings of his bandages.

I gave liberal leave to the Spaniards of his section—with the exception of Moreno. The hospital doorkeepers became accustomed to their cheerful arrivals and chattering departures. Valdes soon looked his normal self and color. The surgeons, knowing what was in store for him when they released him, kept him as long as they mercifully could, and even wasted time in removing the scar of Pidgegood's knife—or mine, rather—by the latest plastic surgery. But at last the week arrived when he had to be passed fit for execution.

I allowed four of the section to take a company truck and pay Valdes a goodbye visit. I met the truck on the road and put Moreno in the back of it, holding a saint of painted wood on a rather large base representing a rock. Inside the base was a sort of cap made of bandages on the thinnest possible mold of plaster of Paris. It needed only one more winding and a safety pin to be an exact replica of Valdes' bandage. Parcels brought by visitors were examined at the door, so we had to use this subterfuge. We felt sure the saint would have no objection to taking part in an errand of mercy.

Beyond providing the party with very precise orders, which I made them learn by heart, I had nothing else to do with the proposed felony. Whatever happened, I knew they would never give me away or even refer to the matter again.

At 14.15 hrs. the detachment passed the lavatories on Valdes' floor. Moreno whipped the cap out of its hiding place and entered No. 3 lavatory. The rest went straight on to Valdes' ward and presented him with the saint.

At 14.18 hrs. Valdes, accompanied by his guard, also entered No. 3 lavatory, sidling in and not opening the door too wide. It was a stable door, but so long as Valdes and Moreno kept their heads down they could not be seen. We simply had to trust that the guard would not look under the door and see four feet instead of two.

Valdes put on Moreno's battle-dress and shoved his bandages in the pocket. Moreno put on the cap, and Valdes' pajamas. Groaning a little and holding his tummy to disguise his height, he trotted back to bed and dived in.

His four visitors made a little doleful conversation and said an emotional goodbye. Then they picked up Valdes and drove like hell for our camp, passing close behind the French sector of the front where they dropped their corporal. I wasn't sure that I had not been too impudently ingenious there. But the plan worked. After all, the last place anyone would look for Valdes was among the French.

He changed into ragged civilian clothes—also provided in the truck—and spent the night crawling through the French forward positions until he was sure that only enemy patrols were ahead of him. Next morning, pretending to have escaped from a German labor battalion, he came in. The French believed him, or said they did. They were always short of good men and pretty un-scrupulous how they recruited them. Six hours later Valdes had enlisted in the Foreign Legion.

Moreno had a much better run for his money than we ever thought he could. He kept up the deception till dawn of the following day and very gladly accepted what I had prophesied— two years reduced to one when the sentence came up for revision. The others swore that they had never known that the man in bed was not Valdes, and the prosecution just failed to prove beyond a reasonable doubt that they did.

Pidgegood enjoyed a happy and idle war in the mental home. As for me, the worst I had to bear was an interview with my colonel who told me privately that I was strongly suspected of knowing more about the escape of Valdes than I had stated in evidence. He had sworn to my character and assured the military detectives that their suspicions were impossible.

"It's an immoral trade," he said, looking me straight in the eye. "One becomes far too fond of one's subordinates."

BEST "FIRST STORIES" OF THE YEAR

Elaine Slater

The Way It Used To Be

*A curious and subtle story, with a surprisingly sharp
bite . . . The author informs us that she is "primarily
a housewife and mother of four children, ranging in age
from 15 to 3." She is in her mid-thirties, has a B.A. from
Smith and an M.A. from Columbia in Comparative
Literature. Her thesis won a prize—it dealt with the
nature of Good and Evil in Cervantes and Dostoevsky,
surely excellent preparation for the writing of mystery
stories!*

*The idea for "The Way It Used To Be" popped into
Mrs. Slater's head "at an odd moment [odd, indeed!],
while feeding or diapering" one of the children. What
better plot origin for a busy housewife and mother? And
certainly other story ideas will "pop" into Mrs. Slater's
head . . . let 'em pop, we say!*

The professor's voice droned on and on in a clipped British accent. A fly, buzzing above her, hit himself repeatedly against the
ceiling as if searching blindly for something.

What was it? Something Marilyn had forgotten was haunting

her. What could it be? It lay stubbornly encased in her un-
conscious, refusing to stir. Why was it causing her so much
anxiety. Damn!

"Miss Clayton"—her name startled her—"we have just dis-
cussed Macbeth's motivations in some detail. Would you care to
expound on the motivations of Hamlet?"

"Well . . . as I see it, Hamlet's motivations were always cancelled out. What I mean is, he wanted to kill his uncle primarily
because he hated him—that is, he was jealous of him. On the
other hand, this violently powerful motive was cancelled out by
his equally violent love for his mother and his desire not to hurt
her. It was a kind of . . . well, a guilty love, I guess. Ummm,
so that I would say that while Hamlet had very strong motivations
which should have led him to direct action, instead of complement-
ing each other, they nullified each other so that he was paralyzed."

"I see. Mr. Ellis, would you care to expand this theory for us?"

Marilyn was pleased with herself. She had really pulled that
off, and she hadn't half heard the question. But her pleasure was
marred by the persistent nagging of that lost thought.

The bell rang. Class was over. Suddenly the shrill clanging released her hidden memories. *When the alarm rang this morning,
she had arisen, dressed quickly, and got everything ready for
breakfast. Dad was not down yet. She gulped her coffee and ran
off to class. Oh, yes. There it was—not enough to have bothered
her this whole hour. There had only been two places set at the
table. She had noticed it without noticing it. Oh, well. It was really
nothing after all!*

She grabbed her books and dashed off to Psych. She loved this
course, and she was a favorite of the teacher who called on her
constantly for the right answers. This morning's discussion was
about the relative effects of heredity and environment. Miss
Hazard was an excellent teacher.

"Scientists have debated this point for years," Miss Hazard
said. "It has engendered such controversy that unfortunately it
has invaded the realm of sociology, and even of politics. Hereditary or environmental traits are called upon to prove or disprove
all sorts of diverse theories, but the fact is that we are still not at

all sure of the exact part each plays in our ultimate make-up. Mr. Jessup, would you please give the class an example of a trait that you feel is purely hereditary?"

"Yes. I would say our appearance is purely hereditary."

"Mmmm, yes, perhaps. But has not our appearance been refined, and in some cases been drastically shaped, by environment? Need I remind you of the example of the giraffe? Miss Clayton, can you give us an example from your laboratory work that might indicate the effects of heredity or environment or both?"

This time Marilyn was ready. "Yes. If you took a baby rat away from one of its parents—its mother, I mean—and separated it from her by a glass wall, you would see some of the effects. I mean, the rat under normal conditions might have been friendly and calm, even while eating from the student's hand. But if you tear it from its mother, letting it see her but not reach her, it would become frustrated and its whole personality structure would change. It would snap at anybody who came near, possibly even stop eating. So you see, environment would have intensified and even distorted emotions that it had inherited, but which might have remained latent all its life under normal conditions."

"Have you made such an experiment, Miss Clayton?"

"No, but I've made similar ones, and I feel positive that I am right."

"A scientist never feels positive about anything," Miss Hazard replied kindly, "until she has made not one but indeed hundreds of experiments to substantiate a theory. However, your point is well taken, and I suggest you do a laboratory experiment such as you describe."

Marilyn was angry. *Of course she was right! And she had been in such a good mood when she left the house this morning. Why was it all being spoiled? She had slept well for the first time in ages, and everything had seemed wonderful. And now that thing about the table being set only for Dad and herself—why had it worried her? Everything was perfect. Dad was fine. She knew that because she had heard him come in late last night after the University Deans' meeting. He had gone straight to the study where he slept when he didn't want to wake his young wife. Marilyn had heard him, but her stepmother hadn't.* The bell rang.

It was too hot for field hockey, but that was what came next. So Marilyn headed for the locker room. She got into her gym things, cursing mildly when she missed her hockey stick. She dashed out onto the field late, incurring a black look from Miss Overbrook.

"Take your positions, everybody."

"Uh . . . I don't have a stick, Miss Overbrook."

"No stick! Where is it? How can you play without a stick?"

"I guess I left it home." *She was sweating now—it was much too hot for hockey anyway.*

"Home! What would you take a heavy hockey stick home for?"

"I don't know." Marilyn was truly puzzled.

"Well, we have no extras, so you might just as well get dressed again, and I shall have to mark you absent."

Marilyn was furious. *Why was this wonderful day turning out so badly? Oh, well, it was almost lunchtime. She'd get dressed and go home and have lunch with Dad. Just the two of them. The way it used to be.*

She ran all the way home.

Rick Rubin

A Gift for Antonietta

*An engaging tale of a long day's honest work in that city
of danger and intrigue, Naples . . .
   The author is in his late twenties and has already
packed in a "typical writer's" background of varied
activity: graduate of Stanford University in 1952 with a
B.A. in journalism; cryptographer in the U.S. Army,
serving in Naples; two years of wandering after his
honorable discharge, working ski resorts in the West in
the winter, Lake Tahoe gambling joints in the summer;
then, in rapid succession, janitor, waiter, bellhop, ski
instructor, shill for blackjack tables—knocking around
in Idaho, California, Colorado, Nevada, and Mexico;
more recently, an advertising copy writer, and most
recently, a free lance fiction writer, with rejection slips
hitting a total of no less than 80 before EQMM
purchased this, his first story, to make the long, hard, and
heartbreaking grade . . .
   Good luck to you, Mr. Rubin—you have had
diversified and colorful experiences—now use them as
story material!*

Here it is the very gnawed out end of the month, thinks Amadeo Corazone, leaning against a lamppost and staring out at the Bay of Naples. Just before payday, everyone broke, and hardly a single rich tourist in sight. All Naples a city of paupers, and nowhere for a poor fellow to turn an honest profit.

Amadeo pities himself. Twenty-five years of age and still forced to make his living catch-as-catch-can on the streets, living by his good looks and his wits. He pities himself for having to allow his mistress Antonietta to support him, and having to take her backtalk along with her lire. He pities himself his frayed suit, his tattered shirt, his battered shoes, his lack of a hat. Poor Amadeo Corazone. He's almost ready to look for a steady job, some despicable and menial work as a porter or an elevator operator. But . . .

But a little American tourist lady gets a crisp new 5000 lire note, on top of a pile of other notes, when she changes a Traveler's Cheque at the Banco di Napoli. The other bills are frayed and tattered, but the fiver seems almost too bright and new to spend. It's about twice the size of an American dollar bill, and folded, it will fit comfortably in one half of the tourist lady's new Florentine leather pocketbook. He does some calculating, figuring 625 lire to the dollar, and comes up with a value of exactly $8.

If the bill weren't so new, so unfolded, Amadeo might not have noticed it as the little American tourist lady comes out of the bank, blinking in the brilliant Neapolitan sunlight.

But Amadeo does see it, and immediately decides it must be his. Among other things, there is the matter of Antonietta. A man supported by a woman finds the woman hard to dominate. But give her a little gift, and even though she's still supporting you she thinks of you as her lord and master. So thinks Amadeo Corazone as he decides that Antonietta must receive a pair of nylons, or some earrings, directly after Amadeo lays his hands on that crisp new 5000 lire bill.

"Ah, dear lady," Amadeo croons, "There is a little thing I must speak to you. Will you please to listen a moment to me?"

The American lady eyes him suspiciously, narrowing her pale-blue eyes. But in a second she decides that he is a harmless fellow, this young Italian man with the broad shoulders and the little boy's shock of dark brown hair hanging over his brow. Such intense black eyes he has! And how polite he is!

"My family, it is fallen on hard times," Amadeo laments to her. "It is the cruel war." He refers to a war fourteen years over and almost forgotten, completed while Amadeo was still a lad in short pants.

"Poor fellow," says the tourist lady, scenting fallen aristocracy.

"Hard times," he continues. "To make the living we are reduced to selling the priceless family heirlooms. The lace, the jewelry, even this cameo of my sainted grandmother."

Here he pulls out a packet of tattered tissue, and unwrapping it, shows the tourist lady a cameo brooch—a cheap, mass-produced cameo brooch worth no more than a few hundred lire.

"Note the beautiful hand carving," Amadeo whispers enticingly. "A remarkable likeness of my sainted grandmother. She was a leader of the society of all Napoli in her day."

The tourist lady sees the remarkable likeness. Her breath quickens.

"Yet hard times force me to sell it in order to buy food for the members of my once proud family. I can expect no more than 5000 lire for it, only a tiny part of its value."

"Only 5000 lire?" A hint of avarice is heard in the lady's voice, visible in the form of an invisible black buzzard crouching on her shoulder—but visible to so perceptive a fellow as Amadeo.

"Ah, perhaps with a little luck I can get more. Perhaps I can find someone so sentimentally disposed as to give me eight or ten thousand lire," sighs Amadeo.

"A genuine heirloom, you say?"

"Many times over, dear lady. Worth more than you can imagine."

She actually begins to reach. Amadeo sees her hand dart into her purse and withdraw a thick wad of paper money, the exquisite fiver on top.

Then in a swoop comes that pork-of-the-morning Giorgio, that swine who preys on the poor visitors, fat and greasy in his fake uriform, with his fake solicitous attitude! A pox on such thieves as he! Spoiling Amadeo's perfectly honest sale. For after all, isn't Amadeo selling the lady something from which she will get more than her money's worth in pleasure? What if she *could* buy the same cameo in any shop for 250 lire? Would the American tourist lady enjoy such a trinket a fraction as much as this priceless "heirloom" from a nearly royal family?

Giorgio swoops like a pig with wings and all Amadeo can do is stand by, cursing softly under his breath.

"Modom," Giorgio shouts, "You must beware of these scurvy street vendors. And beware, Modom, of the counterfeit bills. In Italy they are the great danger. Myself, a custom's Inspector, permit me to inspect your money—to guard you against the counterfeiter!"

"Oh!" says the lady, stunned by the rapidity of Giorgio's onslaught.

Giorgio, that flying pig, already has the money out of her hand, the whole bundle, before she can recover herself. He succeeds in detaching the bright new bill that Amadeo needs so badly for Antonietta's present. He holds it up to his eye, checking it with zeal.

The lady recovers her tongue and demands her money back. It cannot be counterfeit, she states, for she has just received it in the marble-walled Bank of Naples.

Giorgio apologizes most profusely. "Had I but known you had just received it from that most reliable establishment," he says. "A thousand pardons, Modom."

But while he talks he switches a counterfeit bill for the glorious fiver, then hands the sheaf of bills back again to the lady and slips off into the shadows. That pork-of-the-morning!

"Now about that cameo," says the lady, offering Giorgio's worthless counterfeit 5000 lire note.

A mere nothing," says Amadeo, trying to keep Giorgio in sight. "A trinket. Worth no more than a hundred lire. Excuse me please."

He dashes down the alley after Giorgio but slows down when he has him safely in sight. Giorgio is now a marked man. He, perhaps alone among all the citizens of Naples, surely and without question has money. But what can Amadeo do to get that money? What, short of breaking Giorgio's skull? Which Amadeo is capable of, both in anger and in strength, but which would be a most unwise action.

Perhaps then a little shakedown? A threat of exposure? Such a pig of a thief would undoubtedly be easy to scare. Yes, that is it— a threat of exposure to the police. Amadeo will modestly admit that he can be bought off with the fiver. And then Antonietta will have her little gift, and Amadeo will again be lord and master. Besides, it will be a good deed, thus to put the fear of God in the head of such a pork as Giorgio.

Amadeo quickens his pace, hurrying to overtake Giorgio. But before he can close in on him there is a flash of blue, and Pasquale, the neighborhood policeman, has pounced on the counterfeiter. Amadeo turns to flee, but thinks better of it and merely retires into a doorway. He listens carefully to what ensues.

"And how are you today, my dear Giorgio?" Pasquale demands in a voice not at all as cordial as his words.

"Ah, honored officer of the police, how fine to see you!"

"Absence perhaps makes the heart grow fond?"

"Has it been so long?"

"Altogether too long, my friend Giorgio."

"Ah, well, one is busy."

"Busy at your old tricks? I believe I saw you speaking but a moment ago to an American tourist lady."

"A matter of no consequence."

"A matter of exchanging bills, as I saw it."

"No, no, you must be mistaken,"

"A matter of wearing a false uniform."

"Only for parades and celebrations. You know how I love parades and celebrations, Pasquale."

"I too, Giorgio. I too love to celebrate. Perhaps you would like to help me to celebrate?"

"Help you, friend police officer?"

"A small contribution—to buy a bottle or two and perhaps a bit of sauce for the pasta."

"Unfortunately, at the moment . . ."

"The usual size of contribution, Giorgio. Your regular monthly contribution."

Cursing softly, Giorgio passes Amadeo's fiver to Pasquale.

Amadeo curses softly too.

Now it is Pasquale who has a pocketful of money, but how is one to separate the money from a policeman? Antoinietta's gift seems more distant than Capri across the bay. And she becomes every day more difficult to manage, stronger in the knowledge of how it is she who supports Amadeo.

Amadeo follows Pasquale on his rounds, at a respectful distance, racking his brain for a way to separate the policeman from the loot. The sun bakes his brain. He cannot think of even the smallest of strategies. Hitting an officer of the police is considered the worst of form.

Pasquale strolls about the streets, greeting thieving shopkeepers with a smile, patting small children's heads, and tipping his cap respectfully to women in the streets.

Amadeo follows in a fog of concentration.

Then, before the smidgen of an idea has occurred, the necessity of procuring an idea eliminates itself. Pasquale the pouncer is pounced on by Rosa, his luscious wife.

"Pasquale, Pasquale, give me some money for food. Give me some money for wine. Give me some money for clothes. Pasquale, give me, give me . . ."

The very same 5000 lire bill—now growing limp but undeniably the same fiver—passes from the policeman's thin hand to the soft white one of his wife Rosa.

And off down the street, jiggling happily, goes the good wife Rosa. And off down the street, his mind occupied with an entirely new train of thought, goes Amadeo.

What a long day it is becoming, Amadeo thinks. How hard it is for a poor man to make an honest living, surrounded as he is by thieves. What a pity that beating up a policeman's wife is no more acceptable than beating up an officer of the law. That would be so much easier than following her down back alleys and pummeling one's tired brain for some means of separating her from one's rightful property.

Might he offer himself to Rosa as a lover? Yes, surely that might be the way to recover his funds. She must need a handsome, virile young man like Amadeo, living as she does with the stern-faced Pasquale. Maybe he ought to rush up to her and offer his services.

But that would take a long time. He'd never have the fiver soon enough to buy Antonietta a gift today.

No, there must be some other way.

But where is Rosa leading him? Not home certainly. This isn't even the same neighborhood that Pasquale's house is in. Why, the shameless witch! So it's true what they say about her and Bernardo! Yes, right into the building she goes. Right up to Bernardo's apartment. The vulgar, shameless witch!

Amadeo parks himself at the bar across the street. He purchases an espresso and a sweet roll, and discovers that after paying the tab he hasn't a single lira left. And a long afternoon is stretching ahead. He sighs and leans on the bar. Who can tell where his fiver is now?

Rosa could tell, but Amadeo isn't prepared to ask her when she trips out of the apartment house three-quarters of an hour later, light of foot and merry of eye. But there's no need to ask. She orders a mineral water, which she drinks in a gulp, smacking her lips with relish, and then she dives into her purse for money. Looking into her billfold, Amadeo sees no fiver there.

The evil wench has given it to her lover! Without a doubt. The money she has wormed from her poor, hard-working husband given to that loafer and black marketeer, that sallow-faced, money-lending Bernardo.

Amadeo has dubious thoughts. Is that what his Antonietta will do when he marries her some day? When he becomes rich, or gets a steady job, heaven forbid, will she take the sweat of his brow to give it to some lover? Best he give her a good beating too, along with the gift. But first the gift. A beating without a gift and no telling what Antonietta may do. So back to the matter of the gift—or more properly, the separating of Bernardo from Amadeo's rightful fiver.

Now here's a dilemma. Bernardo is familiar with every subterfuge known to the citizens of Naples. In fact, he's used them all himself. A tough nut, this Bernardo. But Amadeo feels himself strong. He'll think of something, never fear.

By the time Bernardo descends from his apartment, natty in a light summer suit and a straw hat, Amadeo has his plan worked out. It is simplicity itself!

"Bernardo," he shouts, running up out of breath, as though from a heated dash clear across the city. "Rosa sent me to you to get the 5000 lire back. Pasquale suspects! He demands either to see the money or the groceries she was to buy. Quick, give it to me, and I'll run all the way and deliver it to her."

"Ha," Bernardo snorts. "Let the baggage suffer. A lot I care. I'm tired of her anyway. Away with you, Amadeo."

What can you do with a vicious sort like that? Knock him over the head and simply take the money? Not likely. Bernardo is of a numerous clan—a clan not shy of vendetta. Not the sort of fellow for a lone wolf like Amadeo to tangle with. Amadeo is reduced to stringing along behind, waiting his chance.

And it is getting late! Amadeo's hopes are falling. It is getting late in the afternoon and not even a hundred lire for dinner, let alone a pair of nylons or some earrings for Antonietta. Amadeo begins to feel queasy in his stomach.

What a city! Full of thieves, cheating wives, counterfeiters, bribed policemen, and every other sort of riff-raff. A poor fellow can't even begin to make a living here. For the hundredth time in the past few years Amadeo thinks of moving to the north. To Florence, or perhaps to Milan. Ah, there an honest Neapolitan can flourish, among the sweet-dispositioned, pure-hearted northerners.

What's this? Bernardo in earnest conversation with a skinny, bespectacled little American soldier? A soldier carrying a bag suspiciously shaped like cartons of cigarettes, and wearing the shoulder patch of Southern Headquarters of the NATO forces, in nearby Bagnoli. Ah, ha!

Bernardo peers into the sack. The soldier indicates the number six with the fingers of his two hands. Bernardo hands the soldier the fiver, plus a 1000 lire note. The soldier hands the paper sack to Bernardo.

Bernardo turns on his heels. The soldier saunters off down the avenue, Amadeo hot on his tail. Such a little fellow. Not at all like the giant Americans who look so fearsome. This one couldn't struggle out of a net of wet spaghetti. Or, for that matter, resist a big, healthy fellow like Amadeo, intent upon recapturing his rightful due.

And it will teach the skinny little soldier a lesson. Teach him not to deal with black marketeers and not to walk unescorted down perilous back streets in Naples, city of danger and intrigue. Really, by doing this, Amadeo will probably save the little fellow's life some day in the future.

But rounding a corner, the soldier goes into a bar and sits with another soldier. They jabber, and as Amadeo watches through the doorway the little soldier passes the fiver to his larger companion. They shake hands, down their drinks, and come out of the bar. They separate.

No chance of strong-arm tactics any more. The soldier who now has the money seems ten feet tall. He's a paragon of American soldier manhood! Broad as the Piazza Plebiscito. Tall as Vesuvius. Fierce-looking as the bad man in an American Western movie.

Well, there's always more than one way to make a lira.

"Hello, Joe," Amadeo says, sidling up to the giant. "You like a girl? A drink? I can fix it for you."

"Get lost, buddy," the giant says. "Anything I want I'll find for myself."

"Ah, but sarge, I can find better for you. No cost! I do it just to be a friend."

"Be a friend and shove off," the giant says, slapping Amadeo on the back with such heartiness that the Neapolitan almost spills to the pavement.

And again Amadeo finds himself hungrily trailing after a man who he knows without doubt possesses at least 5000 lire.

What a tragedy life is! The rich grow richer, the poor grow hungry. The poor are permitted only to look through the plate-glass window of life at the good things on display. Taunted, but never fed.

Amadeo walks, ponders, and waits. Who can tell when fate will give even the poorest of us a bit of luck? The lady of luck is fickle. Then fate does it! Into La Zebra Bar turns the oversized, overstuffed, overstrong American. Amadeo peeps cautiously through the door, walks quickly inside behind the soldier. Amadeo smiles as though he personally has carried the soldier many miles on his back, then directly into La Zebra.

The soldier heads for a table where a slim, dark-haired girl is sitting alone.

Amadeo swaggers to the bar.

"A vermouth with a touch of lemon, if you please," he demands of the bartender.

"And the money?"

"Taken care of. Rest assured, my friend, taken care of."

"What makes you so sure?"

"The soldier I just brought in."

"Ah, poor Amadeo, the sun has touched your head. It's the end of the month. The soldiers are all broke as little matchsticks."

"Not that soldier. Wait and see."

The soldier gulps a whiskey and soda as his eyes take in the exciting-looking girl. The black-haired girl smiles softly up at him.

The soldier puts his arms around the girl.

The girl cuddles against the soldier.

The soldier rests his head against the girl's inviting shoulder.

Suddenly the girl leaps up, slaps the soldier's face, and stalks off.

The soldier shouts his wrath but the bartender cuts him off, threatening to call the military police. He sends the soldier packing.

The soldier gone, the girl returns. She sits down beside Amadeo. She smiles dreamily.

"Give me the 5000 lire you took from the soldier's wallet, bebe," Amadeo says.

"Don't be silly—he had no money. It's the end of the month. The soldiers are broke as peasants."

"The fiver," Amadeo commands, snapping his fingers. "The rest you can keep for yourself."

The girl is mystified as to how he knows. "Why should you have it?" she demands. "I'm the one who got it."

"Didn't I lead the soldier in here? Didn't I send him directly to you, like a dove to a falcon? I've been following that fiver since early morning. It's mine."

Ruefully the girl reaches into her blouse and produces the fiver.

Ah, thinks Amadeo, now things are going to be all right. A long day's honest work—but success at the end!

Tomorrow he'll find a lovely gift for Antonietta, for that's the sort of generous, good-hearted fellow he is. Antonietta can't say he leeches off her, not after he gives her an expensive gift. And to-night—tonight he'll have a good supper and a drink or two. No need to throw away the whole fiver on a gift.

Amadeo pats the girl gently—with the contented air of a man who has worked hard, thought clearly, and rules his own roost with an iron hand.

"Thank you, Antonietta," he says.

June McMahan Roy

A Visit from Brother Thomas

*How long is it since you've read a ghost story? Too long
probably—ghost stories are a wonderful change of pace
in the broad field of mystery, and here is a most
ingenious one, complete with murder, withal charming
and brightly allusive.*

*The author is a Californian, in her late thirties, and
married to a geological engineer; at the time this story
was written, they were living in Livorno (Leghorn),
Italy. Even though "A Visit from Brother Thomas" is
her first fiction sale, Mrs. Roy has had a prolific writing
background: she was first published at the tender age of
six—"The Astonished Elephant," on the Children's
Page of "The Denver Post"; she began writing again in
her early twenties—a full-length book (unpublished),
scientific articles for her husband, publicity in Alaska,
radio scripts and musicals with parody lyrics for various
Army bases, Women's Club skits, verse—Cardinal
Spellman and Monsignor Finnegan collect her religious
verses—and now, with all our good wishes, in the pages
of EQMM . . .*

The lives of great men all remind us that the man nobody knows is the man nobody wants to know. It is only after the public is reasonably well informed about a man that it will buy his "Life." For instance, the career of that extraordinary scientist, Dr. Brian Blossom Bell, became absorbingly interesting only after rockets—and Dr. Bell—shot with supersonic speed into the daily headlines from their relative obscurity in scientific journals.

But B.R.—Before Rockets—the market for a "Life of Dr. Bell" would have been limited to a handful of fellow-scientists, to his elder sister, the captivating Miss Betsy, and to his lifelong friend, the suave and genial Dr. Mayhew. Mrs. Bell, whose beauty was as brilliant as her mind was not, might have taken her sapphire eyes from the field of fashion long enough to skim the bits concerning her courtship and marriage with the eccentric rocket authority. But then, with a delicate yawn for duty done, she would have resumed her contented appraisal of the latest Paris fashions.

After Rockets, of course, when every literate person in the world was familiar with the name of Dr. Bell, every literate person in the world was a potential buyer of the "Life of Dr. Bell."

I got the assignment on the strength of an extended profile in a sophisticated magazine and a not unsuccessful career in the field of biography. I spent less time than I care to admit in gathering information from Dr. Bell and his intimates and then left New York with my wife, my typewriter, and my notes.

We chose Italy mainly because my wife is an artist and I had promised her an opportunity for a leisurely study of the galleries in Florence, but also because we knew not a soul in that whole lovely country. For I would rather talk than write; and with no friends available and conversations with the villagers limited to my seven words of Italian, I worked while my wife spent blissful hours in the Uffizi and the Palazzo Pitti.

It would have been more convenient for her if we had settled in Florence, but I would have been tempted beyond my strength by the sidewalk cafés and the teeming, English-speaking tourists. So we rented a villa by the sea and my wife commuted to Florence by train. This arrangement gave her an opportunity to perfect her

Italian during the hour-long train ride and gave me long and incredibly undistracted days at the typewriter.

At last, however, the end of my bondage was in sight—if one had remarkably keen eyes. I have always groaned the loudest over the closing pages, especially if the subject is still living, when the agony of tidying things up in the last chapter becomes almost insupportable. True, I groan even when the subject is dead. But death *does* make a neater, more satisfying finish. The final period is final indeed.

On the night in question I was moaning rather more than I usually do because it was nearly midnight, because I was both sleepy and at a loss, and because our best friends, the Sullivans, were arriving for a visit. Mike Sullivan was the most entertaining conversationalist I knew and I had to finish the book before he came and wooed me from my task.

I finished my beer and was rereading the last few pages I had written, looking for a bridge to the final chapter, when a movement near the armchair in the corner of the room attracted my attention. I looked up, expecting to see my wife, although she had told me that she would probably stay in Florence overnight and bring the Sullivans back to the villa in the morning.

However, it was not my small, sleek wife in the armchair, but an immense, untidy Franciscan monk, the folds of his brown habit bunched awkwardly over his knees.

I may doze over a book now and then, but never over my own exasperating prose, which tends to keep me awake when I would rather be in bed. So I was certain that I was not dreaming. Strangely, although I felt neither fear nor amazement, nor any other of the emotions traditionally associated with supernatural experiences, I knew at once that the monk was a ghost.

He had a gentle smile and a friendly expression, and when he caught my eye he inclined his head affably and said, "Buona sera, Signore."

Smiling in response I said, "Buona sera . . ."

"Brother Thomas," he supplied in English on hearing my accent. Then, nodding toward the typewriter, he added, "It is hard, is it not, to leave a work unfinished?"

"I suppose it must be," I said after a moment's thought. "Although I have always been lucky enough to finish anything I have seriously undertaken. Not that there aren't incomplete sketches, fragments, ideas," I went on, for it seemed quite natural to fall into a discussion with this sympathetic ghost. "Every writer has his head and notebooks full of those. But the real bread-and-butter stuff has always, somehow, gone through to the very end."

He gave me a sweet smile and folded his hands comfortably over his enormous paunch. "There is that, however," he said, glancing again at the typewriter.

"What do you mean?" I asked, puzzled. I might be momentarily at a loss, but I was confident that I could find the suitable final flourish to the book.

He smiled more broadly and wagged his fine head. "Dickens and Sterne were the same," he told me. "I had to *come*"—and he gave the word an intonation that made me suddenly more attentive—"to accompany them, too. . . . As a writer myself, Signore, I understand your reluctance to leave your unfinished manuscript. But you really must, my dear fellow."

"I don't think I understand you," I said untruthfully, for I had grasped his meaning perfectly. "Unless I am . . ."

I let the sentence trail off questioningly as he raised his bushy eyebrows gravely and finished it for me.

"Dead."

There was a little silence, quite companionable, and then I said foolishly, "My death comes as a great shock to me. In fact, I have been feeling unusually well recently."

Brother Thomas said nothing, but continued to sit quietly, radiating sympathy while I absorbed his astounding news.

I looked at the typewriter with the unfinished page in the roller, at the empty beer bottle beside it, and then out the window where the umbrella pines were silvered by the moonlight. Beyond them the Tyrrhenian Sea was also rippled silver, and I could smell the kelp and hear the surf pounding on the rocky beach below the villa.

With all my senses in operation I found it almost impossible to believe that I was dead.

"Heart, I suppose," I said at last, for one read frequently enough of men in apparently good health who died unexpectedly of heart attacks.

Brother Thomas looked at me sadly. "I fear not."

"You *fear* not?"

"You were poisoned, Signore . . . *murdered!*"

For a long moment I sat dumbly trying to take this in and make some sense of it. I was mature enough to realize that I was not universally beloved, but I honestly could not think of anyone who might hate me enough to undertake my murder. And even those who disliked me were all on the other side of the Atlantic.

"You must be mistaken," I told Brother Thomas. "I should certainly have noticed being murdered."

"A quick-acting poison in your nightly libation would, I think, pass almost unnoticed," he said. Then he frowned a little. "Almost. You should certainly have been aware of the transition from one State to another."

"No," I said, staring at the lethal beer bottle, "I didn't notice a thing. How long has it been?"

Brother Thomas seemed distressed by the question and began nervously to pleat his brown habit as he looked at the clock on the shelf over my desk.

"This is very disturbing," he said worriedly. "It has been a little over six hours—and yet I was just notified."

"Six hours!" I exclaimed, getting up and pacing around the room. "You mean that I've been dead for six hours and didn't even realize it?"

"It seems so," he said apologetically. "Believe me, caro Signore, this is highly unusual. I shall have to investigate when we Return."

"Speaking of investigations," I said, standing before him, "I trust that there will be an investigation into my death. I don't know how the Italian system of . . ."

He shook his head reproachfully. "Vengeance is not yours, you know."

"I wasn't thinking of revenge," I said inaccurately. "But when a seemingly healthy man dies suddenly, there is always a police inquiry. Even here in Italy, where they like to postpone things, there is bound to be. . . . And then there's the poisoner. Who was it?"

My heart turned over as I looked at the monk in supplication.

"I'm truly sorry, Signore," he said, leaning forward and placing his hand on my arm. "It was your wife."

I sat down dazedly, unable to believe it. And yet, who else could it have been? We knew hardly anyone in the village except Annamaria, who came in twice a week to tidy up, and Mario, who hacked about inefficiently in the yard on Fridays.

My wife, too, was the only one who knew my habit of drinking a beer before going to bed. Easy to drop something in it before she went to Florence—I wondered what it was and where she had got it. I had simply taken the first bottle in the refrigerator. Had the cap been loose? I couldn't remember.

"But what motive could she have?" I demanded, bewildered. After twenty years of love and devoted companionship it seemed incredible that she should suddenly have decided to kill me. "Why did she do it?"

Carefully the monk tied another knot in the already knotted white cord about his waist, then he sighed and spread his hands helplessly. "She has been in love with your friend and doctor for a very long . . ."

"Dr. Sullivan?" I exclaimed. "Why, he and his sister are in Italy now. In fact, my wife went to Florence to meet them this morning and is bringing them here tomorrow." I looked at the clock. "Today."

"Exactly. Your own medical man will be on hand to certify your death from natural causes."

"But he can't do that!" I said, my mind spinning. "Mike Sullivan is not only my doctor, he's my best friend. He wouldn't play around with my wife! Besides, he gave me a complete physical less than a year ago," I told Brother Thomas triumphantly, "and he said then that I was so healthy it was disgusting to a doctor who had to make a living!"

"So he told you."

"Do you mean that there *was* something wrong, that he *concealed* it from me?"

"No," said the monk. "But he and your wife already envisioned this occurrence, so he entered a notation on your medical record that you were suffering from a serious heart ailment."

"That's unethical!"

The monk looked as if he were trying not to laugh at me. "So is murder, Signore. But if the question ever arose they were prepared with a year-old entry, verified by his office nurse, that you had a heart condition that might be fatal at any time. He also supplied the poison, which had the virtue, from their standpoint, of simulating a heart attack."

Stunned even more by the revelation of Mike's and my wife's duplicity than I had been at the news of my own death, I could only shake my head in mute disbelief until Brother Thomas stood up and adjusted the white cord about his immense waist.

"And now, caro Signore," he told me gently, "we really must be going."

I, too, stood, and then turned toward the typewriter with some absurd notion of leaving a note for the police. But of course Mike and my wife would destroy it.

Misunderstanding my hesitation, the monk shook his heavy head regretfully. "No, you cannot finish that now. I'm truly sorry. But there has already been, for reasons I do not understand, a six-hour delay and you have certain formalities to undergo. Also," he glanced at the clock and began to move toward the door, "I have my own work to do."

"What is your work?" I asked absently, frowning unhappily at the pages of manuscript on the desk.

Pleased by my interest, Brother Thomas paused and said, "I sustain a tradition at the Abbey on the hill between here and Florence. Every morning between the hours of two and three, the incumbent monks hear the scratching of a pen on parchment in the Abbot's old office in the north tower. Tradition says it is the Abbot," he chuckled, "but bless his soul, he was never a writer. A very sound administrator and a saintly man withal, but as his clerk, I did all the writing. So you see, I am able to go on with my work and yet keep up the tradition. A very congenial occupation."

He smiled, delighted with his recollections. Then he sobered and said, "But come, Dr. Bell. We must leave."

Stupefied with amazement, I stared at him. And then I whirled, flipped out the top page of the manuscript on the desk, and held it out to Brother Thomas with shaking hands.

"As I told you in the beginning," he said patiently, brushing aside the paper, "I know how you feel about leaving an incomplete work. I have, in fact, been working recently on a manuscript I left unfinished nearly six hundred years ago. But . . ."

He stopped then to peer at the title page, which I was holding insistently before him, and then looked at me with the greatest bafflement.

The working title read: *The Autobiography of Brian Blossom Bell.*

"But if it is the story of your life," he said, bringing his bushy brows together in a frown of reproof, "it is up-to-date, surely. Someone else can . . ."

"*My* name," I said quietly but distinctly, "is Francis Xavier O'Neill."

He looked at me blankly and I went on, "I am a biographer by profession, Brother Thomas, but I have recently been working on Dr. Bell's *auto*biography. I think that the source of all this confusion lies in this,"—I tapped the manuscript—"my first venture into *ghost-writing.*"

The poor monk sat down heavily and tied another knot in the white cord. "But that is impossible!"

"We may assume, I take it, that Dr. Bell is the one who is dead?"

"Oh, yes," he said. "Decidedly!"

"It's easily explained, then," I said, moving about the room, wonderfully alive and acute and giddy with relief and love for my wife and devotion to Mike and all the jumble of things and people I had been about to surrender forever.

"You were puzzled by the six-hour delay, but as you arrived at the villa at midnight and there is a six-hour time differential between Italy and Dr. Bell's home in New York, he must have died at six o'clock last evening. If you had gone there instead of coming here, you would have been in at the death, so to speak. . . . You erred in your choice of ghosts."

Brother Thomas absorbed this information rapidly, then stood up, his brown habit swirling about his ankles as he prepared to depart.

"I shall see you later, caro Signore," he said. "At least," he added with a twinkle in his eye, "I most sincerely hope so."

And with a sweet smile and a gesture of benediction he disappeared.

As soon as the village began its leisurely day I telephoned Miss Betsy Bell and told her to insist on an autopsy on her brother, the result of which led to the sensational trial and conviction of Mrs. Bell and Dr. Mayhew.

The Autobiography of Brian Blossom Bell is enjoying equally sensational sales, largely owing, I like to think, to the *Epilogue,* by Francis X. O'Neill.

I have never written a more satisfactory final chapter—thanks to the error of Brother Thomas.

BONUS STORY

Dashiell Hammett

A Man Named Thin

IMPORTANT DETECTIVE DISCOVERY

*We do not know when Dashiell Hammett wrote the
story we have titled "A Man Named Thin" (the author's
original title was a curious one, "The Figure of
Incongruity"). From internal evidence it seems
probable that Hammett wrote the story in the
mid-1920s—in the formative years before* THE
MALTESE FALCON; *and if this is true, the story
foreshadows much of Hammett's mature talent,
especially his originality of characterization and plot.*

*Hammett sold the story to a magazine of the day, but
before the story could be published, the magazine went
out of business. The assets and inventory of the defunct
magazine were taken over by another periodical—
believe it or not, a magazine devoted to love stories!
Since Hammett's story could not possibly be classified
as "a love story," the manuscript (typescript, actually)
languished in the inventory safe for about 20 years.
Seems utterly incredible, doesn't it?*

*We heard about "an unpublished Hammett
manuscript" late in 1945. We negotiated for its
purchase, and acquired the story early in 1946. So far
as we were able to check at that time, the manuscript
represented the only unpublished Hammett story in
existence; and since Hammett has not had, to the best of
our knowledge, a new story or book published since
1934 (all Hammett books after* THE THIN MAN *are
reprints or collections of previously published work),*

we are now offering you the only story by Dashiell Hammett never before published.

So, to continue the history of this important discovery, we came into possession of the story in 1946. Then for reasons too complicated to explain in an editorial preface, the story remained in our own inventory safe, languishing there for 14 more years. Seems equally incredible, doesn't it?

And now, at long last, first publication . . . And who is the chief character in "A Man Named Thin"? If he is not the first of his breed, surely he is one of the earliest. For the sleuth in this "new" Hammett story is a young poet! We do not know if you will consider Robin Thin a better poet than private detective, or vice versa —but surely he was a daring innovation in the 1920s even for the man who is universally regarded as the founder of the hard-boiled school, the man who eventually gave us the rough, tough Sam Spade and the suave, sophisticated Nick Charles (erroneously known, we should point out, as "The Thin Man").

Whether or not Dashiell Hammett will ever write again, we do not know. His last new book was published 27 years ago. But it may well be that "A Man Named Thin," although written more than 30 years ago, is destined to be the last new Hammett story to appear in print. So read it, not only with interest and, we hope, the thrill of discovery, but also with the respect that an unpublished story by Hammett so richly deserves.

Papa was, though I may be deemed an undutiful son for saying it, in an abominable mood. His chin protruded across the desk at me in a fashion that almost justified the epithet of brutal which had once been applied to it by an unfriendly journalist; and his mustache seemed to bristle with choler of its own, though this was merely the impression I received. It would be preposterous to assume actual change in the mustache which, whatever Papa's humor, was always somewhat irregularly salient.

"So you're still fooling with this damned nonsense of yours?"

On Papa's desk, under one of his hands, lay a letter which, its odd shape and color informed me immediately, was from the editor of *The Jongleur* to whom, a few days before, I had sent a sonnet.

"If you mean my writing," I replied respectfully, but none the less stanchly; for my thirtieth birthday being some months past, I considered myself entitled to some liberty of purpose, even though that purpose might be distasteful to Papa. "If you mean my writing, Papa, I assure you I am not fooling, but am completely in earnest."

"But why in"—if now and then I garble Papa's remarks in reporting them, it is not, I beg you to believe, because he is addicted to incoherencies, but simply because he frequently saw fit to sacrifice the amenities of speech to what he considered vigor of expression—"do you have to pick on poetry? Aren't there plenty of other things to write about? Why, Robin, you could write some good serious articles about our work, articles that would tell the public the truth about it and at the same time give us some advertising."

"One writes what one is impelled to write," I began not too hopefully, for this was by no means the first time I had begun thus. "The creative impulse is not to be coerced into—"

"Florence!"

I do not like to say Papa bellowed, but the milder synonyms are not entirely adequate to express the volume of sound he put into our stenographer's given name by which he insisted on addressing her.

Miss Queenan appeared at the door—an unfamiliar Miss Queenan who did not advance to Papa's desk with that romping mixture of flippancy and self-assurance which the press, with its propensity to exaggerate, has persuaded our generation to expect; instead, she stood there awaiting Papa's attention.

"After this, Florence, will you see that my desk is not cluttered up with correspondence dealing with my son's Mother Goose rhymes!"

"Yes, Mr. Thin," she replied in a voice surprisingly meek for someone accustomed to speak to Papa as if she were a member of his family.

"My dear Papa," I endeavored to remonstrate when Miss Queenan had retired, "I really think—"

"Don't dear Papa me! And you don't think! Nobody that thought could be such a . . ."

It would serve no purpose to repeat Papa's words in detail. They were, for the most part, quite unreasonable, and not even my deep-seated sense of filial propriety could enable me to keep my face from showing some of the resentment I felt; but I heard him through in silence and when he had underscored his last sentence by thrusting *The Jongleur*'s letter at me, I withdrew to my office.

The letter, which had come to Papa's desk through the carelessness of the editor in omitting the Jr. from my name, had to do with the sonnet I have already mentioned—a sonnet entitled *Fictitious Tears*. The editor's opinion was that its concluding couplet, which he quoted in his letter, was not, as he politely put it, up to my usual standard, and he requested that I rewrite it, adjusting it more exactly to the tone of the previous lines, for which it was, he thought, a trifle too serious.

> *And glisten there no less incongruously*
> *Than Christmas balls on deadly upas tree.*

I reminded myself, as I took my rhyming dictionary from behind Gross's *Kriminal Psychologie* where, in the interest of peace, I habitually concealed it, that I had not been especially pleased with those two lines; but after repeated trials I had been unable to find more suitable ones. Now, as I heard the noon whistles, I brought out my carbon copy of the sonnet and determined to devote the quiet of the luncheon hour to the creation of another simile that would express incongruity in a lighter vein.

To that task I addressed myself, submerging my consciousness to such an extent that when I heard Papa's voice calling "Robin!" with a force that fairly agitated the three intervening partitions, I roused as if from sleep, with a suspicion that the first call I had heard had not been the first Papa had uttered. This suspicion was confirmed when, putting away paper and books, I hastened into Papa's presence.

"Too busy listening to the little birdies twitter to hear me?" But this was mere perfunctory gruffness; his eyes were quite jovial so that in a measure I was prepared for his next words. "Barnable's stuck up. Get to it."

The Barnable Jewelry Company's store was six blocks from our offices, and a convenient street car conveyed me there before Papa's brief order was five minutes old. The store, a small one, occupied a portion of the ground floor of the Bulwer Building, on the north side of O'Farrell Street, between Powell and Stockton Streets. The store's neighbors on the ground floor of the same building were, going east toward Stockton Street, a haberdasher (in whose window, by the way, I noticed an intriguing lavender dressing robe), a barber shop, and a tobacconist's; and going westward toward Powell Street, the main entrance and lobby of the Bulwer Building, a prescription druggist, a hatter, and a lunchroom.

At the jeweler's door a uniformed policeman was busily engaged in preventing a curious crowd, most of whom were presumably out on their luncheon hours, from either blocking the sidewalk or entering the store. Passing through this throng, I nodded to the policeman, not that I was personally acquainted with him but because experience had taught me that a friendly nod will often forestall questions, and went into the store.

Detective Sergeant Hooley and Detective Strong of the police department were in the store. In one hand the former held a dark gray cap and a small automatic pistol which did not seem to belong to any of the people to whom the detectives were talking: Mr.

Barnable, Mr. Barnable's assistant, and two men and a woman unknown to me.

"Good morning, gentlemen," I addressed the detectives. "May I participate in the inquiry?"

"Ah, Mr. Thin!"

Sergeant Hooley was a large man whose large mouth did nothing to shape his words beyond parting to emit them, so that they issued somewhat slovenly from a formless opening in his florid face. His face held now, as when I had engaged him in conversation heretofore, an elusively derisive expression—as if, with intent to annoy, he pretended to find in me, in my least word or act, something amusing. The same impulse was noticeable in the stressed mister with which he invariably prefixed my name, notwithstanding that he called Papa Bob, a familiarity I was quite willing to be spared.

"As I was telling the boys, participating is just exactly what we need." Sergeant Hooley exercised his rather heavy wit. "Some dishonest thief has been robbing the joint. We're about through inquiring, but you look like a fellow that can keep a secret, so I don't mind letting you in on the dirt, as we used to say at dear old Harvard."

I am not privy to the quirk in Sergeant Hooley's mind which makes attendance at this particular university constitute, for him, a humorous situation; nor can I perceive why he should find so much pleasure in mentioning that famous seat of learning to me who, as I have often taken the trouble to explain to him, attended an altogether different university.

"What seems to have happened," he went on, "is that some bird came in here all by himself, put Mr. Barnable and his help under the gun, took 'em for what was in the safe, and blew out, trampling over some folks that got in his way. He then beat it up to Powell Street, jumped into a car, and what more do you want to know?"

"At what time did this occur?"

"Right after twelve o'clock, Mr. Thin—not more than a couple of minutes after, if that many," said Mr. Barnable, who had circled the others to reach my side. His brown eyes were round with excitement in his round brown face, but not especially melancholy, since he was insured against theft in the company on whose behalf I was now acting.

"He makes Julius and me lay down on the floor behind the counter while he robs the safe, and then he backs out. I tell Julius to get up and see if he's gone, but just then he shoots at me." Mr. Barnable pointed a spatulate finger at a small hole in the rear wall near the ceiling. "So I didn't let Julius get up till I was sure he'd gone. Then I phoned the police and your office."

"Was anyone else, anyone besides you and Julius, in the store when the robber entered?"

"No. We hadn't had anyone in for maybe fifteen minutes."

"Would you be able to identify the robber if you were to see him again, Mr. Barnable?"

"Would I? Say, Mr. Thin, would Carpentier know Dempsey?"

This counter-question, which seemed utterly irrelevant, was intended, I assumed, as an affirmative.

"Kindly describe him for me, Mr. Barnable."

"He was maybe forty years old and tough-looking, a fellow just about your size and complexion." I am, in height and weight, of average size, and my complexion might best be described as medium, so there was nothing in any way peculiar about my having these points of resemblance to the robber; still I felt that the jeweler had been rather tactless in pointing them out. "His mouth was kind of pushed in, without much lips, and his nose was long and flattish, and he had a scar on one side of his face. A real tough-looking fellow!"

"Will you describe the scar in greater detail, Mr. Barnable?"

"It was back on his cheek, close to his ear, and ran all the way down from under his cap to his jawbone."

"Which cheek, Mr. Barnable?"

"The left," he said tentatively, looking at Julius, his sharp-featured young assistant. When Julius nodded, the jeweler repeated, with certainty, "The left."

"How was he dressed, Mr. Barnable?"

"A blue suit and that cap the Sergeant has got. I didn't notice anything else."

"His eyes and hair, Mr. Barnable?"

"Didn't notice."

"Exactly what did he take, Mr. Barnable?"

"I haven't had time to check up yet, but he took all the unset stones that were in the safe—mostly diamonds. He must have got fifty thousand dollars' worth if he got a nickel!"

I permitted a faint smile to show on my lips while I looked coldly at the jeweler.

"In the event that we fail to recover the stones, Mr. Barnable, you are aware that the insurance company will require proof of the purchase of every missing item."

He fidgeted, screwing his round face up earnestly.

"Well, anyways, he got twenty-five thousand dollars' worth, if it's the last thing I ever say in this world, Mr. Thin, on my word of honor as a gentleman."

"Did he take anything besides the unset stones, Mr. Barnable?"

"Those and some money that was in the safe—about two hundred dollars."

"Will you please draw up a list immediately, Mr. Barnable, with as accurate a description of each missing item as possible. Now what evidence have we, Sergeant Hooley, of the robber's subsequent actions?"

"Well, first thing, he subsequently bumped into Mrs. Dolan as he was making his getaway. Seems she was—"

"Mrs. Dolan has an account here," the jeweler called from the rear of the store where he and Julius had gone to comply with my request. Sergeant Hooley jerked his thumb at the woman who stood on my left.

She was a woman of fewer years than forty, with humorous brown eyes set in a healthily pink face. Her clothes, while neat, were by no means new or stylish, and her whole appearance was such as to cause the adjective capable to come into one's mind, an adjective further justified by the crisp freshness of the lettuce and celery protruding from the top of the shopping bag in her arms.

"Mrs. Dolan is manager of an apartment building on Ellis Street." The jeweler concluded his introduction, while the woman and I exchanged smiling nods.

"Thank you, Mr. Barnable. Proceed, Sergeant Holley."

"Thank *you*, Mr. Thin. Seems she was coming in to make a payment on her watch, and just as she put a foot inside the door, this stick-up backed into her, both of them taking a tumble. Mr. Knight, here, saw the mix-up, ran in, knocked the thug loose from his cap and gun, and chased him up the street."

One of the men present laughed deprecatorily past an upraised sun-burned hand which held a pair of gloves. He was a weather-browned man of athletic structure, tall and broad-shouldered, and dressed in loose tweeds.

"My part wasn't as heroic as it sounds," he protested. "I was getting out of my car, intending to go across to the Orpheum for tickets, when I saw this lady and the man collide. Crossing the sidewalk to help her up, nothing was further from my mind than that the man was a bandit. When I finally saw his gun he was actually on the point of shooting at me. I had to hit him, and luckily succeeded in doing so just as he pulled the trigger. When I recovered from my surprise I saw he had dropped his gun and run up the street, so I set out after him. But it was too late. He was gone."

"Thank you, Mr. Knight. Now, Sergeant Hooley, you say the bandit escaped in a car?"

"Thank you, Mr. Thin," he said idiotically, "I did. Mr. Glenn here saw him."

"I was standing on the corner," said Mr. Glenn, a plump man with what might be called the air of a successful salesman.

"Pardon me, Mr. Glenn, what corner?"

"The corner of Powell and O'Farrell," he said, quite as if I should have known it without being told. "The northeast corner, if you want it exactly, close to the building line. This bandit came up the street and got into a coupé that was driving up Powell Street. I didn't pay much attention to him. If I heard the shot I took it for an automobile noise. I wouldn't have noticed the man if he hadn't been bareheaded, but he was the man Mr. Barnable described— scar, pushed-in mouth, and all."

"Do you know the make or license number of the car he entered, Mr. Glenn?"

"No, I don't. It was a black coupé, and that's all I know. I think it came from the direction of Market Street. A man was driving it, I believe, but I didn't notice whether he was young or old or anything about him."

"Did the bandit seem excited, Mr. Glenn? Did he look back?"

"No, he was as cool as you please, didn't even seem in a hurry. He just walked up the street and got into the coupé, not looking to right or left."

"Thank you, Mr. Glenn. Now can anyone amplify or amend Mr. Barnable's description of the bandit?"

"His hair was gray," Mr. Glenn said, "iron-gray."

Mrs. Dolan and Mr. Knight concurred in this, the former adding, "I think he was older than Mr. Barnable said—closer to fifty than to forty—and his teeth were brown and decayed in front."

"They were, now that you mention it," Mr. Knight agreed.

"Is there any other light on the matter, Sergeant Hooley?"

"Not a twinkle. The shotgun cars are out after the coupé, and I reckon when the papers get out we'll be hearing from more people who saw things, but you know how they are."

I did indeed. One of the most lamentable features of criminal detection is the amount of time and energy wasted investigating information supplied by people who, through sheer perversity, stupidity, or excessive imagination, insist on connecting everything they have chanced to see with whatever crime happens to be most prominent in the day's news.

Sergeant Hooley, whatever the defects of his humor, was an excellent actor: his face was bland and guileless and his voice did not vary in the least from the casual as he said, "Unless Mr. Thin has some more questions, you folks might as well run along. I have your addresses and can get hold of you if I need you again."

I hesitated, but the fundamental principle that Papa had instilled in me during the ten years of my service under him—the necessity of never taking anything for granted—impelled me to say, "Just a moment," and to lead Sergeant Hooley out of the others' hearing.

"You have made your arrangements, Sergeant Hooley?"

"What arrangements?"

I smiled, realizing that the police detectives were trying to conceal their knowledge from me. My immediate temptation was, naturally enough, to reciprocate in kind; but whatever the advantages of working independently on any one operation, in the long run a private detective is wiser in cooperating with the police than in competing with them.

"Really," I said, "you must harbor a poor opinion of my ability if you think I have not also taken cognizance of the fact that if Glenn were standing where he said he was standing, and if, as he says, the bandit did not turn his head, then he could not have seen the scar on the bandit's left cheek."

Despite his evident discomfiture, Sergeant Hooley acknowledged defeat without resentment.

"I might of known you'd tumble to that," he admitted, rubbing his chin with a reflective thumb. "Well, I reckon we might as well take him along now as later, unless you've got some other notion in your head."

Consulting my watch, I saw that it was now twenty-four minutes past noon: my investigation had thus far, thanks to the police detectives' having assembled all the witnesses, consumed only ten or twelve minutes.

"If Glenn were stationed at Powell Street to mislead us," I suggested, "then isn't it quite likely that the bandit did not escape in that direction at all? It occurs to me that there is a barber shop two doors from here in the opposite direction—toward Stockton Street. That barber shop, which I assume has a door opening into the Bulwer Building, as barber shops similarly located invariably do, may have served as a passageway through which the bandit could have got quickly off the street. In any event, I consider it a possibility that we should investigate."

"The barber shop it is!" Sergeant Hooley spoke to his colleague, "Wait here with these folks till we're back, Strong. We won't be long."

"Right," Detective Strong replied.

In the street we found fewer curious spectators than before.

"Might as well go inside, Tim," Sergeant Hooley said to the policeman in front as we passed him on our way to the barber shop.

The barber shop was about the same size as the jewelry store.

Five of its six chairs were filled when we went in, the vacant one being that nearest the front window. Behind it stood a short swarthy man who smiled at us and said, "Next," as is the custom of barbers.

Approaching, I tendered him one of my cards, from perusal of which he looked up at me with bright interest that faded at once into rather infantile disappointment. I was not unfamiliar with this phenomenon: there are a surprising number of people who, on learning that my name is Thin, are disappointed in not finding me an emaciated skeleton or, what would doubtless be even more pleasing, grossly fat.

"You know, I assume, that Barnable's store has been robbed?"

"Sure! It's getting tough the way those babies knock 'em over in broad daylight!"

"Did you by any chance hear the report of the pistol?"

"Sure! I was shaving a fellow, Mr. Thorne, the real estate man. He always waits for me no matter how many of the other barbers are loafing. He says— Anyhow, I heard the shot and went to the door to look up there, but I couldn't keep Mr. Thorne waiting, you understand, so I didn't go up there myself."

"Did you see anyone who might have been the bandit?"

"No. Those fellows move quick, and at lunchtime, when the street's full of people, I guess he wouldn't have much trouble losing himself. It's funny the way—"

In view of the necessity of economizing on time, I risked the imputation of discourtesy by interrupting the barber's not very pertinent comments.

"Did any man pass through here, going from the street into the Bulwer Building, immediately after you heard the shot?"

"Not that I remember, though lots of men use this shop as a kind of short cut from their offices to the street."

"But you remember no one passing through shortly after you heard the shot?"

"Not going in. Going out, maybe, because it was just about lunchtime."

I considered the men the barbers were working on in the five occupied chairs. Only two of these men wore blue trousers. Of the two, one had a dark mustache between an extremely outstanding nose and chin; the other's face, pink from the shaving it had just undergone, was neither conspicuously thin nor noticeably plump, nor was his profile remarkable for either ugliness or beauty. He was a man of about thirty-five years, with fair hair and, as I saw when he smiled at something his barber said, teeth that were quite attractive in their smooth whiteness.

"When did the man in the third chair"—the one I have just described—"come in?"

"If I ain't mistaken, just before the hold-up. He was just taking off his collar when I heard the shot. I'm pretty sure of it."

"Thank you," I said, turning away.

"A tough break," Sergeant Hooley muttered in my ear.

I looked sharply at him.

"You forget or, rather, you think I have forgotten, Knight's gloves."

Sergeant Hooley laughed shortly. "I forgot 'em for a fact. I must be getting absent-minded or something."

"I know of nothing to be gained by dissembling, Sergeant Hooley. The barber will be through with our man presently." Indeed, the man rose from the chair as I spoke. "I suggest that we simply ask him to accompany us to the jeweler's."

"Fair enough," the Sergeant agreed.

We waited until our man had put on his collar and tie, his blue jacket, gray coat, and gray hat. Then, exhibiting his badge, Sergeant Hooley introduced himself to the man.

"I'm Sergeant Hooley. I want you to come up the street with me."

"What?"

The man's surprise was apparently real, as it may well have been.

Word for word, the Sergeant repeated his statement.

"What for?"

I answered the man's question in as few words as possible.

"You are under arrest for robbing Barnable's jewelry store."

The man protested somewhat truculently that his name was Brennan, that he was well-known in Oakland, that someone would pay for this insult, and so on. For a minute it seemed that force would be necessary to convey our prisoner to Barnable's, and Sergeant Hooley had already taken a grip on the man's wrist when Brennan finally submitted, agreeing to accompany us quietly.

Glenn's face whitened and a pronounced tremor disturbed his legs as we brought Brennan into the jewelry store, where Mrs. Dolan and Messrs. Barnable, Julius, Knight, and Strong came eagerly to group themselves around us. The uniformed man the Sergeant had called Tim remained just within the street door.

"Suppose you make the speeches," Sergeant Hooley said, offering me the center of the stage.

"Is this your bandit, Mr. Barnable?" I began.

The jeweler's brown eyes achieved astonishing width.

"No, Mr. Thin!"

I turned to the prisoner.

"Remove your hat and coat, if you please. Sergeant Hooley, have you the cap that the bandit dropped? Thank you, Sergeant Hooley." To the prisoner, "Kindly put this cap on."

"I'm damned if I will!" he roared at me.

Sergeant Hooley held a hand out toward me.

"Give it to me. Here, Strong, take a hold on this baby while I cap him."

Brennan subsided. "All right! All right! I'll put it on!"

The cap was patently too large for him, but, experimenting, I found it could be adjusted in such a manner that its lack of fit was not too conspicuous, while its size served to conceal his hair and alter the contours of his head.

"Now will you please," I said, stepping back to look at him, "take out your teeth?"

This request precipitated an extraordinary amount of turmoil. The man Knight hurled himself on Detective Strong, while Glenn dashed toward the front door, and Brennan struck Sergeant Hooley viciously with his fist. Hastening to the front door to take the place of the policeman who had left it to struggle with Glenn, I saw that Mrs. Dolan had taken refuge in a corner, while

Barnable and Julius avoided being drawn into the conflict only by exercising considerable agility.

Order was at length restored, with Detective Strong and the policeman handcuffing Knight and Glenn together, while Sergeant Hooley, sitting astride Brennan, waved aloft the false teeth he had taken from his mouth.

Beckoning to the policeman to resume his place at the door, I joined Sergeant Hooley, and we assisted Brennan to his feet, restoring the cap to his head. He presented a villainous appearance: his mouth, unfilled by teeth, sank in, thinning and aging his face, causing his nose to lengthen limply and flatly.

"Is this your baby?" Sergeant Hooley asked, shaking the prisoner at the jeweler.

"It is! It is! It's the same fellow!" Triumph merged with puzzlement on the jeweler's face. "Except he's got no scar," he added slowly.

"I think we shall find his scar in his pocket."

We did—in the form of a brown-stained handkerchief still damp and smelling of alcohol. Besides the handkerchief, there were in his pockets a ring of keys, two cigars, some matches, a pocketknife, $36, and a fountain pen.

The man submitted to our search, his face expressionless until Mr. Barnable exclaimed, "But the stones? Where are my stones?"

Brennan sneered nastily. "I hope you hold your breath till you find 'em," he said.

"Mr. Strong, will you kindly search the two men you have handcuffed together?" I requested.

He did so, finding, as I had expected, nothing of importance on their persons.

"Thank you, Mr. Strong," I said, crossing to the corner in which Mrs. Dolan was standing. "Will you please permit me to examine your shopping bag?"

Mrs. Dolan's humorous brown eyes went blank.

"Will you please permit me to examine your shopping bag?" I repeated, extending a hand toward it.

She made a little smothered laughing sound in her throat, and handed me the bag, which I carried to a flat-topped showcase on the other side of the room. The bag's contents were the celery and lettuce I have already mentioned, a package of sliced bacon, a box of soap chips, and a paper sack of spinach, among the green leaves of which glowed, when I emptied them out on the show-case, the hard crystal facets of unset diamonds. Less conspicuous among the leaves were some banknotes.

Mrs. Dolan was, I have said, a woman who impressed me as being capable, and that adjective seemed especially apt now: she behaved herself, I must say, in the manner of one who would be capable of anything. Fortunately, Detective Strong had followed her across the store; he was now in a position to seize her arms from behind, and thus incapacitate her, except vocally—a remaining freedom of which she availed herself to the utmost, indulging in a stream of vituperation which it is by no means necessary for me to repeat.

It was a few minutes past two o'clock when I returned to our offices.

"Well, what?" Papa ceased dictating his mail to Miss Queenan to challenge me. "I've been waiting for you to phone!"

"It was not necessary," I said, not without some satisfaction. "The operation has been successfully concluded."

"Cleaned up?"

"Yes, sir. The thieves, three men and a woman, are in the city prison, and the stolen property has been completely recovered. In the detective bureau we were able to identify two of the men: 'Reader' Keely, who seems to have been the principal, and a Harry McMeehan, who seems to be well-known to the police in the East. The other man and the woman, who gave their names as George Glenn and Mrs. Mary Dolan, will doubtless be identified later."

Papa bit the end off a cigar and blew the end across the office.

"What do you think of our little sleuth, Florence?" he fairly beamed on her, for all the world as if I were a child of three who had done something precocious.

"Spiffy!" Miss Queenan replied. "I think we'll do something with the lad yet."

"Sit down, Robin, and tell us about it," Papa invited. "The mail can wait."

"The woman secured a position as manager of a small apartment house on Ellis Street," I explained, though without sitting down. "She used that as reference to open an account with Barnable, buying a watch, for which she paid in small weekly installments. Keely, whose teeth were no doubt drawn while he was serving his last sentence in Walla Walla, removed his false teeth, painted a scar on his cheek, put on an ill-fitting cap, and threatening Barnable and his assistant with a pistol, took the unset stones and money that were in the safe.

"As he left the store he collided with Mrs. Dolan, dropping the plunder into a bag of spinach which, with other groceries, was in her shopping bag. McMeehan, pretending to come to the woman's assistance, handed Keely a hat and coat, and perhaps his false teeth and a handkerchief with which to wipe off the scar, and took Keely's pistol.

"Keely, now scarless, and with his appearance altered by teeth and hat, hurried to a barber shop two doors away, while Mc-Meehan, after firing a shot indoors to discourage curiosity on the part of Barnable, dropped the pistol beside the cap and pretended to chase the bandit up toward Powell Street. At Powell Street another accomplice was stationed to pretend he had seen the bandit drive away in an automobile. These three confederates attempted to mislead us further by adding fictitious details to Barnable's description of the robber."

"Neat!" Papa's appreciation was, I need hardly point out, purely academic—a professional interest in the cunning the thieves had shown and not in any way an approval of their dishonest plan as a whole. "How'd you knock it off?"

"The man on the corner couldn't have seen the scar unless the bandit had turned his head, which the man denied. McMeehan wore gloves to avoid leaving prints on the pistol when he fired it, and his hands are quite sunburned, as if he does not ordinarily wear gloves. Both men and the woman told stories that fitted together in every detail, which, as you know, would be little less than a miracle in the case of honest witnesses. But since I knew

Glenn, the man on the corner, had prevaricated, it was obvious that if the others' stories agreed with his, then they too were deviating from the truth."

I thought it best not to mention to Papa that immediately prior to going to Barnable's, and perhaps subconsciously during my investigation, my mind had been occupied with finding another couplet to replace the one the editor of *The Jongleur* had disliked; incongruity, therefore, being uppermost in my brain, Mrs. Dolan's shopping bag had seemed a quite plausible hiding place for the diamonds and money.

"Good shooting!" Papa was saying. "Pull it by yourself?"

"I cooperated with Detectives Hooley and Strong. I am sure the subterfuge was as obvious to them as to me."

But even as I spoke a doubt arose in my mind. There was, it seemed to me, a possibility, however slight, that the police detectives had not seen the solution as clearly as I had. At the time I had assumed that Sergeant Hooley was attempting to conceal his knowledge from me; but now, viewing the situation in retrospect, I suspected that what the Sergeant had been concealing was his lack of knowledge.

However, that was not important. What was important was that, in the image of jewels among vegetables, I had found a figure of incongruity for my sonnet.

Excusing myself I left Papa's office for my own, where, with rhyming dictionary, thesaurus, and carbon copy on my desk again, I lost myself in the business of clothing my new simile with suitable words, thankful indeed that the sonnet had been written in the Shakespearean rather than the Italian form, so that a change in the rhyme of the last two lines would not necessitate similar alterations in other lines.

Time passed, and then I was leaning back in my chair, experiencing that unique satisfaction that Papa felt when he had apprehended some especially elusive criminal. I could not help smiling when I reread my new concluding couplet.

> *And shining there, no less inaptly shone*
> *Than diamonds in a spinach garden sown.*

That, I fancied, would satisfy the editor of *The Jongleur*.

POSTSCRIPT

Dashiell Hammett's *A Man Named Thin* was the "discovery" story in the 20th Anniversary Issue of "Ellery Queen's Mystery Magazine" (March 1961), which went on sale February 1, 1961. Just 21 days before *A Man Named Thin* appeared in print for the very first time—indeed, while the story was actually on the press—Dashiell Hammett, the thin man himself, passed away in Lenox Hill Hospital in New York City. And so *A Man Named Thin* did prove to be the "last" Hammett story, even though it had originally been written about 35 years before its creator's death.

With the passing of Dashiell Hammett we lost one of the really great mystery writers, who may some day be acknowledged one of the great writers (without the "mystery" label).

Who will take the place of the man who wrote such novels as THE MALTESE FALCON and THE GLASS KEY and THE THIN MAN—who created such authentic characters as Sam Spade, Nick Charles, and The Continental Op—who gave us such memorable short stories as *A Man Named Spade* and *The Gutting of Couffignal*—who, as we once wrote, did not invent a new kind of detective story, but did invent a new way of telling it—who was the most important modern originator in the mystery field, giving us the first 100 per cent *American,* the first truly *native,* detective story, thus founding a school whose influence was, is, and will continue to be colossal, not only among mystery writers but among all writers—who will take Dashiell Hammett's place?

Who *can* take his place?

The king is dead . . .

A DETECTIVE STORY TO END

A DETECTIVE STORY ANTHOLOGY

Anthony Boucher

The Ultimate Clue

TO READERS: *an extremely clever short-short* . . .
TO WRITERS: *an "object lesson" in technique* . . .

They do happen once or twice in a detective's lifetime—the neat perfect story-book puzzles; and the neatest one that ever happened to me was the Magini-Coletti problem—or The Case of the Two-Word Solution.

This is a football story, but you don't have to know a punt from a pontoon to figure out the answer. It happened while California was having that great series of teams under Steve Sealy, the shrewd old 280-pounder whom the sports writers called the Sagacious Seal. This was the year Cal was rated sixth nationally by the AP and fourth by the UP and all because of a couple of grape-tromping Italians from the Napa Valley.

Jack (for Giacomo) Magini was a runt of a quarterback with an aim like William Tell's. Game by game he was tearing up all Paul Larson's varsity records, and his favorite target was a rangy alp of an end named Tony Coletti, who had adhesive pads on his fingers like a gecko. They'd been playing together since the tenth grade; and a Ph.D. candidate in the psych department was wondering if he could use them for a thesis on ESP in athletics.

Cal was a 20-point favorite in the Big Game—and in Northern California the Big Game means Cal-Stanford. Oh, there are other games of some bigness in their own regions, like Yale-Harvard and Army-Navy, but the Big Game is . . . well, it's the Big Game. Point-spread never means too much, and sometimes the smart money goes on the underdog; so nobody was surprised when the 20-point favorite only just squeaked by at 26-20. But plenty of people were surprised by how it happened—including the Pacific Coast Conference, which hired me to look into it.

Three times Coletti was in the clear without a defender between him and the goal line, and Magini had all the protection in the world to get his pass away . . . but the ball and the receiver didn't connect. The pass was too long—or the end was too slow reaching his assigned spot. The pass was short—or the receiver had gone out too far. The old rapport, the ESP, wasn't working. And who could tell whose fault it was?

Excepting Magini. And Coletti. And possibly the gambling syndicate.

For the pure among you, let it be noted that gambling on football games isn't usually on a win-or-lose basis. It's by point-spread —that is, by the margin of victory. And those three incomplete passes, each of which would have been a sure touchdown, meant that the underdog-betters collected, probably in six figures, even though Stanford still lost and Cal racked up an undefeated season.

When the PCC gave me the assignment, the first man I wanted to talk to was old Steve Sealy. But the Seal stalled. "Give me eight hours," he said. "Come around late tonight, O'Breen, and maybe I'll have earned your fee for you. I'm *talking* to those two boys—talking like I never talked between halves. I know them better than their fathers—the ones they were born with *and* the ones that hear their confessions. And if one of them sold out, I'll know which."

He did, too; but he never lived to tell me. Not directly. He'd been dead about two hours when I let myself into his unlocked home after ten minutes of doorbell pushing. Why will an otherwise intelligent man equip his desk with a paper cutter as lethal as a switchblade? It had gone through all that flesh straight to his heart and your guess is as good as mine as to how long he lived with that steel in him.

There was a book on the floor beside him. It was a biography of Knute Rockne and it had left a gap in a shelf of books about the football greats. The shelf was crowded; the Rockne book couldn't have fallen.

I looked at it while I was waiting for the police. The lower half of the last page was torn out. What was left seemed to be the full text of the last page with some white space under it.

In the ashtray on the desk there were paper ashes, powdered beyond any possibility of reconstruction.

So I could see what had happened—and I knew who killed him.

He had been still barely alive, unable to pull his 280 pounds off the floor. He couldn't get to the desk to write, so he grabbed a book and tore out what made the exact message. But the killer hadn't gone yet; he came back and ripped the message out of the dying pudgy hand and burned it.

But I knew what the message was. For perfectionism I had to check an undamaged copy of the Rockne book and prove what was on that destroyed half page; and then, once we knew which boy to concentrate on, it was easy enough for the police to establish the gambling contacts and piece together the rest of a perfect case for Murder One.

All that took time; but the story-book puzzle solved itself as soon as it was stated. For of course that missing half of the last page told me that the murderer wasn't the quarterback. He was

THE END

ABOUT THE EDITOR OF EQMM

The team of Frederic Dannay and Manfred B. Lee—who, as everyone knows, are Ellery Queen—has written fifty-one books, including those first published under the pseudo-pseudonym of Barnaby Ross, and has edited forty-three more. A conservative estimate has placed their total sales in various editions at nearly 50,000,000 copies. And millions of listeners agreed when *TV Guide* awarded the Ellery Queen program its National Award as the best mystery show of 1950. Ellery Queen has won five annual "Edgars"—the national Mystery Writers of America awards similar to the "Oscars" of Hollywood—and both the silver and gold "Gertrudes" awarded by Pocket Books.

Ellery Queen's most recent successes are *The Finishing Stroke* and *Inspector Queen's Own Case.* He is internationally known as an editor—*Ellery Queen's Mystery Magazine* celebrated its 20th Anniversary in 1961—and his library of first editions contained the finest collection of books of detective short stories in existence.

These facts about Queen may account for the remark by Anthony Boucher, in his profile of Manfred B. Lee and Frederic Dannay, that "Ellery Queen *is* the American detective story."